PALACE TRASH

Essential Translations Series 60

Canada Council for the Arts
Conseil des arts du Canada

ONTARIO ARTS COUNCIL
CONSEIL DES ARTS DE L'ONTARIO

an Ontario government agency
un organisme du gouvernement de l'Ontario

Canada

Guernica Editions Inc. acknowledges the support of
the Canada Council for the Arts and the Ontario Arts Council.
The Ontario Arts Council is an agency of the Government of Ontario.
We acknowledge the financial support of the Government of Canada through
the National Translation Program for Book Publishing, an initiative
of the *Roadmap for Canada's Official Languages 2013–2018:
Education, Immigration, Communities*, for our translation activities.
We acknowledge the financial support of the Government of Canada.
Nous reconnaissons l'appui financier du gouvernement du Canada.

PALACE TRASH

ROGER FODJO

GUERNICA
EDITIONS
TORONTO • CHICAGO • BUFFALO • LANCASTER (U.K.)
2025

Original title: *Les poubelles du palais*

Guernica Founder: Antonio D'Alfonso

Michael Mirolla, general editor
Sonia di Placido, editor
David Moratto, cover and interior design
Front cover: Mirko Fermani

Guernica Editions Inc.
1241 Marble Rock Rd., Gananoque (ON), Canada K7G 2V4
2250 Military Road, Tonawanda, N.Y. 14150-6000 U.S.A.
www.guernicaeditions.com

Distributors:
Independent Publishers Group (IPG)
600 North Pulaski Road, Chicago IL 60624
University of Toronto Press Distribution (UTP)
5201 Dufferin Street, Toronto (ON), Canada M3H 5T8

First edition.
Printed in Canada.

Legal Deposit—First Quarter
Library of Congress Catalog Card Number: 2024948891
Library and Archives Canada Cataloguing in Publication
Title: Palace trash / Roger Fodjo ; translated by Kwoh Molen.
Other titles: Poubelles du palais. English.
Names: Fodjo, Roger, author.
Series: Essential translations series ; 60.
Description: Series statement: Essential translations series ; 60 | Translation of: Les poubelles du palais. | In English, translated from the French.
Identifiers: Canadiana (print) 20240501438 | Canadiana (ebook) 20240507797 | ISBN 9781771839594 (softcover) | ISBN 9781771839600 (EPUB)
Subjects: LCGFT: Novels.
Classification: LCC PS8611.O455 P6813 2025 | DDC C843/.6—dc23

For Caroline, Alex and Indira

 1

FRANCE IS IN turmoil. The great country is in the eye of the storm. A quiet turbulence that moves forward without a bang. Only the wise know that this apparent calm of ordinary days is being shaken by an unprecedented earthquake. Political circles are well aware of it. They have taken the measure of the problem and are committed to trying everything to quell it. This is not a new wave of mad cow disease or avian flu that is hitting the Republic. It is not a suspicious package dropped by an Axis of Evil activist at a crowded intersection, or a tailspin announced on the Paris stock exchange. It's much more than all these little nuisances combined!

The mustachioed Commissioner, Laurent Fournier, in charge of tracking down the fugitive, gets angry. He pulls out what hair he has left, screaming with impatience. The investigations have barely begun, and he can already see them stalling. His men deployed discreetly in the field have covered every nook and cranny of the Île-de-France region to prevent the game from slipping away. The intelligence agents, more alert than ever, are putting all their brain power to the test. They are also supported by the most advanced technological tools. But still nothing! Where is the man who stole secret documents from the National Archives? The "professional", as some people call him in the police world, was able to get his hands on original parchments dating back to the Old Regime! If these writings are famous, it is not so much because of their age. It is not so much because of the illustrious signature of the powerful King Louis XIV that appears on them. It is only because of the secrets they contain! Secrecy is all that is exciting about these original parchments. Secrets are the prominent part of the history relief. One is mistaken in thinking that they create holes in history, but they are rather mountains turned upside down. Buried, secrets become abscesses that fester under a fragile bandage.

And how many centuries have passed since this event? Three and a half centuries! Man can torture history as he pleases, like clay in the hands of the potter, but facts are stubborn. Marie-Thérèse of Austria, Queen of France in her time, fell in love with her black slave—hold your breath—and ended up offering the French court a little half-breed baby as evidence of their romance. This is not a novelistic artifice. It is not another story woven out of nothing, which jumps with both feet onto the burning realities of humanity. This is France, this is Versailles.

She was born on an autumn morning in 1664. Beautiful and cute. The little Louise-Marie in her mother's arms dreamed of a life in a castle like all princesses but could not yet imagine what would happen to her in the following days. The maternity wards of the Kingdom had never considered babywear for, if you please, purple children! So, Louise-Marie had, or would have been thrown in the garbage by order of the King as food for scavengers. If to this day questions about the method used to erase the newborn persist, her sudden disappearance from the palace, however, is not in doubt. Was she buried alive, given up to a wild beast, thrown in the garbage, or stolen and hidden by an anonymous courtier? The answer can be found in a parchment that has just been stolen. The author of the theft is not alone. Reports claim that he is supported by accomplices, actors in the dark, media organizations, associations of the aggrieved, occult foreign powers, all ready to open fire on Paris when the time comes. Do not forget! The English people are not about to lose the memory of their idol who was crushed in Paris under a tunnel while she was pregnant, lest she too give her lineage such a child. Monarchies are alike, you see!

Commissioner Fournier is a tracking machine launched on the fugitive's trail. By all the gods, the beast must not cross the border! All the holes in France are plugged. The only way out for him is to make the courageous decision to surrender.

Why so much silent noise? Why so much panic? Cyprien Ghezo doesn't at all have the look of a bomber. He is a saint without a halo. He has a gentle and docile temperament. However, he is giving the highest authorities of the State a hard time. The phone does not stop ringing between the Élysée Palace, the Quay d'Orsay, the Beauvau Square, and the French embassy in Porto-Novo. For four days, he has been on the run with a precious document stolen from the National Archives Center. He can't wait to find out what happened to the purple child he claims he is related to. Did she live? Was she rescued by a benefactor? Is she living in the stomach of a carnivore in the Versailles woods? He doesn't know, at least for the moment. The heap of information he holds has not yet been sifted. Perhaps this child has left traces in history—and why not! Anonymous traces that only God can reveal to those he loves. The father of the missing baby, the Queen's lover, had come from Dahomey to serve as a slave at the French court. But the roles were soon reversed, and Nabo's new life became quite different from his original destiny. His talent as a court entertainer had brought him to the attention of Her Majesty the Queen. A queen's will is God's will. And out of this tender clandestine love between the slave and Her Majesty was born a girl tinted with the colours of the countries of sun, in the court of the Sun King!

If one starts to recall that wax melts in the sun, one would not have made any discovery. Let us rather leave to La Palisse the task of saying his truisms. But these obvious facts are not ideas to throw away. Everything has a meaning. Each word finds its place in the sentence, as each idea finds its place in human philosophy. So to speak, little Louise-Marie was a soft wax that did not resist the fury of the Sun. Her traces in the history of France were quickly erased. A storm blew over her life and swept away the memory of her in the mind of the historians who were accomplices.

From the depths of his hole, Cyprien convinces himself. "Since no one testified to having seen her body, she did not die at birth as it was claimed."

He opens the stolen box. It is a small black rectangle with a lid secured by a buckled strap. It looks like a miniature coffin. Inside it are fossilized documents. He reexamines the contents, piece by piece. Skeptical! "What had they done with my ancestress?" he wonders. Suddenly, a siren's wail breaks the harmony of the ambient silence. It comes from passing cops. It is undoubtedly on his account that this terrifying concert is being sounded. He must get himself to another niche, right now!

Very far from there, the screaming vehicles converge towards the same point. Soon, they all become silent and can be seen hastily entering the parking lot of a shopping mall. This is where the wanted man has just been reported. But what? It's all in the wind! The cops soon realize that they are victims of a hoax. Another hoax!

From a secret location, Commissioner Fournier radios his men.

"What happened to the hunt?"

"It was only a false alarm, Commissioner!"

"You make me laugh! Don't tell me that a nigger in sandals is routing our National Police! We are watched from the top. Two more hours without success, and we'll be going to settle accounts! You got me!"

Radio stop.

2

Cyprien Ghezo had left his native Benin a few years before. Like any young person, he had dreamed of becoming useful to his country through a distinguished position. His ideals led him to cross the Mediterranean in search of an education worthy of making him a man of the future. As an intelligent and curious student, he has built a perfect track record and has earned numerous degrees along the way. Today, he is working on a doctorate in molecular biology. This is not without its worries. He is afraid of getting his noble parchment, because not all goals are good to achieve. To stop being a student in France is to become "undocumented". Everything happens like in those epics where the knight must face a monster to rescue the princess. The more the hero approaches his goal, the more he is afraid to reach it. To graduate is to choose the forced return to the fold where companies will ask him: "Sir, if you have learned how to put Paris in your pocket, why have you returned here? We are afraid that we have no occupation to entertain you."

Destiny is wicked! To pay for studies and life, he has often endured the shit of odd jobs, sometimes outdoors, sometimes in offices. In such offices, bosses ring a bell to call an employee of Cyprien's category because his name is not worth remembering. The most prestigious of these positions is the one he filled as an employee of a cleaning company. His role: to snoop around offices in the capital's upscale neighbourhoods. This is called industrial espionage. In business, all tricks are allowed, and the most painful are prized. It is only the fault of those who suffer it. Unfortunately, his small fortune did not last long, and he soon fell back into precariousness.

Now a notorious fugitive, he has traded the tranquillity of his sober life for an involuntary nomadism that does not allow him to spend an entire night in one place.

In Cotonou, as in Porto-Novo, French police helicopters constantly crisscross the sky. They are flown by French soldiers from the Abidjan base. The inhabitants of these cities wonder what other political maneuver is going on behind their backs. From time to time, colonies of crows, dislodged by the roar of the engines, circle over the city and land on the rooftops. Something is definitely going on. The situation requires this deployment. The fugitive, they think, would have found the best refuge in his native country. He will ascend into the realm of invulnerability if a steamroller is not quickly put in place. On the ground, raids and silent searches are conducted in various places. Travellers are taken off buses and submitted to identity checks by squads of gendarmes. Along borders, invisible ants in fatigues close their ranks. The people of Abomey don't know what's going on either, but they are untroubled. They trust this powerful hand raised on a pedestal at the entrance of their city, on the Goho Square. This hand has the knack for repelling any foreign intrusion attempt. It is King Behanzin's hand, the monarch who keeps a keen eye on the horizon, while from his mouth fall heavy words that claim: "I WILL NEVER ACCEPT TO SIGN ANY TREATY SUSCEPTIBLE TO ALIENATE THE INDEPENDENCE OF MY ANCESTORS' LAND." Not having the courage to desecrate this shrine, the recon patrols retreat at the entrance of the city of Abomey.

☙ Two days of combing Benin produced nothing. However, at Orly Airport in Paris, Cyprien Ghezo boarded the plane. He then landed at Cotonou-Cadjehoun airport in Benin and regularly passed through the police station before an international search was launched against him. He is now on the loose and is holding documents highly compromising to the French Republic. If he lets out their contents, there would be chaos! Manuscripts classified as "State Secrets" at the National Archives Center must not be left at the foot of a tree in the equatorial forest, or in a sloping ghetto that has never had electricity. These are documents capable of shaking the foundations of the Republic if they are disseminated. Many of these texts, originals and copies as well, have a restriction of thirty, sixty, ninety years, and even more! The fugitive student does not do things by halves. He has seized a file with a hundred-year restriction! This is the time limit the National Archives Center gives itself before allowing a researcher to access the file. This measure applies to all files likely to disturb public order, to provoke racial hatred or to settle scores. In this case, public order is not the only risk. Above all, it is the deep soul of a Republic itself, held on a leash by

Freemasonry, the esoteric order called the Builders, that is at stake. If the freemasonic Republic produces so many homeless people, let's conclude that these builders are not free! And yet, they have infused the French Republic with their motto and forced it to bark empty words like Liberty, Equality, Fraternity.

Liberty? Yes, it exists! It is the freedom to do what you want, to throw a child in the garbage because she is of mixed race. All the rest is hollow. For Equality and Fraternity, let's look elsewhere, under the banana trees.

Commissioner Fournier has rarely been given such an important responsibility. He is engaged in a real race against the clock. He has only three days to arrest the criminal. The documents were transferred to the National Archives and added to the existing inventory in November 1910. Only three days left, and the hundred-year restriction will be lifted! After that time, it will no longer be possible to prosecute the student for violating a state secret. This takes all the salt out of the soup. In this hypothesis—the one Fournier doesn't want—the man will only be prosecuted for setting off firecrackers in a public reading room, causing the hospitalization of a dozen elderly people who collapsed, and for taking away without permission a small dusty coffin containing papers yellowed by three centuries of waiting.

The Commissioner is actively repositioning himself in the field. From time to time, he calls to know how the case is progressing.

"Is there anything new?" he asks.

"Yes, Commissioner," his Lieutenant replies. "Everything suggests that he has not travelled. I am sure of it."

Lieutenant Toulon is used to keeping his statements in proportion. But, in this case, he has left no doubt.

"Who are you talking about, Lieutenant?"

"Cyprien Ghezo has not crossed our borders, Commissioner. He is within our walls."

"Unbelievable! And what about the boarding pass provided by Orly Airport? Is it a fake one?"

"Far from it, Commissioner! This same name was also recorded by the border police at the landing in Cotonou, but it was a different person who travelled instead of our man."

"I understand ... Why didn't we think of it before? ... You mean that he had his passport used by someone else!"

"That's right!"

"Track down his friends. I'm waiting for the list right now."

"We don't have his address book, Commissioner. It's going to take us some time to compile this list."

"Do whatever you can, Lieutenant! Send men to the campus. We only have thirty-six hours left."

3

NORTHERN SUBURB OF Paris, Saint Ouen Gate. Jules Bartoli, Cyprien Ghezo's friend, gets off his motor scooter and parks it against a plane tree. He takes off his helmet and places it under his armpit. His pace is slow. He looks at everyone suspiciously, as if all the passers-by were plainclothes policemen. He goes down to a basement and tries a large door. It is locked. His finger presses a doorbell. The door unlocks and Cyprien's figure suddenly appears. The two men greet each other like troopers, clapping their palms and hitting their fists.

"I'm glad you came on a motorcycle," Cyprien says as he sees the helmet. "I was afraid you would take your father's Sedan."

"No, this is not the time to play the spoilt child," Jules says. "We have to do everything discreetly. And yourself, are you all right?"

"I'm not worried, buddy."

Cyprien lets out a laugh. Jules gets rid of his coat and hangs it in a corner of the wardrobe. His friend serves him coffee to get him in shape. Outside, a cold of minus fourteen degrees crushes bones. Jules' gaze hits the black box on the shelf.

"Did you find what you were looking for in there?"

"Partly," Cyprien replies. "The relevant information isn't there. I want to know where this child went after she was born. Everything you see here is about her first days in the palace. There are also some strong traces of His Majesty the King's anger, as well as a surprising description of his wife's grief. I also understand that the French troops were no longer progressing on the various fronts they were holding at the same time, because of this marital dispute of the royal couple. His Majesty, who used to fight in the vanguard on the fronts, had suddenly lost his warrior strength after this shameful birth. A cuckolded king has no pride. It is normal that he had lost all his bravery. He had withdrawn to his royal apartments and spent days and nights melancholic."

"I think he was up to something fishy."

"You are right, my dear Jules! I wanted to hear someone say that!"

"Have you gone through the whole file?"

"It's a mess you could read for days. The box contains everything. The organization of the State, credentials, ennoblements of numerous mistresses, legitimations of the King's natural children, copies of decrees, arrest orders, and even his own will. A document placed at the bottom of the box is lost."

"How come?"

"It is completely wet. The ink in it has run in a diffuse stain. It is irrecoverable."

"I'm sorry! I think I know why: in a rush, the box might have been held upside down and rainwater would have seeped through the ventilation holes in the bottom. Remember that it was lightly raining that evening."

"That's clear, I get it now."

"So, did we work for nothing?" Jules asks.

"Oh, no! We worked for that. It is a treasure. Only one paper is lost. I have to restart the investigations on this subject, until my final goal."

"What would be your final goal, Cyprien, you that nothing stops?"

"First of all, it is to bow down on Louise-Marie's grave, of course, if she was offered a burial somewhere on this earth. I don't believe that she ended up in the mouth of a wild beast in the woods of Versailles. Then, if France copies good examples from other humbly powerful states, it will be able to apologize for this historical crime."

"You will need to bring evidence. We are only at the stage of suspicion at the moment."

"Yes, you understand what is at stake in our efforts. This evidence is hidden somewhere. We will get it, whether it is buried under the waters of the Seine or on the top of Mont Blanc."

"Does this seem like a small matter to you? The streets are mined, though everything seems normal. Of all the people you see these days, there are more cops than civilians. When you ask someone for directions, you don't know if they're going to follow you next."

"I am well aware of all those risks, Jules. But you see, it's finding the truth and making it public that counts.

"In my opinion, you should drop this case, Cyprien. I helped you because I thought you were only seeking answers to a couple of questions."

"I want to get those answers for myself and raise public awareness."

"That's all in the past, after all. Why are you willing to risk so much for a supposed crime committed more than three hundred years ago?"

"Look, Jules, this is a crime, not a misdemeanor. Time is not a rag that erases crimes. And if you want to know my interest in the case, I will remind you that I claim to be related to the missing child. That's no small thing. We are both, she and I, descendants of the King of Dahomey, the ancestor of Behanzin. The blood that flowed in the veins of that girl flows in mine."

"I understand that it hurts you. It is the disappearance of a relative that is at stake."

"It's more than hurting. It makes me furious!"

"At this pace, dear friend, you must be falling into a vindictive spirit worthy of classical tragedies."

"This is a matter of justice and honour. Don't you realize that Nabo, who came to serve as slave in the court of another king, was himself a crown prince of the Kingdom of Dahomey? This is an affront that must absolutely be cleansed!"

"You make me hate these people, Cyprien!"

"For three and a half centuries, this ember has been smoldering under the ashes. It is time for the truth to come out."

"Then you will become a messiah!"

"Or an antichrist if you will. It all depends on which side you're on."

"But tell me, are you one of those who think that the twenty-first century is the century of great revelations?"

"I don't believe in the New Age discourse. However, I hear more and more people talking about the great revelations of the Aquarian Age."

"Let's move on! Tell me more about Nabo."

"Gone! Him too. Perhaps quartered."

"Yes, or rather decapitated, somewhere in the south of France. Isn't his head on the Corsican flag?"

Cyprien laughs out loud to ease the gloomy atmosphere around them.

"It's not the same thing," he says. "The Moor's head you're talking about dates from the thirteenth century. And besides, in the administration of capital punishment in the past, they did not behead for this kind of felony. Criminals of lese-majesty were rather quartered by horses, thieves were hanged, nobles were beheaded, heretics were burned."

"So, what about the guillotine?"

"It only appeared during the Revolution, proposed by Doctor Guillotin, to shorten the suffering of people sentenced to death."

"You have a lot of work to do, dear friend. You are looking for the daughter and the father."

"I will go in stages. First the daughter, then the father."

"I support you. You can count on me. Wherever you go, I will be with you. I hate human bondage."

"Are you serious, Julio?"

"Yes!"

Jules gets up and goes to the coffee pot. He shakes the tank, which is empty. There is no more coffee, no more tea. Empty packages are lying in the trash can. He opens the fridge, nothing to nibble on!

"How did he live here, our friend Jean?"

"He lived like a refugee, in his own pad."

"It looks like a church."

"It looks less like one. In a church you can eat the hosts and drink good altar wine."

Jules takes off his coat with a sudden gesture, showing a certain nervousness.

"War is not declared yet," Cyprien says to him. "Please kiss your beautiful Yasmina for me."

"I will," Jules says, without smiling.

The two hit each other in the palms and the fists, then Jules walks through the door. Cyprien latches it shut.

Jules Bartoli is a twenty-one-year-old gentleman, born in Ajaccio. His parents owned a luxurious duplex near Campo dell'Oro Beach, where they retreated two seasons out of four each year. The rest of the time the family lived in a spacious apartment in the heart of the city. Jules was the model of a little boy who never complained about life. He still jealously keeps his childhood photos, showing him on his father's shoulder on the way to the Sanguinary Islands, or hanging from his arms like a crucified boy between mother and father. The Parata Tower was his main fascination. He imagined that at the top of this rock one would have the world at their feet. He was an extroverted boy, while his sister rather liked to withdraw into confined spaces. So, their parents offered them the pleasure of visiting caves, museums and mountains, so that they didn't harm anyone. This happiness lasted until the day a blast of unknown origin blew a wing of the building that housed their apartment. There was talk of a terrorist act that no one claimed responsibility for. Jules will never forget the fright that this explosion gave him. He will always remember the sinister images he saw in the morning when he woke up.

Bricks filling the courtyard, cribs thrown away, paramedics picking up shattered bodies. It was the seed of an insecurity that would blossom over the years in Ajaccio. This phenomenon, that looked like unstoppable, forced his father to make a wise decision. He sold the apartment and the duplex of the Campo dell'Oro and moved to Paris with wife and children.

It was in this new city that Jules met Cyprien in a squash club at the university. They extended their friendship beyond the campus, although today they attend two different institutions. Clearly, Jules is becoming more idle than studious. When he borrows a book from the library, he pays particular attention to its thickness. He likes books less and less, calling them "bricks" because of their thickness. The more he studies, the bigger the books get. He no longer measures them in pages, but in centimeters. Discouraging! Today, he has found in the Louise-Marie case a good opportunity to give another meaning to his life: lending a hand to a friend. That, he knows how to do!

4

LIEUTENANT TOULON'S MEN have gleaned some information on the campus. But at times, they have heard people objecting: "A doctoral student is not a high school student. We haven't seen him for weeks. Go and check with the librarian." And from the library, nothing good would come. How can they pull their badges out to show that they are cops coming after the student? If they do, they will see hordes of goons rush out of classrooms and come down on them hard. In these campaign times, when immigrants and young graduates are at the center of all debates, it's best to walk away from a campus empty-handed.

Within the hour, Toulon receives a call from the bank. The fugitive's bank card has just been used in Cotonou. He immediately informs the Commissioner. Rather than rejoicing over it, this news ends up confusing their judgment. But Laurent Fournier does not let the new information fool him.

"If the passport is in Cotonou and its holder is in France," he says, "why wouldn't he have handed his bank card too?"

"He could do that to distract us," the Lieutenant remarks.

"His cell phone hasn't worked so far?"

"Not at all, Commissioner. His last call was to the Institute of Archaeological Studies in Grenoble, three days ago."

"And what happens when we try to call him?"

"Right to voicemail."

"He's a smart and forward-thinking guy. The most urgent thing is to ask our local Embassy there to immediately mobilize the police in that area."

He checks his watch and does a mental calculation, his lips moving. Then he says: "Thirty-three hours, Lieutenant! Thirty-three hours ... You understand what I mean!"

The General Intelligence, known as GI, has provided a detailed file on the student. Signatures, addresses lived at since he entered France, jobs held, health status, sexual orientation, list of last phone calls, etc. At his last known address, another tenant has been living there for a year.

He started his last job only two weeks ago and didn't show up for the last three days, according to the foreman. He doesn't know if the worker is coming back, he adds, recounting details of some actions he personally witnessed.

It is a restoration company that has won the contract to refurbish the old Château de Versailles, southwest of Paris. Seen from the outside, Versailles is not an architectural jewel. It is rather sober as a seventeenth century castle. It does not have spread out towers and ramparts like other monuments of the same rank. Its fame, eternally engraved in stone, is based on the tenacious endeavour of the powerful Louis XIV who designed it.

Versailles is not a fortress surrounded and isolated by a moat with a drawbridge. Louis already had ideas of freedom and transparency. It was he, the sovereign, who in 1670 had the walls of Paris demolished and who declared the capital an "open city". The imaginative genius of the builder of Versailles is reflected in the unparalleled magnificence of its long Hall of Mirrors and its Great Waters. Its acres of gardens and hunting grounds give an idea of His Majesty's extravagant spirit. He wanted to be on a par with the gods. He wanted to rise as high as the firmament, to bestride Nature, to bestride the world. He had too big of an ego to admit any humiliation. Yet, he was the very one who saw a mixed-race child from his wife's womb fall into his arms. Three and a half centuries later, Cyprien Ghezo arrived on the scene, pushed by the wind of chance. He was hired by this restoration company two weeks ago. The work is now progressing at a steady pace. Under the imposing mass of the standing monument, the machines rumble. The repeated hammering sends its echo into the surrounding woods. In the dungeons adjacent to an underground gallery, the one that leads to the carriage room, black dust rises, swirls in the dungeons and escapes through the window wells. The basement of the castle contains an important network of galleries that resembles our modern subway system. Their main crossing is under the Royal Chapel, which rests on the ancient Thetys Cave. The longest of these galleries extend beyond the southern ramparts. One of them wisely connects the castle to the Grand Trianon, a retreat dedicated to the King's amorous escapades. It was through this tunnel that Queen Marie-Antoinette managed to escape from the wild horde of insurgents who attacked the palace on October 6, 1789.

Ghezo is holding an electric sander in both hands. He applies it with all his strength on the stony walls to remove the black dirt accumulated over centuries. This dirt is the collective and everlasting imprint from several generations of prisoners who happened to be housed here. After completing the renovation work on this part of the building, this living expression of human suffering will be swept clean. The protective helmet he is wearing has lost its blue colour. His mask has turned black. He can't help breathing in the filthy dust that finds its way in through the sides of his mask.

When the tourists come later, they will not know that a worker has sacrificed his life expectancy for their pleasure. The sanded areas gleam in the light of the sweeping lamp introduced into the dungeons. Everything is moving at a steady pace when suddenly, he notices an engraving carved in a stone. The writing has become exposed upon removal of the layer of grime from the stone. The engraving is prominently visible in its groove, as if someone had reinforced it with black ink. The worker stops the machine and tries to decipher the inscription. Only the first few words appear. "TO THE MEMORY OF ..." The engraving is not deep. It is so shallow that another stroke of the sander would have smoothed it out.

It is clear the engraver did not have a piece of equipment sharp and rigid enough for a deeper work. The engraver was doubtlessly a prisoner. The walls of prisons are not made of cardboard or cellular concrete that can be dug out with a fingernail. Never mind, prisoners have always managed to write on their walls. Ah, how stubborn revolutionaries are! Moufdi Zakaria did not beat around the bush when he wanted to get his message out. He wrote his revolutionary poem using his own blood as ink, in his Barbarossa Prison. Prison walls are undoubtedly the jaws of a vice that crush the body of the prisoner to death, while offering him a magnificent medium that favors the expansion of his eternal spirit. This is how many prisoners manage to escape one day, leaving their jailer with a pile of empty bones.

Cyprien restarts the machine and cleans a large portion of the wall. The whole engraving appears—clear and neat! He gets down on his knees and reads it several times. Shaking! What does it mean? Two names are mentioned. He knows one of the characters perfectly well. But the second one, who is female, does not awaken any memory in him. The engraving says that they were condemned and dispatched. But where were they sent to? He doesn't know. He takes up the machine again and in the blink of an eye, scrapes off the whole remaining portion. A sudden madness takes hold of him. He seems to have been stung by a terrifying venom. All the walls of the dungeon are scraped, but no other clue! He leaves the place and dashes towards the gathering lodge. On his way, he comes across the foreman who shouts at him. The young man proceeds without turning his head. The foreman follows him into the changing rooms. When he gets there, Cyprien has already got rid of his helmet and gloves. He puts on his jeans with surprising speed. The foreman who has seen his movement, follows him to the gathering room.

"What are you doing, sir? It's not time to leave the site!"

"Sure! But excuse me, I'm going home. It's an emergency! I'll be right back. I have the feeling that my apartment is on fire."

"You don't live across the street, Mr. Ghezo. How can you see your apartment?"

"Believe what I'm telling you, Mr. Bonnot! A 1,500-watt hot plate is burning near my closet."

"Ah … I understand … You forgot to unplug it after making your coffee. Go check it right away!"

He runs out and catches the bus at the nearby stop. His heart is pounding. He is afraid that the foreman will come down to the workstation before he returns. Bonnot is a young man in his thirties, lively and light. He is not like those sluggish supervisors who lock themselves up in their cabins to record workers' complaints. He has an eye for everything, and with his boots he treads all corners of the site. If he were to resume his rounds before Cyprien returns, he would certainly see the strange engraving and report it to his boss. The boss would in turn inform the monument's curator who, as a last resort, would give an order for these writings to be erased immediately. Cyprien starts envisioning the worst. With what he has discovered, he could be considered as someone who knows too much. As a result, he would be at the risk of having someone cause him to disappear or to suffer an accidental "fatal fall" from the scaffolding. Don't blame me, that's the language they use on construction sites!

After a few minutes, Cyprien returns with a digital camera. As he passes by, he notices the foreman's absence. Perhaps he has started his rounds of the site? But further down, the foreman appears standing by a wall. He is raging against a worker for acting like a mule.

Cyprien wonders: has he visited the dungeon in the meantime? Their eyes meet. Cyprien quickly goes down into the cellar. His camera is armed. He hears the foreman's boots trampling the gravel behind him. Inside the dungeon, he takes several photos of the engraving. The foreman enters unannounced as he takes the last picture. Cyprien puts the camera away.

"And your apartment, were you able to prevent the fire?"

"Yes, fortunately! Don't worry about it. Just a smell of melted metal and overheating in the room."

The foreman looks at him suspiciously.

"Tell me what you're shooting in that dungeon."

He inspects the room.

"What do you think one can shoot in a dark and filthy prison? Do you take this place for Côte d'Azur, Mr. Bonnot? Tell me! You see tourism everywhere! Even in the bowels of the earth where human misery is hidden."

The foreman walks towards the wall. Cyprien seizes the sander and destroys the engraving with diabolical violence.

"I don't understand you anymore, Mr. Ghezo! What is going on in your head? What is this way of doing things?

"I have to make up for lost time," he explains, getting back to work.

A cloud of dust rises and forces the foreman back. He rushes outside coughing terribly.

Shortly after, from the doorsteps, he insists, "I don't understand what's gotten into you, sir. Tell me what you read on these walls."

"It's not your business, I believe," Cyprien says.

"Yes, it is! I'm your boss!"

"So what?"

"You're fired!"

Cyprien grabs a flashlight and walks around the sanded dungeons. He inspects the walls, but no more signs appear. After walking a few steps back, he falls to his knees in front of the wall that had the engraving. His boss gives him a look, furious and surprised at the same time. It feels like the worker is in full meditation in this position. An intimate communion seems to be going on between him and the ground. The foreman thinks the worker is hearing voices from the beyond. Standing still, his boss witnesses one surprise after another of this unheard-of show.

Cyprien gets up.

"I need a jackhammer!" he shouts. "I'm going to exhume them, right now!"

"Who do you want to exhume?"

His question remains unanswered.

The worker quickly goes to get a pickaxe and brings it into the dungeon. Under the frightened eye of his boss, he grabs the tool with both hands and lifts it. Big blows begin to crackle. The concrete screed breaks up under the powerful strikes of the sharp metal that penetrates its heart. Overwhelmed, the foreman goes to alert the site manager to what is going on. When the two men arrive at the dungeon, the laborer has made a big hole. A pile of rocks stands next to the excavation. They see him reaching out to clear clods of earth. His fingers dig down. No bones found! He hears the two men shouting his name, but his madness prevents him from paying attention to them. He pulls out his cell phone and calls an information center, asking for a number. He immediately calls the number he has received. It is the Institute of Archaeological Research of Grenoble. Nobody answers at the other end of the line. He leaves a short message:

"Tell me, sirs, how long can the ground keep the skeleton of a buried baby? Thank you for calling me back."

"He is crazy, this boy!" the site manager remarks. "What is he looking for?"

"He wants to exhume an alleged body," the foreman replies. "He is convinced that there is a grave there."

"How long has he been with us?"

"Two weeks, but that doesn't matter anymore. He's fired!"

"Let's call the police."

The same evening, Cyprien goes to his university library. He occupies one of the research stations and begins to search through the electronic material. The computer invariably responds to his queries: "No result for *Louise-Marie, Nabo's daughter*," "No result for *Nabo, Louise-Marie's father*," "No result for *Louise-Marie, natural daughter of Marie-Thérèse of Austria*," "No result for *mixed-race child born to the Court of France*," "No result for *Nabo, black slave and Queen of France's lover*," "No result for *Louis XIV, cuckolded king*." A strange feeling grows in the student that the library is empty; that historians are nothing but big braggarts who deserve to be burnt at the stake.

He feels that this is a long walk that has just begun. The road ahead will be gruelling.

5

CYPRIEN HAS PLANNED to meet with Jules at Georges Pompidou Center, the huge cultural facility called Beaubourg. He is sitting on a subway train. During the journey, his eyes are riveted on his digital camera, which scrolls photos endlessly on a small built-in LCD screen. The photos of the dungeon are the last three. The whole enigma of the Louise-Marie case is contained in these images. The engraver of the message was a prisoner, undoubtedly. What was the nature of his involvement in the case? A snitch? A traitor? An innocent victim who knew too much and whom the King had silenced? In any case, the prisoner had not yielded to his fate. His message to posterity sounded like a cry of innocence and a desire to disclose the disappearance of the two characters. He certainly knew that his action bore heavy responsibility. As for his ambiguous words, when reading them, one wonders if he had not deliberately wanted to maintain misunderstandings.

The subway arrives at Rambuteau station. He gets off and emerges above ground. In front of him stands this gigantic center which, from outside, looks more like an oil patch than a temple of knowledge. Cyprien allows himself a few minutes to contemplate this building that responds to the style of functionalism. According to this architectural trend, the law of preponderance is simple: down with the ornaments! Only the useful is considered to the detriment of the pleasant. For, at Beaubourg, the pipe that carries shit is transparent so that no one doubts its role as a transmitter between the toilets and the sewers. If we were to compare Beaubourg to automotive engineering, we would see it as a military Jeep.

Bartoli, faithful to the appointment, is there under the porch. The two friends hit each other in the palms and clench their fists. Cyprien turns to the topic at hand without wasting a minute.

"What do you understand in 'condemned and dispatched'?"

"It depends on the context, in my opinion. But in our case, I tend to believe that to dispatch is to kill. Latin is specific in its expression by clearly saying *'to dispatch ad patres.'* Meaning to send to the ancestors. In Latin, there is no possible ambiguity. If you think that dispatching was geographical, it is not excluded. At that time a whole family could be exiled for nothing."

"And the fact that no written testimony was left in the history books?"

"It's because there was a necessity for discretion, obviously. Hence the predominance of the first hypothesis: to kill. But let's not jump to the conclusion so quickly. Nothing is decided yet. Perhaps books will speak."

They enter the room. Some research stations are free. They take seats in front of those screens and start typing keywords on keyboards. Nothing good comes out immediately. Many volumes, however, talk about King Louis XIV, his many mistresses and illegitimate sons, his unbridled love affairs, etc. Beside all this profusion, only one volume is dedicated to the legitimate Queen, Marie-Thérèse of Austria, daughter of King Philip IV of Spain. Cyprien calls his friend who has also noticed the same scarcity. He clicks the title to order it. Then he goes to join Jules. While waiting for the fifteen-minute time window allowed to get the material out of the shelf, the two get back to the images of the dungeon. Jules examines the three photos and rereads the engraving. Despite the shine of the LCD screen, it looks musty.

The book comes out. A large five-hundred-page volume to consult on the spot! Jules is flabbergasted. "It's a brick," he says. Unfortunately, borrowing rare documents is not allowed. They immediately move to the reading room. The table of contents describes the Queen's life from her sumptuous wedding on Pheasant Island to her tragic death at the Versailles Palace.

Maternity chapter: Out of six children born, only one survived. The one who is pointed out, the Great Dauphin, first-born, crown prince of France who will never reign. He is the only child who came under the spotlight. Honour to whom honour is due. At his birth, endless parades were organized. Melun prisoners were released on the King's order. What remains unsaid, like an omission, is the birth of the third child, Louise-Marie. This has been left as a hole in the story, but in reality, it is the only protrusion in the history of royal motherhood. If this little half-breed baby was not killed, she is therefore the only surviving child of the legitimate offspring of the couple, because the Dauphin was poisoned young.

Until then, the author remains methodical and credible. A birth precedes or follows a death. So, the parents will get used to the sinister devotion of going at each death to deposit the corpse of their dear child in the Bourbons' Vault, the royal family's tomb, housed in the underground crypt of Saint Denis Basilica, in the northern suburb of Paris. What is surprising in Louise-Marie's case is the stunning silence on the usual devotion of the burials. There was none! Hence the suspicion that there was no death at all. Where did the child go shortly after her birth? The enigma remains.

Cyprien flips the page with a sudden gesture that rustles papers. Jules awakes from a drowsiness.

"Have you come across anything?"

"No, nothing good for the moment. But I must tell you that the absence of a clue is a very interesting clue."

"Explain what you mean," Jules asks.

"From The Queen we have six births against five burials. There is one birth too many or one death too few."

"That is clear. It is a matter of disappearance."

Cyprien approves the thought. "Yes, a concealment, to be precise. According to the historian, the child was born in November and stopped living in December of the year 1664. Judging by the titles, other books would say less about it, I'm sure. However, let us take them and see."

They order at once four books on the royal couple. After fifteen minutes, they have the volumes on the table. But to their great disappointment, they discover nothing about the mysterious girl.

"Libraries are so silent," Jules says.

"It's not the librarians' fault. It's the politicians who have censored publications on the issue from the Old Regime to us. Do you know what I'm thinking?"

"Tell me!"

"I'm sure that at the National Archives Center we can find traces of the character, if we ask for her birth and death certificates, for example. What do you think?"

"That's a brilliant idea, my friend!" Jules exclaims. "Why are we still here? Let's go right away!"

6

THIRD DISTRICT, 11 Quatre-Fils Street. This is the address of the CARAN, the National Archives' Reception and Research Center. By chance, Beaubourg and the National Archives are two neighbouring institutions, so they got there on foot. Cyprien pushes open the metal gate and enters, followed by Jules. They find themselves in a large and apparently deserted area. To their left, under the columns, a glass door leads inside. They let the security guard search their backpacks, as is customary. Cyprien is already registered with the CARAN. He has a reader's card. Jules pays for a registration at the reception desk. As he is completing the transaction, his friend spots a painting hanging behind the cashier. The picture represents the Queen's bedroom at the Versailles Palace. It is facing Cyprien, as if someone has put it there to tease him. The predominant element in it is a huge four-poster bed standing on one side of the room, partly covered by a thick hanging that falls from the ceiling. A gilded balustrade forms a border between the bed and the rest of the room. Cyprien recognizes the decor. By imagining that the little missing baby was conceived on this bed, he perceives this display as a provocation.

They leave their belongings in the checkroom, keeping only blank sheets. Jules goes quickly to ease his bladder and catches up with his friend who is waiting at the top of the stairs.

"This is the inventory room," Cyprien says.

Pushing the heavy wooden door reinforced with copper stripes, they enter this large room on the second floor. The section allocated to the Old Regime is sparsely furnished. A panoramic glance is enough to assess its extent.

"Where do they hide the books?" Jules asks.

"CARAN is not a library. The inventory room only provides us with registers that locate our research topics in specific series. It is up to us to find the series and the call number of a document. Then we will ask for the document in the reading room. Another thing: registers are neither classified in alphabetical order, nor by topics. They are recorded based on the chronological order of their admission to the Center."

"Isn't that a bit boring?"

"No more than a stat paper ..."

Jules resigns himself.

Cyprien takes a blue register that compiles the general state of the repository. As usual, the two friends sit side by side. The O series appears under the title "House of the Kings". It begins with O1, which describes the copies of documents issued by King Louis XIV, and ends with O3713, which is titled "House of Queen Marie-Thérèse". Cyprien smiles as he scans the numerous subheadings in this series.

"It looks like luck has rewarded us."

"Yeeeesss!" Jules exclaims quietly, raising his arms in a V-shape.

Cyprien dictates the subtitles and the quotes. Jules takes note. They put the register away and go up to the reading room on the same floor. They are given seat numbers and sent to the order room. It is a small glassed-in booth held by a skinny and baffling woman who plays the psychologist.

She hesitantly enters the data, then declares the documents out.

"Out!" Cyprien exclaims.

"Yes, out, gentlemen!"

He turns to his friend.

"Julio, someone has preceded us. We are now going to have a competitor."

"If it's not a teammate, it must be an enemy. I hope luck will allow us to meet."

"What is your interest in an old subject like this?" the woman asks.

"We are researchers, madam."

"Ah! I understand. You are writing a thesis. Why don't you carry out your research in libraries?"

"We know what we want. Boxes 281 to 283: 'Genealogical documents'. The subtitles are about princes of the blood, legitimated children, natural children, and other family affairs."

Leaning forward, she says, "The royal family! You are researching the King's descendants!"

"We don't cover the whole field," Cyprien explains. "We are only interested in the third child, Louise-Marie, born on November 26, 1664. The document we want to consult talks about her, we are pretty sure."

She shudders.

"You have balls, young people! Sorry! My apology for using such a word ..." With her hand, she scrapes her face out of shame, before continuing. "You know, this is a very sensitive subject. You don't touch this matter as if you were playing chess. There are currently a lot of people who claim to be heirs to the throne of France in case of a possible return to monarchy. I don't know if you will find much here. I would recommend you go to the Central Registry of Paris Notaries. There, they will provide you with the birth certificates of all the children of the King. If I am not mistaken, such documents must be in the ARNO database. There are only two of them, ARNO and MIRIAD. Do you know the address of the Registry? 60 Francs-Bourgeois Street. Go there quickly before they close."

"We would like to consult the document we gave you the number for, madam."

"In that case, wait for it to return to shelf. If you're lucky, it will not be extended by the reader at the end of the day."

They exit the booth.

"I feel like she's taking us for a ride," Jules says.

"Me, I don't feel like riding with her! It will not work with me."

They use the stairs again and go down to the checkroom from where they collect their belongings and hit the street.

At the reception desk of the Central Registry of Paris Notaries, things take on the appearance of a Court hearing. Finally, a supervisor comes out to explain that a good part of the documents has been stolen or destroyed.

What they were able to save, he adds, was sent to CARAN, which is the sole owner of paper documents. Well, he just managed to escape unscathed! Everywhere in France, when someone wants to prevent you from accessing an ancient treasure, they invariably declare it was destroyed during the Revolution.

The two friends return to CARAN the next day. A man is serving in the ordering room. They hand him their reference.

"Hello, sir, has this document been returned yet?"

He grabs the reference.

"You can't talk about returning," he says. "It never went out."

"Sorry?"

"You guys are asking for a box. There is a different procedure for ordering boxes than for registers and microfilms. Fill out this *Request to consult a box* and drop it at the manager's office. I do not guarantee a favourable outcome."

Cyprien fills out the form and hands it to the man.

"How long before we get an answer?"

He doesn't say a word.

"Tomorrow?" Jules asks.

"Yes, tomorrow, tomorrow! Let's hope so!" he says.

The next afternoon, three young people arrive at CARAN. Yasmina, nineteen years old, is Jules' girlfriend. She asked to come with them. She is a student like her boyfriend, an active member of an association dedicated to child protection. When Jules told her about the Louise-Marie case, it did not leave her insensitive. Without thinking twice, she promised her help to get the truth out.

Tonight, the three friends did not come with the candour of choirboys. They have hatched a scheme to take the documents by force if the management refused to make them available. As none of them carries a backpack, they passed without suspicion the security check conducted by the security guard. The poor guy doesn't know what the three young people are hiding in their pockets. Yasmina takes a one-day pass. She is determined not to return later for the same cause. They climb to the second floor and appear in front of the distribution counter where three or four agents serve the ordered documents on an ongoing basis. They are assigned reading room numbers. They kindly thank the agents.

Cyprien hands his card, but instead of receiving the box, he is served an unfavourable notice signed by the manager. "Dear reader, the document you have requested cannot be authorized for consultation, as it is subject to a one-hundred-year restriction that will run until November 25 inclusive. However, the Center reserves the right to lift the restriction or to extend its validity at the end of the mentioned period. Yours sincerely."

After this more-than-clear wording, the student finds he has no questions to ask. He pretends he has surrendered to the distribution agents, who move on to the next user.

Cyprien turns to his co-conspirators and asks: "Where will you go on vacation next Christmas?"

It's a code, a password, according to their plan.

"To Poitiers, perhaps," Yasmina answers.

This answer means that they are ready to proceed to attack.

Quickly, they break apart, each one to a preassigned place. They are reading their own newspapers. Christmas is the time for firecrackers and fireworks. They are not reading for real, but they are rather working on shaking up the calendar. Their Christmas is coming in a moment.

When the clock strikes, Cyprien makes a sign. Yasmina gets up and goes to the bathroom in the lobby. Jules lights up two firecrackers and throws them under the chairs. His friend does the same. A chain of deafening explosions shakes the building. Readers flinch. What a panic!

"Bombs! Bombs! Help!" the people shout. A huge plume of fireworks rises and licks the glass roof. The effect gives the feeling that it is a gigantic fire worthy of the Last Day. Amidst cries of extreme distress, people shove tables and scramble away without taking anything. On the first floor, a female finger presses a big red button on the wall. The fire alarm goes off. The CARAN is now a vast field of pyrotechnic experimentation where the artificial and the natural become one. People are running, trampling each other, some jumping over others, some riding others. Those who cannot run crawl. Those who cannot crawl roll on.

Cyprien has jumped over the distribution counter during this mess. He is in the shelving. He's quickly looking for the O-series, and there it is! The box is already in his hands. Is it the real thing? He quickly reviews the quote. Yes, this is the beast! Using the record keeper's stepladder, he shatters a window and leans out. Yasmina runs along the wall and grabs the cardboard box that comes down vertically. She dashes out the gate. Jules is already waiting for her on a humming motor scooter. They take off via Quatre-Fils Street, while Cyprien hastens to merge into the bewildered crowd.

7

MINUTES ARE TICKING away. The clock has accumulated hours, the calendar has accrued days, but there is nothing concrete on Laurent Fournier's desk. He groans when he thinks that he has less than two days to hand in his report. And yet, leads are getting tangled. Sometimes he thinks that the ministry has assigned him wimps instead of policemen. Then, after the storm has passed, he feels better when he acknowledges that his men had the misfortune to run into unforeseeable difficulties. Winter is tricky weather. At this time of year, everyone walks around gloved and hooded, much to the delight of escaped convicts and wanted individuals.

It is the first hour of the morning. On his pocket calendar, which serves as a day planner, he tears out a page overcrowded with notes and arrows. The one for November 23. It is this same gesture that he performs like a ritual each time he starts a new workday. He needs to have the day's page right under the cover, to avoid rummaging around to find it. He smooths out the page of the 24th with his hand and begins to note down the operations of the day in the order they are to be executed. This is where his methodical qualities come in handy. At the top of the list is a raid on Bartoli's home, a decisive raid. He decided to take part in this visit, because he has high expectations of Mr. Bartoli's son, Jules. He will then let Lieutenant Toulon lead the rest of the operations. The day before, they learned new information from several people associated with Cyprien Ghezo. From his telephone provider, they got the full list of his contacts. The host of his e-mail account also provided all the information requested. It is bitter to know that one can be exposed in this way. We often feel that we are shielded behind these numbers, these codes and these screens that seem to offer some privacy. It is nothing of the kind! These tools are only hands that draw our deepest secrets and spread them far into the world of the unknown. To our friends, to our opponents, to our worst enemies.

The cops arrive. Bartoli Sr. is on the couch, with the day's newspaper held in front. He usually starts reading the last page, to get the latest stock market news as quickly as possible. It has been a long time since he had a cop at home. So, he has lost good habits. He no longer knows whether they are served spiced tea or extra strong coffee. The cleaning lady has left, and Bartoli Sr. is in charge of welcoming the strange visitors.

"What can I do for you, Officers? Are you sure you are at the right address?"

"Absolutely," the Commissioner replies.

"Take a seat, please."

"No, thank you, sir. That's nice of you. We won't be long."

The father looks at them, one after another, as if to indicate that he is fully available.

"I'm all yours," he says.

"No, Mr. Bartoli, don't bother. We've come for Jules."

"Jules! What did he do that was so serious?"

Mr. Bartoli's eyes widen. Jules, aware of the situation, screams from his room.

"Dad! Dad! Let me handle this. I know they've got the wrong target."

"We are well informed," the Commissioner says with a perverse smile. "Is this your picture, young man?" He shows him a half-card.

"Yes, this guy looks like me. So what?"

"Where were you on Monday, November 22, between three and five pm?"

"I don't remember. I've been doing so much lately!"

"Think carefully."

"I don't want to waste your time thinking. You see, at school, I never do without cheat sheets. I have a very poor memory. Ask me some other questions."

"When was the last time you saw your friend Cyprien Ghezo?"

"It was Monday, or Tuesday, I think so ..."

"Where was it?"

"Oh, somewhere over there, in the Third District."

"Where exactly?"

"At the Archive Center."

"All right, we're getting there! Were you present during the incident?"

"Yes, yes, that ... I have never been so terrified like I was that night. Bombs everywhere! Windows shattering! A giant fire!"

He claps his hands to express astonishment.

"Then, what happened?"

"There was no aftermath! We ran away like everyone else. Then Cyprien took his flight the next day to Cotonou."

"Has he contacted you since he left? By phone, email, or text?"

"None of the above! It will cost him an arm and a leg if he calls France. As for email, yuck! I heard that the Internet there doesn't flow. Its speed must be less than one mega. To open a window, you have to wait five to ten minutes after clicking. Put yourself in his shoes! Besides, I don't know what he will be doing in the city. There he lives in a seventeenth-century donjon. Didn't the General Intelligence tell you that he's a son of a king?"

"Okay, that's all."

"Thank you, Commissioner. Don't hesitate to come back if you think it's necessary."

The Commissioner turns taking a step away, then stops and turns back to Jules.

"Another thing: what did you have in your hands when you left the Archive Center?"

"Nothing!"

"Nothing, you say?"

"I swear it's true!"

"And your friend, maybe he had something?"

"Something like what, Commissioner?"

"Like a cardboard box, or a document of some kind that he forgot to put down before escaping like everyone else."

"There you go! You mean he stole documents, don't you?"

"Not at all, young man, we just want to know."

"Yes, you suspect him! Admit it, Commissioner! I remind you that Cyprien would never take anything that doesn't belong to him. He is as gentle as a lamb. But when he is falsely accused, he becomes a tiger. When he returns, leave him alone."

"You seem to know him very well!"

"Yes, I do. I make no secret of it. My buddy is a tattooed guy. If you want to force him to confess things, he won't fit the mold. I advise you not to provoke such a confrontation."

Mr. Bartoli is staring at them without saying anything.

"Have you ever seen him dealing with a false accusation?"

"Yes! One day, I went to the construction site where he was doing a job. It was at break time. A visually impaired man was walking through the protected area, feeling the sidewalk with his white stick. As he ran straight into a pole, Cyprien shouted: 'Sir, obstruction! To the right! To the right!' The man understood that the obstacle was on the right, so he went left instead. There afterward, he was picked up from wire rolls, fortunately not barbed ones. Some boys in the neighbourhood who had sympathy for the man attacked Cyprien, accusing him of having misdirected the victim. He responded fiercely, and one after another in the fight that followed, he put their backs to the ground."

"How many were they?"

"Four ... just like you guys."

"That's a pretty great story for someone with a short memory," Toulon comments.

"But are you saying I'm lying to you, Lieutenant? I swear it's true!"

"We would have liked to hear you give a more detailed account of the CARAN incident."

"I have nothing to add to my statement. Why are you going after us? Just check the recording from the surveillance cameras in the building."

The commissioner receives this backlash like a stab in the heart. Talking about cameras! It was only after the incidents that they discovered that the cameras were transmitting images to the monitors without recording them. The whole system was reduced to a set of mirrors that let images scroll by. And for how many years? No one would ever know. Ah, these public buildings!

The team feels a little disgusted by this failure.

"Thank you for your cooperation, young man. Thank you for having us, Mr. Bartoli."

The slap is taken. They leave.

Mr. Bartoli discovers his son. Since the latter came of age, the father has never had the opportunity to see him in a delicate situation.

"You fought well, Jules," he remarks. "But what are you meddling with?"

"I swear to you, Dad, that I'm lying!"

"Just an instant ago you swore to tell the truth!"

"You're not a cop, Dad. You forgot that a cop is served black pepper instead of coffee!"

"You didn't tell me that you witnessed the drama of the Archives Center, come on!"

"Ah, I can't tell you everything, Dad! I am twenty-one. You see that I am old enough to manage my own life."

"And my car, when you borrow it without telling me, what do you think of your concept of autonomy? You should buy a car of your own, rent your apartment. Being of age also means doing that!"

"Ah! Dad! You can't blame me for that. When I drive your car, I play the big man. I think I'm big, and that's what counts today. Thinking I'm great feels really good. That feeling is what keeps me going. Many young people are just like me. You can't understand the problems of our generation. We are a sacrificed youth. To be able to live, we need to be in high spirits."

"You, to play the big man, you drive at the speed of light, you get flashed everywhere and you park anywhere."

"Dad, can't you see that your 6-door sedan is too long to easily fit in Paris parking lots? It is time for you to start liking short cars."

"But, in the meantime, I'm the one who pays for your violation tickets."

"Dad, if you're unhappy with me driving your car, I'll settle for my scooter. I'll leave your junk to rust in peace in the garage."

"Don't talk to me like that, Jules!"

"Because you're pissing me off with your car! That's it!"

"Let's turn the page on the vehicle. Answer me clearly. Did your friend take these documents?"

Jules says nothing. He has his head down and is rubbing his forehead with his right hand. His father is also keeping an apparent calm, but in his heart, he is talking a lot. To himself. *Everyone is after something*, he is thinking. *Life is a goal that flees before man. A child imagines himself great. A teenager projects himself into an adult that he thinks he is. And this adult, when he realizes that he is ready to hug his future, he grows afraid of the dead end and turns back to his past to embrace again the joys of his childhood. That's what being human is all about.*

Mr. Bartoli repeats his question after a moment.

"He's innocent, Dad! This whole story is rooted in racism. They're looking for a reason to stop him from continuing his research on an engraving he discovered in the royal palace of Versailles."

"An engraving! An engraving that has waited for so many centuries without an eye passing over it? Has your friend switched to archeology?"

"No, he's still in *mol bio*."

"Where do you get this saucy story from, son?"

"It's the truth, Dad. He has the pictures. The engraving depicts a State crime committed under the Old Regime and covered up century after century until the Fifth Republic."

The father puts a hand to his chin and looks at his son. He looks at him with the attention one lends to an archaeologist who has returned from an excavation and is about to unpack his finds.

The doorbell rings.

"They are back, for sure!" the father whispers. "You will tell me the rest later."

Jules opens the door.

"It's Yasmina, Dad!"

He kisses her briefly, their kiss sealing a pact as he whispers in his girlfriend's ear:

"We don't say anything about the cardboard box. Nothing!"

8

GHEZO APPLIES HIMSELF to his new life, which he never imagined for himself. His visit to the mall this morning was fast, fleeting! He came back with a few groceries to provide for his keep while conducting his clandestine quest.

At the foot of the bed lies the box. He has gone through all the files it contains, one by one, until late at night. As he now feels fatigue destroying his body, he manages not to fall asleep. He is simply sitting on a footstool, with his hand under his chin. In his mind, imprecise forms appear. Boots trample children, girls are being raped, prisoners are getting thrown to beasts, blindfolded hostages stand facing the wall, hanged men swing from the gallows, boats move across the Sahara Desert toward a war objective, bombs go off uprooting hope ... He dozes off, jumps back to reality from time to time.

The box looks at him, insensitive, unable to say what he wants to hear. It is funny to want to converse with an inert thing. All the documents have already delivered their message. But knowing where Louise-Marie had been taken remains the major enigma. Was the wet paper her birth certificate, or her death certificate, or something else related to her story? It is impossible to know! Posterity has lost this information, unless it is engraved somewhere in some other dungeon.

A crazy idea crosses his mind: To go back to CARAN and check other documents. But he is crazy, this guy! He would throw his head into Fournier's mouth. There's a police saying: a criminal always returns to the scene of his crime. It's very true! And if you doubt it, ask yourself why the tongue always goes back over the tooth that hurts.

Cyprien pours himself a coffee while waiting for Jules to arrive. They are going to take stock. He finished reading the documents late last night. The final file contained Louis XIV's will. The King wrote this huge one-hundred-and-eighty-nine-page volume several years before his death. Throughout the pages, one has the pleasure of admiring the author's methodical mind, as well as his sense of foresight. He has a very noble idea of politics, and undoubtedly, a patriotism that very few French statesmen have been able to equal until this day. He also speaks about the Great Dauphin, his heir. He pictures him as a species preselected by nature for a great mission. His preparation for succession takes the highest place in the King's mind. For this reason, he has never closed his eyes to the young prince's shortcomings. From the dawn of his life, the little scion is initiated into the art of power and authority. To this boy rather inclined towards laziness and superficiality, the King is determined to instill sublime qualities. His tutor, Bossuet, had a hard time choosing between the rigour that the education of a future king requires and the small concessions that can be granted to a son who has become an only child, having lost five siblings.

The one who did not know the earthly paradise was Louise-Marie, very much an innocent victim of social considerations. Her whole existence is summed up in two adjectives: condemned and dispatched.

What happens to children who are dispatched without love, without an identity card, without a recognition badge on their chest, without a bell around their neck to signal their position? Do they become animals without hair or tail, or quadrupedal humans? In which species of beings should they be classified?

Finally, he hears steps in the hallway. Then, the sound of the doorbell. It is Jules. He has his own way of ringing different from that of unwanted visitors. As soon as Cyprien opens the door, the sight of Jules' helmet reassures him. Instead of greeting each other like troopers, Jules offers him a limp hand.

"Is that you, dear friend Cyprien?"

"It certainly is! Did someone say that I was arrested?"

"No, no one said that. I am only confused. I don't know where you really are anymore. By lying and making people accept that you have travelled, I end up believing you are in Benin."

"I encourage you to keep going that way."

"You don't know how much such a game can destroy one's bearings. I understand now that our brain is a blank medium on which anything can be imprinted. Cult gurus, shrinks and other mind manipulators know it very well and take advantage of it at their own sweet will."

Cyprien stares at him, surprised at his behaviour. He suspects something has happened.

"If you've understood the phenomenon of mind control, I think you'll find it easier to get your brain to accept statistics."

Jules laughs. The two greet each other again, this time like troopers. Cyprien is eager to know what happened. Jules sees the questioning in his friend's wide eyes that are shooting at him.

"Do you know the best one?" Jules says. "They came home this morning."

"No kidding!"

"Yes, they did."

"I knew it!"

"I told them everything I could, and it seems to have worked."

"I know that, with you, I have little to worry about."

"Have you found another avenue of research?"

"I'm going to the National Library. Right away. I still need your help, dear friend. If all goes well, we'll come up with something new."

"You can count on me. As long as your search continues, I'll be by your side. But ... the cops ..."

"Don't worry about the cops. Can they stop the river from flowing? You've been great. They're more confused than ever. You were successful in covering up the tracks."

"The plan worked. The day before yesterday, they thought you were in Benin; yesterday they believed you were in France; today, they don't know where you are. It is Jean-le-Mec who should be congratulated. You see, it's all thanks to him. What a brain! What a success!"

"It's thanks to all of you. Yasmina worked a lot too."

"Yes, but none of us could find you a hell of a hiding place like this. It all happened when Jean was going on vacation. Oh! I wish I were him! I imagine him constantly immersed in sunbathing."

Jules gets up and goes to the window. He pushes aside the hanging curtain with one hand. The glass has a film of condensation that prevents him from seeing through it. With his finger, he wipes off part of the condensation and looks through the clear portion of the glass. Outside, fluttering snowflakes fall obliquely. Winds frantically toss branches about.

"The weather is hellish," he says. "I don't like riding my bike in the wind."

"You just have to park the bike; we'll get around another way."

Jules leaves the window and goes to the coffee pot where he pours himself a coffee.

Jean-le-Mec is the nickname of one of Cyprien's acquaintances. He is a very special man. He has no telephone, no computer, no bank account in his name. He is a little rich guy well established in the so-called underground economy. No one knows him, except Ghezo, whom Jean considers to be akin to a younger brother. He has set out to Benin and travels under the innocent title of a doctoral student in molecular biology, while Ghezo, the real student, occupies his apartment in Saint Ouen, a northern suburb of Paris. It is a sacrosanct room located in a basement, isolated from any communication network. Two men, two lives. Ghezo believes in virtue, in the strength of knowledge, in the capacity of man to dominate perverse instincts. Jean-le-Mec lives on small and large smugglings which bring in immediate profits. He is a privileged customer of the capital's upscale restaurants. He loves the company of beautiful women whom he always brings to hotels and forgets about them immediately after the flirtation. The cabaret dancers of the Champs Élysée are the ones who gave him his nickname, Jean-le-Mec. He never pays by cheque, only in cash. For him, the future is not sought in a chimerical projection of a time that one is not sure to live. He likes to say that the future is given to one in the palm of the hand, in front of the eyes. Ready to be taken. Jean and Ghezo do not often speak French when they meet. They express themselves in their mother tongue, Fon, uncontaminated by colonization. The majority of Beninese use this language, which they see as an element of pride and a symbol of resistance to the occupier. Abroad, it is the unifying link between the sons of the motherland whose destinies happened to have met. This is fraternity. The real one! The one that is not carved to decorate the coat of arms of a state, but the one that is lived every day in its raw status. It is only abroad that the word brother takes on its full meaning and is worth its weight in gold.

Although the student knows the month-end anguish, he has always resisted changing his behaviour. Yet, he had been courted when he lost his penultimate job. That was when he was working at a cleaning company as an industrial spy. After eight months of fruitless waiting, the boss, impatient, called him one day and spoke to him very harshly.

"Mr. Ghezo," he said. "When I recruited you, I thought that your education level would make things easier. But I realize that nothing is moving forward. Are you a noob in this city's affairs?"

"You can count on me, sir. With a little luck, I'll get there."

"I'm not asking you to tell me about luck. Empires are not built through luck. It's the fruit of hard work and wisdom. Hey! I mean pugnacity!"

His first task was to rummage through the trash cans of his target customers, looking for bits of information about their products. This method did not work, because the paper shredder was increasingly being used in offices to destroy discarded sensitive documents.

Other times, other customs. The boss switched to a more modern and more refined method. He gave his employee a booby-trapped storage disk that they simply needed to insert into computer drives. He explained to the young man how to use it.

"You're a great PhD student, and our clients understand that you got a cleaning job to earn some funding for your studies. You are far from being considered a stooge. You have value. Go ahead and say this to a secretary, or to a boss himself: 'Sir, could you print me a little document from your printer? I have mine at home that's giving me a hard time.' No one will dismiss you. You know that people are very happy to do small favors that demean the recipient. A secretary who is far inferior to you, will gladly do you this favor to show you that you are not superior. Nonetheless, while she is printing your little doc, magic will happen. This disk contains spyware that will automatically get installed onto her hard drive. Call it a virus if you like. Then you'll be done playing your part. Next, the spyware will allow us to enter the computer's system via the Internet to get information that we can sell to their competitors."

"It's so easy, sir!" the young man said on the spot.

But months went by and Ghezo didn't have any success in trapping a secretary. Everywhere he went, he was told by secretaries that he couldn't be granted the favour of having anything printed, for fear of dangerous viruses such as Trojan Horse, Serwab and other raptors that are raging through computer systems. The manager got so fed up with Ghezo's failure that he threw him out.

"But I'm excellent in cleaning tasks!" he said. "Customers are proud of me. You could keep me for that."

"I'm sorry! I didn't hire you to scrub shitters. You're fired!"

By telling his misadventure to Jean-le-Mec, the latter threw him a golden line. In reality, it is necessary to say powdered line, because the whole business was all about cocaine. His benefactor wanted to initiate him into the traffic networks right away. With tons of arguments, he demonstrated to Ghezo the virtues of the path he recommended.

"You don't need to do crazy studies to get by in our current society. What is the use of being a scholar who is struggling? Leaders are dirty liars. There are no more jobs for graduates. I must admit that I am unable to say how many years the Hundred Years' War lasted. But what do I care?! I'm making money anyway. What use is it to you to know how to calculate the age of the Earth if you can't even afford a short vacation in your own country? Among those bums who live on the streets and pick up discarded cigarette butts on the sidewalks are graduates. Think about what I am proposing to you, because you are at a crossroads. A bad choice will make you regret your whole life. Do you want to be like those other young people who are starving in the suburbs with a bunch of degrees in the closet? Do you? In the end, they earn their living by becoming shit collectors in old people's homes. The luckiest ones work as mail carriers in consulates. You always see them grumpy, always ready to go at someone's jaw, because they know they deserve better. If you agree, I'll get a schedule set up for you and you will come to see how things work out. Don't be a nerd, buddy!"

From argument to argument, he tried to enroll Ghezo. The latter thought about the offer, like any reasonable person would. The temptation was strong, very strong. For weeks, he underwent a struggle with the tyranny of the two masters: need and conscience. He fought against himself, until he reached that glimmer of light hidden in the depths of his being and which the most total carnal corruption cannot overcome. Relying on this spark that contains the inextinguishable flame of conscience, he fanned it, nourished it, and it enlightened him in the decision that he then took, as his conscience prevailed. He would not sell drugs. No! Nonetheless, coping with the tyranny proved to be no small challenge.

After several difficult months, Cyprien was hired by a building renovation company. He was assigned to the Versailles construction site, where he found Pandora's box. This came after he had sifted and re-sifted through the garbage for a long time in vain. Now, it is the dawn of a new day.

9

THEY GET OFF a bus and step onto the sidewalk on Richelieu Street. The snow has melted, leaving the road soaked. A steady hissing occurs under the wheels of cars speeding by, only to huddle in a line as the red light brings them to a stop. On an aged building, a tricolor flag flies in the breeze. Suddenly, a large portico appears on the left wall. It is the National Library. The guards search the two men at the entrance. Nothing to report. They cross the courtyard and push open the first glass panels. The air becomes warm in this intermediate space. As they push open the second panels, a pleasant warmth envelopes them. Just across from the entrance is the reception desk. To the left, a staircase entirely covered with red carpet stretches out. It is framed by two rows of golden railings. A man and a woman welcome the visitors.

"What can I do for you?" the woman asks.

"We are here to do some research," Jules says.

"Is this your first visit to the National Library?"

"Yes," they answer in unison.

"You must first speak to a librarian who will make a decision on admitting you."

"This is not a private foundation, as far as we know!" Cyprien says, feeling insulted. "Is it possible that we are denied access to a public library, ma'am?"

"It depends on who you are and what you want. The librarians will evaluate your case. If you agree to meet them, go down that hallway to the right, open the glass door and speak to one of them."

They obey without further questioning. Opening the glass door, they enter a narrow hallway with a scattering of offices on either side. In each of them, a huge computer occupies a quarter of the space. As they walk along the hallway, they notice no one in any of the offices. Unexpectedly, a man opens one of the doors and signals to them. They join him. The man sets them up, walks around the table and sits down in his deep chair. He almost disappears behind his huge screen, explaining why they couldn't see anyone as they walked.

"Yes, gentlemen, what can I do for you?"

"We need to access the archives of the Old Regime," Cyprien says.

"Do you know what the conditions are?"

"No, we do not."

"To access our reading rooms, you must be either a researcher, an instructor or a journalist, and you must show proof of your title with a professional ID. Are you from one of the three professions?"

"Yes, sir, I am a researcher. A doctoral student in history."

"And you?" he asks Jules.

"Same as my buddy!" Jules replies.

"Good! The first condition is met. The second is about your research topic. I hope you know that this library is an institution of last resort. It is not an ordinary library where you search the catalogue and help yourself on the shelves. Only those who could not get satisfaction elsewhere come here. Since nineteen ninety-six, this Richelieu site has been broken up to supply other ultra-modernized free access libraries. As a result, the remaining documents that make up our inventory are unique. We only allow access to them when they can't be found in any of the other libraries in France. I believe you understand the rules of the game!"

They nod.

"Good! Give me the references: name of the author?"

"I don't remember," Cyprien says.

"Title of the book?"

"Euhhhh ... *genealogies of the XVIII century.* I'm not sure of its accuracy. It's a title that an instructor whispered to us in class, and I've been dragging it around in my mind like this since last year."

The librarian nods as he types on his keyboard. Cyprien's eyes sparkle with surprise. Is the lottery won, perhaps?

"Excellent!" The librarian says. "The document is obviously with us. It is a large set of more than ten books. We are the only ones to have it. I can assure you that you knocked at the right door."

He smiles to congratulate the researcher. The two friends smile too. But Cyprien is very much afraid of disappointing him later. He knows that the worst is yet to come. The famous identification!

"Well," the librarian says, "I need your student IDs to register you, then I'll send you over to my colleague across the street, who will take your picture and issue your reader's card."

"Uh, sir ..." Cyprien says. "We're sorry, we didn't think to bring the student IDs."

"That's okay. Just show me any other official document with your picture on it."

Jules makes a veiled appeal to Cyprien. They don't have to show anything. If they have already been so bold as to set foot in this institution, they will not go so far as to hand in their identities to the interconnected networks of libraries, banks, and telephone services, all of which are under the State's watchful eye.

"You have nothing, young people?" the man asks.

"We're sorry," Cyprien says. "We left our IDs as collateral at a disk rental store. We won't get them until tonight when we return the rented products. Please, sir, do us the favour."

"I can't do that. I'm so sorry for you, but the computers are not merciful at all. Without prior registration, no researcher can access our departments. What is your name?

"Stanislas," Cyprien replies.

"What's yours?"

"I'm Berenger," Jules says.

They give unusual first names to make the librarian uninterested. But instead, they see their interlocutor's eyes widen.

"What a coincidence!" he exclaims. "My first son is named Stanislas. He often gets into situations like yours. So many times, he must bow and scrape to get what he deserves. Tell me today. What is wrong with the Stanislas?"

"Fate made us like this," Cyprien says.

"And you, Berenger, you must be a good boy. Honest and generous, but also rigorous, like the man who is talking to you. Berenger is my first name too. We are like homonyms."

He holds his hand out and gives him a shake.

"Nice to meet you, sir!" Jules says.

He also shakes hands with Cyprien, calling him "son".

"Let me see if I can help you in any other way," he says. "What name are you looking for in this huge 18th century genealogy?"

"We are looking for Louise-Marie of Bourbon."

The man's eyes widen again.

"It looks like a new sesame! Someone asked me the same name this morning at the opening. Who is this Louise-Marie?"

"She is the third legitimate daughter of Louis XIV."

"Why is she so interesting for research this Wednesday?"

"Each researcher has their own motivations."

"What did she have in particular?"

"Oh, what do I know!" Cyprien replies. "She disappeared shortly after her birth at the Court of Versailles. We are looking for her tomb."

"Does this story have anything to do with the man named Nabo?"

The two young men are struck dumb.

"Do you know him too?" Cyprien asks.

"No, the researcher this morning told me about him. I never heard that name until he told me. Nabo, the lover of Queen Marie-Thérèse of Austria, he said. The Queen cheated on her King with her slave who, to make things worse, was a Black."

"All the slaves at the Court were black at the time."

"What does it matter, my son! Six Blacks or half a dozen of slaves make no difference!"

What an old pig! Cyprien thinks. *This pun is his parody of the idiom 'Six of one and half a dozen of the other'. He doesn't know he's talking about my ancestors.*

"Two miserable social conditions combined in one person!" the librarian says. "Notwithstanding, he was the chosen one for our great Queen's thirsty heart. Love is what it is! I hope that you will not go out there and dump such an aberration on the shelves of our bookstores!"

"Of course not. Our research is not intended for publication."

"If not, why are you conducting this investigation?"

"Louise-Marie is my ancestress," Cyprien says.

"Did I hear correctly? Your ancestress, you say? And how could that be possible?"

"She is Nabo's daughter. Nabo was the King of Dahomey's son at the time. I am also descended from the King of Dahomey."

"Are you the son of a king?"

"Yes, Mr. Berenger! It was at the beginning of the 20th century that the Kingdom of Dahomey, having reached its peak under King Behanzin, succumbed to French imperialism."

"Was he the invincible monarch nicknamed Shark King?"

"You are on the right track."

"But this relationship with Louise-Marie does not make her your ancestress!"

"What do you want me to call her? Refer to our traditions."

"What a mess! It brings tears to one's eyes, son! May God one day give you back what the colonizers took away from you. May he guide your steps to Louise-Marie's grave." A brief moment of meditation settles in the room. Great moments impose particular attitudes.

No one is intelligent enough to decree them. Joy, sorrow, recollection, they fall on all consciences, when necessary, as rain falls on all roofs. During this minute of silence, a century of history plays before Cyprien's eyes: French barges sail the seas towards Dahomey. Soldiers engage in pillage, massacre, rape, and all sorts of bestial sins. The King of Dahomey bends but does not break. The invader reinforces his troops and wins a short victory. The Shark is stubborn, so, he refuses to sign treaties. French and Dahomeans fight at sea, on land and in forests. In aerial battle, above the ground, the Dahomeans are brave. Their totems turn into swarms of bees to dislodge enemy sentries from their towers, leaving the field open for surprise attacks. French soldiers at times see the water recede beneath their anchored ships, and then the Dahomean troops pour down onto them on dry land over the ocean bed. On the beach, the invaders have erected a colossal statue of their own leader, Emperor Napoleon. They go there every morning to give him military honours. They do the same every time they return from victorious expeditions, brandishing severed heads they have chopped, to Napoleon.

In front of the librarian, with his eyes closed, Cyprien hears the songs of those soldiers. They chant their anthem and stampede like bulls, lacerating the ground with their big and indestructible boots. On one of those days when they have razed many villages and captured their leaders, soldiers have gathered in euphoria at the foot of their concrete master. Then, while they are singing, hand on heart, in an unparalleled military devotion, a silent wind comes out of nowhere, pushes the concrete colossus, uproots it toppling it down over them with a big bang. This violent hug kills a good thirty soldiers. While fleeing towards the sea, a number of survivors are caught by a giant tidal wave which swallows them the way the Red Sea had swallowed Pharaoh's soldiers.

Dirty war! When the enemies had slaughtered many women and children, when they had burned half the houses, King Behanzin offered himself as a bargaining chip to save the rest of his people. So, he surrendered. This was no suicide, no! He had a plan. The French ship that was taking him as a prisoner to Martinique was to be attacked by a school of sharks. These sharks were conjured to sink the boat and rescue King Behanzin. Unfortunately, this plan did not work. A venal servant close to the King sold the secret for a piece of broken mirror and an empty bottle of West Indian rum, which the French had given him as a reward. Since crystal did not abound in Dahomey by then, he saw these trinkets as a precious treasure. The venal servant also received a hunting rifle and ammunition. At his instigation, the King's sacred ceramic pipe was replaced by a fake one. When the captive Monarch got on the open sea and started to smoke his pipe to call the sharks, nothing happened. No shark came to his rescue! Too late he understood that he had been betrayed. Eventually, the King found himself in Martinique, then in Algiers, where he lived thirteen years in captivity, without cursing the traitor, without cursing his people, before dying in 1906. Thus, he went down into the grave, with his body and all the glory of Dahomey that is present-day Benin.

Cyprien knows the story by heart. His grandmother never tired of telling it to him. She taught him that his country, unrecognizable today, was one of the most powerful kingdoms on Earth. When he told this barely lucid old woman that he was going to France to study, this announcement rekindled her intelligence. She asked the young man if he would return from this exile. Curious, Cyprien asked his grandmother for the reason of her concern about his return. The old woman without hesitation told him about Nabo. Nabo was a son of King Houegbadja who had lived in a very distant era, she told him. To make it clear to him, she deftly placed multiple knots on a rope and explained that each knot represented a century. She said that a white merchant had taken Nabo as a slave and had entrusted him to the French Court because of his talent as a public entertainer. He was snatched by the same people, namely the French, who came back three knots later to destroy Dahomey. Nabo had never returned and had left no trace.

Cyprien saw the old woman weep at all that decadence, after she had told him the story.

Now Cyprien has found traces of Nabo in France, and much more! The ancestor had descendants!

❧ Upon opening his eyes again, Cyprien seems troubled. His immersion in the past has made him aware of the immensity of his dream and how too weak he is to face it. How too weak he is to restore the pride of a humiliated people. Troubled too is Jules, this poor rich boy who, for two days, has successfully applied himself to understanding an existence and a heritage, in short, a whole world, that is different from his.

The librarian sighs.

Cyprien is the one who first breaks the silence.

"Did the visitor get any documents this morning?"

"I don't know. I signed him up as a researcher, and he went to the Western Manuscripts Department to fend for himself. I doubt very much that those genealogies speak of your ancestry. At the time they were compiled, the concept of blood purity was in vogue throughout the West. Any mixture of blood was considered impure and eliminated. What chance did a mixed race female had, to flourish in the royal court in those days?"

"Eliminated in the pages of history too?"

"Isn't history a human fact? It is the victors and not the wise who make history. Napoleon stated that history is a legend accepted by everyone. Listen, I would advise you to look elsewhere. On the François Mitterrand site for example. It is possible that the historians of the Renaissance or those of later times have talked about it. Don't expect anything from the reports of the Old Regime. Look for François Bluche's books. If this author says nothing about it, don't bother. He is the best specialist of the Great Century."

The telephone rings and interrupts him. He picks it up. At the end of the line, he hears a female voice. It is the Director who speaks, the chief curator. The librarian repeats the woman's words in a high-pitched intonation to show his surprise. Thus, one can hear him exclaiming: "... A student!" Then, "... wanted!" Then, "... network put under monitoring ..." The telegraphic message is complete. The two friends don't need to have the conversation explained to them. When the man hangs up, he tells them:

"I am sorry I cannot keep you any longer. I have an emergency to deal with. We have just received an order to record and monitor anyone who does research on the Great Century, especially on the royal family. This is indeed your case, if we understand each other correctly. I'll let you go, in virtue of the fact that you didn't register. But please leave now."

"You wanted to guide us to François Mitterrand Library."

"Yes, I told you to ..."

The phone rings again and cuts him off. It's the woman from earlier who has returned to the attack.

"I received the photo of the suspect as an attachment. I made several copies and I'll come down to give them to you in case of physical identification. You don't have to leave your desk. I'll be right down."

The librarian turns to them. "Young men, we have finished. The chief curator will be down in a moment. She's a little nosy. I don't want her to question you. I will carry your misfortune on my conscience if anything happens to you. Get out of here at once."

"And the François Mitterrand library? ... Please!"

"Ah! You keep coming back to the same things! I told you that you will go to the new Tolbiac business park. If you catch the subway line 14, get off at François Mitterrand Library station. It is a terminus. Emerge and turn right, then left at the first traffic light. Now you got it all!"

They are standing and paying attention to the movements under the hall through the glass door. Cyprien has noted the directions. On the second floor, a door slams. They step out, walking down the long hallway toward the exit.

"Come back!" the librarian shouts.

They come back quickly and stand at the door.

"Sir?" Cyprien asks.

"Wherever you go, avoid touching the digital catalogues. This is valuable advice. Go now, clear out and good luck!"

They turn around and go back into the hallway. At the reception floor, they see a woman at the top of the red-lined stairs. Their eyes meet as she sets foot onto the second step. She stops dead and glances at the papers in her hand, somewhat puzzled. The two friends push open the glass doors, cross the snowy courtyard, pass under the portico and get lost in Richelieu Street.

"Someone has overtaken us," Cyprien says.

"Who could it be, this famous researcher?"

"It looks like the treasure hunt is on."

"I love treasure hunts," Jules says. "I don't know what I'm going to do when you find your ancestress' tomb. I love everything we look for and don't find."

"Stop saying nonsense, Jules! We must find it now. The vise is closing in on us dangerously."

10

IT IS THE end of the lull. Balls of cotton start to fall from the sky again. Soon, Paris is wrapped in its white shroud. Dead! Its inhabitants, all dressed in black, execute their funeral march along the sidewalks. The roofs are bristling with chimneys that spit out their smoke to combat the greyness.

Alongside a street, a police car is parked. Toulon's men are the ones who parked it. They enter a convenience store to try their luck at games of chance. They have the damn habit of consulting the horoscope delivered in the pages of many daily newspapers. The astrologers have agreed this morning to give them each a precious gift. "Lucky day! What a lucky day! Today you will find what you have been seeking for a long time. You may win big at the games! Try your luck today." And there they are, all of them, playing Lotto, playing Keno. The most ambitious bet on the Euro Million and don't stop at two or three tickets. They go far beyond. The stars have spoken! Even the one in the group who was chosen to drive and who usually remains tied to his seat behind the wheel, ready to take off at the slightest signal, has joined in. He cannot resist the call of the stars. Entrusting his wager to a colleague with the numbers to be ticked off often ends very badly. The middleman will shamelessly grab the prize, claiming that he filled in the grid, and will simply want to refund the stake. These are confusing situations that often end in head-butts. Many people share Zidane's talent, you know! The driver doesn't want to give or receive blows. He has joined his companions in order to have his ticket validated in person. All of them respectfully line up, according to their order of arrival.

Once the grids are filled out and validated, they contemplate their receipts as they leave. They all have plans in mind.

"If I win this jackpot, I'll take my wife on a vacation to the Hawaiian Islands."

"I like to call them the 'Sandwich Islands' as they were originally called."

"You can feel Conrad's stomach drop."

Everyone laughs.

"If I win, I'll retire early," the oldest says.

"I'll find the money to pay for my divorce. She makes my life hellish every day."

They arrive at their car.

The driver is disgusted by something he sees. "Look at that, guys! Do you see how people treat us?"

"What is it?"

"A banana peel on the roof."

"If he doesn't like the police, that pain in the ass can go fuck himself."

"Fuck him!"

He takes the garbage and throws it in a nearby trash can, then they open the doors.

"We've had it up to our asses!" another says. "Look! He also left us a tag on my door."

"That's something we can't let the bosses know about. We're going to erase that shit by all means."

"What if the culprit isn't a pain in the ass?"

"What else can the son of a bitch be?"

"It all sounds like a code."

"A code! A code of what?"

"Doesn't that tell you something about the idiom 'To throw a banana peel under somebody's feet'?"

"Oh, yeah, they want us to slip, don't they? You mean they're planning another fucking riot?"

"Exactly! What about the tag? What do we do about it, guys?"

"We'll deal with that shit later! Let's just go!"

A mile away, Cyprien and Jules head for an ATM. Being penniless does not give them any security in their situation. Jules pulls out his bank card and inserts it into the slot. He dials his code and orders bills. The machine displays: "Please wait while we process your transaction." The operation takes an abnormal length of time. One can hear it suffering from inside like a mill grinding stones. Then comes the message: "Do you want a receipt?" He presses NO, to limit the waiting time. The mill continues to grind, but the trap door does not open to deliver the bills. He bangs on the wall. The next display tells him: "Sorry, we cannot process your operation." Just then, the message: "Get your card back" begins to flash. He presses the eject button. The card does not come out. He presses the button several times in rapid strokes. Nothing happens. He hits the wall again in complaint.

Cyprien is the first one to understand what's happening, when he sees the final message displayed in red: "Card held, please contact your bank."

"Let's get out of here quickly," he says.

"You're joking!" Jules replies. "I'm going to the front desk right now to claim my card. Without it, I'm completely broke. What can you do in this city without money?"

He moves on, ready to push the revolving door. Cyprien holds him back.

"Your card was taken to invite us to wait here. Don't you understand the game?"

"Do they need to be on the lookout everywhere to get me? If they need to confront me again, they know where I live. Fournier paid me a visit this morning."

"Things have changed, Jules. They now know you're coming with me. Do you want me to explain more? Look at this!"

Cyprien points to a small camera the size of a fisheye embedded in the top of the automaton.

"It's a snitch's eye," Jules says.

Immediately, they cross the road without worrying about the colour of the light. Vehicles brake suddenly and skid on the slippery road. A few meters away, they plunge into a subway mouth and get lost in the guts of the warm ground.

A group of policemen arrive at the bank, guided by Lieutenant Toulon in permanent communication with the branch manager. The customer did not come to claim his card. No matter! They know at least that the fugitive and his friend are in the zone. From this knowledge of their well woven complicity, both of them constitute one and the same person, in the eyes of the law. Now, Jules is also a target.

They are under the ground.

Jules looks up at the vaulted ceiling and shakes his head.

"I feel that big eyes are watching us," he says.

Cyprien in turn scans across the ceiling above the platform. There are cameras everywhere! They are no longer fisheyes, but big remote-controlled pivoting machines that are able to twist and readjust their angle of view over a 360° amplitude.

"They will catch us here like two little moles in their burrows. Let's clear out!"

At this very moment, the subway arrives. They mingle with the crowd of people getting off and return to the street by another exit. Assuming that they would take the subway, Toulon has got all the stations of the line on the alert. From terminal to terminal, the exits are being discreetly screened by cameras.

Cyprien hails the first cab that passes without a customer.

"Where are you going, gentlemen?"

"Uh ... Just drive away, go straight ahead!" Jules says.

They don't even know where they are going. They are more interested in leaving one place quickly. As the cab drives away, they pass several motorized police patrols that have occupied the zone like flies attracted by a putrid smell.

11

"I DON'T THINK the results are very good, Lieutenant," Laurent Fournier says.

"We are fighting, Commissioner," Toulon replies. "We have done everything possible to reach the goal. But so far, luck has not smiled on us."

"Here you are, coming here to talk to me about luck. I expect you to be more aggressive on the field than you are. Come up with new methods, come up with new leads."

The Lieutenant nods.

"Do you know what time it is, Lieutenant?"

"Quarter to eleven."

"I'm not asking you to tell me that it's quarter to eleven. I'm asking you to see that time is moving forward while we're stalling. We have only one and a half days left to prove ourselves. The Quai d'Orsay keeps calling me to find out where we are. I have huge difficulty in answering each time that no lead has yet proven conclusive. At least, we have been lucky in that some leads have eliminated themselves. Our embassy, which coordinates operations in Cotonou, has dropped the search. Cyprien Ghezo never left France. But knowing who travelled under his name is not a priority for the moment. Our man is under our beard. I mean in Paris! Cameras have shown him in front of a bank and on a subway platform. But so far … He keeps slipping through our fingers. Is that a manpower problem, or an experience problem, Lieutenant? You tell me. Do you need more men?"

"I don't think so, Commissioner. The men are experienced. The problem is the weather, which is working against us. With a slippery road, we can't get to a place as fast as we want."

"This villain is the devil himself. He has chosen the right moment for his move."

Fournier takes a deep breath and clenches his fists.

"I've been thinking about something since this morning," he says.

"What, Commissioner?"

"I'm going to put out a call for witnesses in various media, with the promise of a reward. I want that boy nailed, right now."

"Isn't it too early to take that step, Commissioner?"

"I rather regret doing it late. I should have thought of it long before."

"The discretion with which we work may suffer. Wouldn't this be a way of publicizing what the authorities want to cover up, Commissioner?"

"The authorities have entrusted this matter to me with all due confidence. It is up to me to set in motion all the mechanisms that I deem useful to accomplish my mission. If we fail, we are disowned. We must succeed. Do you understand me, Lieutenant? We must succeed …"

The cab arrives in front of the house.

"This is it," Jules says. "Park well, because we're going to get your money from the house. It may take a few minutes."

"Okay, then we won't stop the meter. I also need a guarantee that you will come back and pay me."

"My friend is here," he replies. "He's not getting out. I'll be right back."

He slams the door and starts moving up the stairs. A piece of curtain is parted in a window. He sees his father's face watching, his forehead and lips flattened against the glass. Seen from outside, he looks like a Plantu's cartoon. The father has seen the parked cab and his son arriving. He opens the door, then goes to sit down.

"Hi Dad," Jules says as he enters.

"Jules, where did you leave your motor scooter?"

"The scooter is parked somewhere. I don't like to ride on it when it's snowing and windy at the same time."

"So, cab is what you choose for your trips in the city?"

"Dad, it was an emergency. Buses are jam-packed."

"Yeah, I hear you. Did you know that the police came back for you?"

"Again!"

"Yeah, the cops just left here. Right before you arrived."

"What business do I have with the cops? They just have to come and spend their days and nights here."

"They took a look in your room to make sure you weren't there."

"Why are they persecuting me as far as under my sheets? Did they show you a search warrant, Dad?"

"They didn't do that on their own. I'm the one who asked them to look in your room. I wanted them to see how absent you were."

"Why did you do that, Dad?"

"Because you're innocent. We're not to blame, son!"

"You were wrong, Dad! You shouldn't open my door to that French Gestapo."

"What are you hiding in your room, son?"

"Nothing! That's all! No more talking about it. I need money to pay the cab."

"Don't you have any money left? Didn't your transfer come through?"

"Dad, it's a long story. I'll explain later. First, give me some money to pay the cab and let him go."

"How much is he asking?"

"Maybe fifty, maybe a hundred euros."

"Doesn't he have a meter?"

"He's a bad guy, Dad. He'll keep the meter running until I get back."

"Go and get some money from one of the drawers in my desk."

Jules goes and opens all the drawers. He comes out with not only enough to pay for a cab ride, but also enough to buy a cab. At the car, the driver is not in any hurry.

"You! Stop your fucking meter right now!" Jules orders.

The driver complies and tells him the fare. Jules pays without a word of complaint, adding a generous tip. He gives the rest, a good part of the booty to Cyprien.

"Take my friend where he wants to go," he says to the driver.

The two friends hit each other in the palms and clench their fists.

"See you soon," Cyprien says.

"You can count on me."

The driver turns on his meter again and drives off.

As Jules gets back into the house, he finds his father no longer the cuddly daddy he was two minutes ago. When Jules starts walking towards his room, his father stops him.

"I want you here, Jules."

The father waves him into a chair opposite his own. Jules heads to the chair and sits down. Ouch! This suspicious father has a face like thunder! His furious look is questioning before he even opens his mouth.

"Is there a problem, Dad?"

"There are several of them. Let me be blunt. The first is that you lied to me about your friend Cyprien. I thought he was in Benin, according to your tale. But I am surprised to see that you are moving around Paris with him. The second is that you have drawn the police to yourself, and the whole family may suffer as a result. Thirdly, you're being targeted to the point you no longer feel free to move around. You are forced to take a cab, because otherwise the authorities would get ahold of you."

The father brings into the conversation all the little shenanigans that the young man has been trying to keep secret. Before him, Jules is listening religiously without interjection. Everything is true. He did not imagine that his father would know all these things. He had forgotten what a great economist his father is. When you are able to predict a rise or fall in the stock market from abstract data, you would find it easier to know what your kid is up to.

"Why are you doing all this, Jules? Why are you meddling in a problem that isn't yours at all? I know that your friend Cyprien has an interest in it. But he is who he is, and you are who you are."

"He must find his ancestress' grave. Family is sacred in Benin. Moreover, the racial injustice that underlies this despicable crime must be made public."

"I can understand your friend behaving this way. But what do you have to do with it?"

"Dad, I can't leave him alone. He needs help to achieve his goal. Once again, you are ignoring the problems of our generation. Outside the group, we are worthless. We need to stick together to succeed. In your day, all you had to do was go to school and graduate. Things are different now."

"You are my son. I have to tell you that your future is less problematic than that of many of your friends."

"You want to talk about money, don't you? I'm not as interested in your wealth as I am in my friends. I want to live a different life than you. I don't want to be heartless like you. It's because of your disregard for other people's feelings that Mom left us."

"Jules! Don't talk to me about mom! You don't know anything about it. You are becoming insolent. Is this, according to you, what living another life means?"

"I don't want to be a slave to money like you. You spend your day glued to the TV, watching the stock market jitters live. When the European and American stock markets close, you switch to the Asian ones that have just opened. This way, day or night makes no difference for you. I don't want to live on speculation. I want to work differently. To find a job today, you have to be in a network. That's why friends are useful. On campus, we don't just build classmate relationships that only last until the scoreboard at the end of the year. We form bonds that extend beyond the boundaries of school life."

"I'm not stopping you from having friends as far away as Tibet. But what is embarrassing and therefore worrisome is that you have put us in the crosshairs of the police."

"Come on, Dad! Are you afraid of the police at your age? If you are, you'll see that by receiving them constantly, they won't make you worry any more in the long run. My pet peeve was dealing with injections when I was a kid. But later on, by dint of receiving them, I ended up becoming indifferent to needles."

"That's what I don't want. Don't talk to me about needles. The cops don't come here to treat us. That's different. If you're old enough and you think you can do anything you want, I suggest you get your own place. You don't know why we moved from Ajaccio. You were still a toddler, but your mother and I often explained it to you. When we moved to Paris, we needed to live in peace. This peace, we obtained it. Nothing bothered us until you came to get us in trouble with your story of a mixed-race child who disappeared when the Earth was created. Do you think your friend is facing the same risk as you? If the police get hold of him, his government will demand his repatriation. Don't be stupid. If he is repatriated, when he gets off the plane, they will roll out the red carpet for him. He will be considered a national hero who was seeking to rehabilitate the history of his people. But what will happen to you? Remember those stories you loved to read as a child. If you are arrested, you won't even go to jail. You will be chained to the top of a high mountain, where an eagle will come every day to peck at your liver. No one, no matter if they are as powerful as Heracles, your favourite hero, will be able to free you. And there is where you will die. It was not a hollow myth."

Jules doesn't blink anymore. His gaze is fixed at an imprecise point of the ground. He seems to be dreaming. He sees himself transported to Ajaccio, the mountainous city. An eagle flies over the peak of the Parata, which is one of his best childhood memories. The bird of prey glitches noisily as it visits the rocks in search of a chained prisoner. His body shudders.

His father resumes: "I want to tell you that in all things, you must know how to measure your interests. You can call me a materialist if you please. Those who pay the most are always those who have earned the least. You mustn't let yourself be used. What do we do with a cigarette butt when we've finished smoking?"

Jules does not react. He is still on the summit of his hometown.

"What do we do with a cigarette butt when we've finished smoking, Jules? Answer me. I'm serious."

Jules rubs his eyes as he answers: "We throw it away."

"Good! We don't just throw it away; we throw it away and crush it. You have never observed smokers well. I do not wish to see you one day under the heel like a cigarette butt."

Jules immediately gets up and heads for his room. He slams the door, which echoes over hundreds of meters around. His father says nothing.

12

CYPRIEN WALKS BACK and forth on the completely wooded esplanade. Freezing drafts of air coming out of the Seine storm the immense complex. The François Mitterrand Library is a vast carpet of Ipe wood, on which four large glass towers stand facing each other. Altitude: two hundred and fifty meters above the Seine! It was made to celebrate knowledge that is elevated to the clouds here. In addition to his thick coat, Cyprien is wearing a chapka that covers his forehead and ears. A scarf surrounds his neck and mouth. He must have already killed more than thirty minutes at this point. However, Jules still does not appear. He strides along the balustrade that limits the central garden housed in a ravine. The setting resembles a giant flowerpot. Winter-hardy Scots pines extend their branches that barely overhang the sky bridge.

Jules didn't show up at the meetup; perhaps he will no longer come. He's never broken his promises before. What could have happened to him?

Cyprien waits. Hours pass. He decides to enter the library alone. He is so close to his goal, he must not fail to attain it. Inside the library, he sets off on the long conveyor belt that leads to the reception desk. No control, no search.

"Hello ma'am, would you tell me where the History department is, please?"

"Go down the long hallway and look for Ward J."

"Sorry?"

"Ward J, as in "Justice".

"Thank you."

He wished that J stood for "Jules". What has happened to the guy?

Cyprien walks down the red-lined hallway. In various corners, security guards shoot their sleep-deprived red eyes at users. The right wall is invaded by giant portraits of the twelve apostles in the presidential elections. Rebellious hands have added their touches to the posters. After their passage, some candidates have their eyes gouged out, others wear horns, the smiling socialist female candidate has a blackened tooth, the anti-GMO candidate has his moustache thickened, the postman is in tears, and the extreme right-winger has had his left arm amputated.

At the end of the hallway, he turns left. Ouch! He realizes that the shorter way should have been to go by the west entrance. Under the J pavilion gantry, there are so many guards! What are they protecting, those men with red armbands? Red like their sleep-deprived eyes. Cyprien buys a ticket and goes to the entrance. A queue of about ten people stretches out in front of the elevator. For every person who leaves, another enters. This is the rule.

While waiting, he reads the slogans posted on a board: "Room with two hundred and seventy seats, more than thirty-five thousand books, more than two hundred magazines, etc." Imagine what it feels like to be exposed like this in front of a public building while hiding. People come out in dribs and drabs, but with more joining than leaving, the line is getting longer and longer.

Finally, Cyprien reaches the elevator. The second floor is a boiler room where life is good. The bag check is a digital process, no rough search. Inside the room, the shelving is immense. The pilgrim remembers Librarian Berenger's advice, "No digital catalogue!"

He sinks into the shelves. The sword of Damocles hangs over his head. He feels as if at any moment, someone is going to inveigh against him. How difficult it is going to be to find one's way through this forest of information without the help of a computer! The manual catalogues that were stored in drawers in the days of our ancestors have been thrown into the Seine. But, in order to go unnoticed, he must refrain from electronic magic.

Here is the history of the whole world from the dawn of time to the latest news item reported in the daily papers. Where to start? He blindly chooses the hallway that opens before him. As he walks, he sees the great geographical regions pass by. America, Africa, Asia, Oceania ...

In the European zone, he targets France. This is a whole area to explore! Sub-groups such as Prehistory, Antiquity, Middle Ages, and others, are visible. The organization is meant to be rigorous. At this pace, the French Old Regime cannot hide for long.

The seventeenth century is here, at last!

The books are piled up in eight rows of shelves, erected two meters above the ground. A few people walk around the shelves and consult titles randomly. Others come up with precise references and reach for the book of their choice without missing a beat. At the end of the shelf, someone else is rummaging through the books like Cyprien. He must be a storage clerk. The troubling thing is that the man's hands are gloved, and his head is lost in a hood. Cyprien has not yet found his reference. There are so many publications on the reign of Louis XIV. Some titles are repeated, to the nearest comma, by three or four authors. The person in the hood is close to him. Is it a man or a woman? Is he a police informer, a spy? Is it the specter of Louis XIV who has come to take his revenge, or to provide a hint? The stranger has no book in his hand. Everything seems unsatisfactory to him. He goes over the spines of the books. He pulls out some titles and puts them back after a look. But why should such a natural situation look dramatic? He is doing this manual search maybe because he didn't find his reference in the digital catalogue. That must be it! The two are standing side by side when the miracle happens. The same book has caught their attention. It is the very book, Cyprien notices, that he is looking for.

They both reach for the book as they cry out: "François Bluche!" It is a puzzling scene. The stranger pulls the book out first. Cyprien looks at him astonishingly. He does not recognize him.

"Here you are!" The man says. "I had not thought of meeting you here, Cyprien!"

He unzips his hood and lets it fall behind his back.

"Mister Bonnot! Is it really you? What are you doing here at a time like this? I couldn't imagine you being away from your construction site in Versailles!"

"And you, I thought you were stuck in your classroom at the university!"

"Let's say that we both invented this unusual meeting. Tell me what brings you here, Mister Bonnot."

Cyprien looks at him suspiciously. Bonnot is for sure the one who left traces at the National Library, site of Richelieu. That's him!

"Dear Cyprien, you're not the only one on a treasure hunt. You took me for a simpleton, didn't you? The least a foreman can do is to visit all the workstations on site to see what workers are doing. You thought that by leaving your station in a hurry, I would refrain from going down to the dungeons."

Cyprien remains silent as Bonnot speaks. Only three days ago, he was still Cyprien's boss. He briefly revisits the scene where the brutal rupture between them occurred.

"What exactly did you see on the wall, Mister Bonnot?"

"You can rest assured that we saw the same thing. The proof is that we are both here to find out more. This means that we were guided by the same message."

"Does that mean you had read the engraving before I destroyed it?"

"For your information!" Bonnot says, handing Cyprien an empty cigarette pack on which he had written some words.

Cyprien reads it silently with moving lips: "IN MEMORY OF NABO AND HIS DAUGHTER LOUISE-MARIE BORN OF THE QUEEN, CONDEMNED BY THE COURT OF FRANCE AND DISPATCHED."

He keeps looking at the message with disbelief. Then he says: "Mister Bonnot, you are a genius!"

"The genius is you, Cyprien. And please, don't call me Mister Bonnot. Call me James."

"Thank you for the offer, James."

"Dear friend, by destroying this engraving, you wanted to send me packing, didn't you?"

"James! Never mind. Once fate has brought us together; we become teammates. Tell me how you went from technician to researcher."

James shakes his head.

"I hope I'm not stepping on your toes!"

"Not at all! In my opinion, everyone is free to conduct research on any subject."

"To cut a long story short, I would like to inform you that the Versailles construction site is now closed. Because of the hole you left in the dungeon floor. As soon as you left, the works manager and I brought the matter to the attention of the palace curator. He was very surprised and worried, and he came down to make a report. No more engraving on the wall, only a gaping hole in the floor! He wanted to know what you had read, a good way to find out if we knew about it. I hid the message from him. I never saw anything! Nothing!"

"Well done!"

"When I read his mind, he seemed to attest by his attitude and gestures to something that was indeed hiding in that hole, or not far from it. If not, why stop the construction without notice? In all likelihood, the national curator of the monuments of France is updated. He must be the one who has ordered the site to be put on halt."

"I'm sorry that you are unemployed because of this!"

"It's not a real unemployment, mind you. I will be assigned somewhere else soon. I'm taking advantage of the break to find out more about this case. For me, it is serious."

"What's the purpose of your research?"

"I want to find Nabo's traces in the history of France. He is the one I am interested in. That cause will make a lot of noise. It is a scandal that we must not try to avoid. We have not invented Nabo, Louise-Marie, or Queen Marie-Thérèse of Austria. All of them lived in Versailles under Louis XIV. All are interconnected. In my opinion, it is time to let people of our time know about it. A column published on this matter could make us famous, or downright rich. Maybe I'll stop swallowing dust from sanders on construction sites and listening to the cacophony of jackhammers all day long."

"Okay then, brace yourself for the long trek."

"I know! I was at the Richelieu site this morning, after having drooled uselessly in other libraries."

"I know about your visit to Richelieu."

"What a guy! You're a real cop, Cyprien!"

"I don't think you're putting it right. We're the ones who have the cops after us. It's a very delicate matter, as you know. Have you got anything on Nabo yet?"

"It's a total desert! What about you?"

"I'm investigating his daughter, Louise-Marie. But I haven't got much so far. I found a footnote in a book by Cortequisse. This author is so cautious in his statements. He puts everything in the conditional."

"Hush! Someone is following our movements."

"Who?"

"No idea, but he has an ugly face."

"Let's get out of here! You quickly go through the book, then pass it to me. I am under the golden candelabra, on the garden side."

"Okay!" James whispers.

Three minutes later, James Bonnot comes back with the book.

"You're a reading machine!" Cyprien says.

"Check this out! This *Dictionary of the Great Century* is a directory of proper and common names with explanatory notes."

"Is Nabo in there?"

"You don't have to dream. The letter N begins with 'Naissance' and continues with 'Namur'. Mr. Bluche forgot to mention Nabo at the very beginning."

"Louise-Marie too, perhaps."

"It's not worth wasting your time. I've checked. There is no trace of her. Louise-Marie is not Louis XIV. And the unknown place of her rest is not the Bourbon Vault. Let's take off before it's too late!"

The suspicious-looking agent is back. He takes a few steps into the room without saying anything to anyone, without looking anyone in the face. He goes to a window and looks at the pine forest outside.

"This gentleman is waiting impatiently for something," Bonnot says.

"I would say for someone," Cyprien replies. "Tell me, James, did you find the reference of this book in a catalogue?"

"You really amaze me. What can you do in a library of this size without consulting the catalogues?"

"Did you do it, tell me clearly!"

Bonnot feels pressured. "I did, that's it! François Bluche, *The dictionary of the Great Century*. Quote: 944.033. Located in the upper garden. Does that suit you? I hope so, dear friend!"

"Let's clear out immediately," Cyprien says. "I can confirm that your traces on the electronic catalogue have triggered an alert. I wasn't worried when I saw you digging in the huge repository like me."

"It's just that the book was misplaced by the last reader."

"I can tell you no. It was moved around on purpose!"

"Why would someone do that?"

"To keep you here for hours looking for it."

"What would be the point?"

"By spending more time looking for it, you give the police the opportunity to come here and capture you without any effort."

"I don't get it. Am I wanted?"

"You have Pandora's box in your hand. They don't want you to open it. Look at the tricks this man is doing. He is part of the enemy's machine that's being set up."

James suddenly rights himself. His ears seem to pick up a siren's wail from far away. He gets up immediately.

"What does this mean, Cyprien?"

Cyprien pushes him towards the door.

"We're going downstairs, I'll explain everything to you when we get to a safe place."

"You see, I remember a title I found by chance while searching. *Louise-Marie of…*

He stops abruptly to recall the title.

"We don't stop, James!"

"Oh, I don't like it when my memory plays tricks on me!"

James wants to go back quickly to see the exact title. Cyprien blocks his way.

"I think you want to talk about Louise-Marie of Orleans."

"Exactly! That's the title I'm trying to recall."

"No, it's not our Louise-Marie born in 1664. The one you are talking about belongs to the 19th century and she was the Queen of the Belgians."

"What is this book doing among publications on the Great Century?"

"It is a mirror that has been placed in front of us. You now have confirmation that the books have been moved around."

"Nothing is clearer to me now."

They go into the hallway and call the elevator. The machine, located on the fourteenth floor, continues its ascent. The light marks fifteen, then sixteen, and so on.

"We are toast!" James says.

"There is always another way," Cyprien replies. He looks at the emergency door. They don't waste a moment. Soon they are taking the stairs. On the first floor, they quickly open the exit door. They come face to face with the security guard who simply asks them: "Break or final departure?" It is a question he asks mechanically to all those who leave, so he knows whether to allow people in to take the vacated seats. "Break," Cyprien answers. "We're having a coffee next door!"

They take the conveyor belt that carries them over the pine trees, like in a children's story. At the top, they cross the large wooden esplanade and run onto the Simone de Beauvoir footbridge laid over the quiet Seine. The bridge, lined with Ipe wood too, vibrates intensely under their steps. Cops pass on the other side going the opposite way up the Tolbiac bridge, while the two brave men soon get lost in Bercy.

13

NOON. THE TABLE is set. The housekeeper alerts her boss. She then goes to knock at Jules' door to invite him to the dining table too. She gets no response. A deafening silence comes from Jules' room. The employee keeps on knocking, in vain. The father signals for her to stop.

"He's not ready yet," the father says.

"Probably needs to rest," the young woman says.

She withdraws. She knows that what she calls rest is not rest. Jules has almost fallen out with his father. Their sky is cloudy.

Mr. Bartoli sits down at the table and begins to eat his meal alone. The first bite tastes insipid. He finds the second bitter, the third revolting. He lets the fork fall into the plate and holds his head in both hands. How dare his son blame him for his mother's departure? The father cannot escape feeling some remorse. After a brief moment of immobility, he stands up abruptly. He steps alertly towards his son's room, slowing down as he approaches the door. He knocks, calling out the boy's name. From inside, Jules responds and says he is not hungry.

"It's noon. Why aren't you hungry?"

"No reason."

"Come and have a glass of wine."

"I'm not thirsty."

"Open the door for me, please."

"No, I'm resting. I don't want to see anybody."

The disappointed and confused father withdraws. As he walks slowly to the table, he notices Jules' cell phone in an armchair. He takes it, admires it, then turns it on. A small light at one corner starts to flash like a plane looking to land at night. He opens the flap. Yasmina's picture appears on the screen. Her enlarged face occupies almost the entire frame. He finds the girl's number in the phonebook and sends her a beep. She calls back immediately. He wisely lets it ring.

"Jules, you have a call!" he shouts.

"How come I have a call?" he yells from inside his room.

"Why is it surprising you do?"

Jules unlocks the door. He walks out into the living room with a haggard look. His father confesses and apologizes.

"I'm the one who turned on your phone, assuming you left it off by mistake."

"You betrayed me, Dad! You should never do that to me! They're going to catch me!"

"Who's going to get you? Are you hallucinating?"

"This is not about hallucinations. The cops who come to this house every minute are not imaginary figures. They are demons who want to kill me."

"Your friend Ghezo is the one they're looking for, not you. You have nothing to do with it. Don't worry."

"You keep betraying me, Dad. I wonder how far you'll go. It's clear you don't love me."

"I'm sorry, Jules. I shouldn't have turned your phone back on."

"You're annoying, Dad."

"I'm sorry, Son."

"It's too late to say that. I'll leave your house."

"Did I hear right, Jules? I hope you're not serious. Don't do this to me, Jules! I need you here."

His son returns to his room, slamming the door.

The doorbell rings. The father opens a curtain to see who it is. *They were so prompt*, he says to himself. Confused ideas cross his mind. He starts crafting an alibi as he descends the stairs. Looking through the peephole, he recognizes Yasmina's thick hair.

"It is good to see you here, sweetheart. Your boyfriend is not doing well. He is in a bad mood."

"Did you have an argument with him?"

"Not really. Just a little exchange."

"Mr. Bartoli, I know what parents call a little exchange."

"What do you mean, Yasmina? You're taking sides without understanding."

"Yes, our problems are similar. You can call it generational solidarity."

"You're giving me a new word. Until I was old enough, I only heard about generational conflict. I expect a lot from you, my dear. Go and see him right away, please!"

"Don't worry. His sad face will not last long. I am a remedy for his mood swings."

What a role women play in our lives! he thinks.

She knocks at Jules' door. The lock clicks and the door squeaks. The father returns to the table, but he has no appetite. He remains attentive. Whispers from the room reach him, but only from the girl's discreet voice. Then complete silence reigns. The father conjures images. Torsos undressed on the fly. A bra projected above the wardrobe. The sweat of jiggling. And so on.

Minutes later, Jules opens the door and presents himself to his father. He is all sheepish, his step heavy. He is coming to apologize. Mr. Bartoli can't believe it. But why not? That the magic of love could undermine the arrogance of his son and heal his heart, is something he should well expect. However, it is simply incredible how quickly the boy is asking for forgiveness! It is the very image of the prodigal son. Jules must have understood that one doesn't die from their sins, but from refusing to be forgiven.

"Dad, I'm sorry for what happened. Please forgive me."

"You are already forgiven, son."

"Are you being honest?"

"Yes, I am."

The father gives his son a big hug. Yasmina appears and rushes to take a picture with her cell phone. The scene ends with bursts of laughter, confessions, promises, vows. The fact remains that the boy has not given up on supporting his fugitive friend. It is a matter not to be raised.

"Sir," Yasmina says, "our son was a little down in the dumps. Nothing serious. He just needs to relax, and he'll be fine. We want to go on an outing."

"Is that true, Jules?" his father asks.

"Yes, I wasn't really mad. I can't leave the house, Dad."

"Do you have enough money to go out?"

"Yes," Yasmina replies. "We have enough to satisfy our desires."

He looks at Jules, who says nothing. The girl smooths her hair. "Jules wants to take one of your cars."

"Jaguar or sedan?"

"Sedan."

"Take it," the father says. "It's yours. But be careful with everything. Don't do anything crazy, please. And above all, don't get me another little pack of violation tickets."

The father's look is imploring. Jules is stunned to see him so accommodating. He wishes he were like his father, gifted with the heart of a dove. But the ardor of youth leaves him sometimes with hot blood bursting his veins.

They leave right away.

They have no sooner disappeared around the curve than the police arrive from the other end of the street.

"Mr. Bartoli, you are trying to protect an offender wanted by Justice. Do you know that you're facing serious consequences yourself?"

"What are you talking about, Lieutenant?"

"Your son is in this house. He just placed a phone call, and he received one."

"What if I prove you wrong?

"Go ahead."

"I was the one who used his phone."

"For what reason?"

"He didn't show up for lunch. I want to know where he is, trying to contact some random friends in his phone book."

"Bring us just one piece of evidence and we'll leave you alone."

Mr. Bartoli picks up a phone and hands it to them. The Lieutenant grabs it with a skeptical look. He sends a beep to one of his own men.

"What number is displayed?" he asks.

"06 ..."

The man recites the entire ten-digit litany. Right!

The Lieutenant's face undergoes a change, defeated by this simple proof made available. He didn't expect it. Men of his rank never accept to lose without a fight. He nods.

"Sorry for the inconvenience, Mr. Bartoli."

Just then, the Lieutenant receives a screaming radio message: "Another phone call from the same location, but to a different contact."

Mr. Bartoli's eyes widen.

"You bugged my son, didn't you?"

"That's none of your business, Mr. Bartoli."

14

YASMINA DRIVES UP Arago Boulevard with Jules on the passenger seat. The snow has completely melted. One can hear the chirping of the wheels which lacerate the sheet of water spread out on the roadway. The black sedan moves forward quietly in a line of cars moving at a slow pace.

"It's a real pleasure to drive this car," she says.

"My father chose it more for its length than for its comfort. Before this one, he drove an extravagantly large American car. He could never find his way on our Parisian streets. In parking lots, he often used the bumper to create his own space."

"He must like to stand out from the crowd."

"It's clear, that is my father!"

"Here we are, Jules. I turn after the light."

Jules looks up and sees the arrow that points to the François Mitterrand Library.

"What an imposing monument!"

Yasmina finds a parking lot between the young plane trees protected in wooden forms. They get out and take a look at The Avenue Café. Everything smells new in Tolbiac. The asphalt covering the streets is impeccably black. Roads are open and free. The horizon is not at the end of the nose like in the streets of the old city. You can see several kilometers in front of you. As far as one can see, cranes bristling here and there swing their long metal arms into the sky, driving pulley blocs.

They step onto the Ipe wood platform and enter the long hallway of the south entrance. Jules stops abruptly and thinks.

"What's going on? Any problem?" Yasmina asks.

"Let's not get buried together. Stay at the wheel. We don't know if we're going to leave this place quietly or with a bang."

"I was thinking that, too."

She returns to the car.

He goes in, up to the reception where he is shown the J pavilion. This time, it's J for Jules. But he feels so lonely, so small in this vast unknown world full of suspicion. Would it have been better if he had let his girlfriend come with him? With her he always feels stronger and more confident. On the red carpet, he walks with measured steps. The gigantic portraits of the election candidates are there to distract him, like those malicious sirens who tried to divert Ulysses from his war mission. But he walks coldly, attentive to the slightest signal that could come from Cyprien. He proceeds to Pavilion J. A number of people swarm under the portico. The security service interrupts him as he heads for the elevator.

"Remember to get in line, sir," the lady in uniform tells him.

"I'm sorry, ma'am."

"It is obvious that you're not a regular visitor. Did you get a ticket at the reception desk?"

"I forgot."

"Get one right away and come back immediately so that you don't lose your position in line."

From the second floor, the hall supervisor sends a succinct radio message to the woman: "Send two people upstairs, please!"

Usually, the number of people exiting the elevator determines the number of substitutes allowed to go up. Her response is a thinly veiled refusal: "I don't see anyone leaving the room, sir."

"Don't worry about it. The last two who went down are not coming back."

"They made it clear that they were going for coffee!"

"They lied to you. They didn't go downstairs for coffee, but to head for the hills."

Everyone around the woman is listening to this message at the same time as she is.

"Are you talking about the young black man and his friend?"

"Yes, of course! They're the ones the police came for earlier."

"Were they wanted?"

"Yes, since this morning. We just forgot to forward you the message downstairs."

"They managed to get away, I think."

"Oh dear! They are foxes. They were able to leave the premises two minutes earlier."

"All right! I'll send you two substitutes."

"Thanks a lot!"

Jules withdraws from the line. The woman kindly shows him a ticket machine, as well as the reception desk located a little further on, at the west entrance. He then turns around and disappears. As soon as he slams the door of the sedan, Yasmina starts off with a bang.

15

THE CLOCK STRIKES thirteen hours. In a convenience store in the Twentieth District, men are gathered. Their eyes are riveted on a small screen embedded in a metal cage. The lotto winning numbers scroll by. It is here that luck crowns nameless people and dethrones many others who had royal dreams. Toulon's men have observed a truce to attend the draw live. Their car is in the neighbourhood, parked in front of a silk-screen printing shop. The technician is trying to find the most suitable product to remove the tag without damaging the paint.

The convenience store is full of people. Those who have played are holding their tickets in their hands. They look from their tickets to the draw screen and back. Ups and downs! A good start that arouses keen interest suddenly turns into bitter disappointment. This is lottery.

Far away, in the northern suburbs of Paris, on a street in Saint Ouen, a black sedan tries to find a parking space. Many of the parking lots are of the parallel type, which doesn't really fit with the length of the sedan. The trick is to manage to park without attracting anyone's attention. A few streets away, fortunately, a shopping mall generously offers them its space. They leave the vehicle there and walk. The scooter, chained to a plane tree, patiently awaits its owner. They take the small slope that leads to the building. The door of the basement is closed. Jules presses the buzzer. No answer! He renews the chime and waits. Silence persists. Yasmina has a strange bad feeling.

"I feel like I'm being spun," she says.

"You cannot call it a feeling, my chick! We are well and truly being spun."

"I feel like someone is watching my back."

"If you think you're being watched from the back, then it's just a feeling. Behind your back you only have this closed door."

"We were fools to come and look for Cyprien in this hiding place at this time. Do you think he could have escaped from the library to come and hide here in broad daylight?"

"Let's leave before it is too late. Your premonitions are always right."

As they are leaving, a whistling causes them to stop and turn. It's Cyprien standing under the frame of a door he has just opened. They go back.

"You played a joke on us, my friend. What's the matter with you?" Jules asks.

"I was watching you through the keyhole. I had to make sure you were not being followed."

He kisses Yasmina and shakes his fist with Jules.

They all get in. Three coffees are served.

"We missed you at the library," Yasmina says.

"I was worried about Jules," Cyprien replies. "I knew he must have had a setback."

"No, Cyprien," Jules says. "*You* were the one *I* was worried about. I heard the security guards saying that you left without warning. They talked about the young black man and his friend. Which boyfriend did you go with?"

"I never told you I was gay?"

"What! Are you serious?"

"I'm joking."

"He is just kidding," Yasmina says. "He doesn't have a gay man's features."

"So, who was he?"

"It was James Bonnot, my ex."

"Your ex-what?"

"My ex-foreman on the Versailles site."

"I thought you were in a fight!"

"No, far from it. He's also interested in our investigations. He's the one who stole a march on us at Richelieu. We found ourselves in Tolbiac in a funny situation where we caught our two hands reaching out for the same book."

"Won't this wolf get in our way?"

"He's not a competitor. We have to see him as a teammate. There's a lot to exchange with him."

"Now I don't have to worry. And as for your gay story, I had a hard time imagining you in tight clothes, with your zipper positioned rather behind."

"Now you're passing on some exaggerated popular imagery. And if that were the case, would you disown me as a friend?"

"So, my dear, you are testing my tongue. Everyone is playing at being a hypocrite when it comes to the matter of balloon knot. But I wouldn't blame you if you were gay. Life is such that you never know how you'll get into certain situations. You never imagined that you'd end up in drag one day. But now you have to wrap yourself in a female down jacket to save your life. I'm sure you're ready to put on makeup and lipstick. The longer this situation lasts, the more you end up finding your new attire normal. Then, you'll be approached by the drag club who will offer you something better. Look, whether you are gay or not, you are still a friend and nothing less. Everyone is free to choose their own path. As for me, I have my own way of expressing my manhood."

"Jules is a real male," Yasmina says.

"Yes, I acknowledge it, sweetheart. You're in a good position to say so. I love your beautiful secret flower."

"I too dream of a beautiful flower in full bloom," Cyprien says. "But I don't often have time to smell the flowers."

"What are you doing that is so constraining to the point you can't enjoy your youth? Don't you know that life is a meteor?"

"You speak like Horace. *Collige virgo rosas.*"

"Translate that for me so I can understand."

"*Enjoy your youth,* or else, word for word, *Pick roses while you're young.*"

"Well, there you go!" Jules says. "Horace proves me right. Realize that I didn't even need to know my master to apply his teachings."

"Don't be such a loudmouth," Yasmina says. "If we have to be practical, Jules, this week you haven't collected a single little bouquet."

"You're right, my dear. But you do know what our focus is right now."

"You're on the wrong track, Jules," Cyprien says. "There is no explanation you can give to a love-thirsty heart. I would have liked to hear you say, for example: 'Ah! My love! Your forgiveness I call upon! Don't be quick to make me pay the price of this negligence. If my efforts in the scale of your desires have not met the weight you expected, to make up for it I am eager! A basket or a tote of flowers do you want, my sweetheart? Your inexhaustible garden invites me. Be mine!'"

Jules takes up the last lines. "Your inexhaustible garden invites me. Be mine!"

Yasmina approaches Jules and lets herself be caught in his open arms. She clings to his chest. He sighs, nibbling her lips. Cyprien cheers, covers them with good wishes. He grabs a handful of rice from a storage can and sprinkles it over them as confetti.

As the couple kisses, he returns to sit on the footstool. His imagination catches fire. If he could also stop chasing the shadow of the dead for a moment to pick a little rose, what would be the harm? It is proven that good feelings as well as bad ones are contagious. He cannot indifferently watch this wiggling of bodies. But how long ago was his last kiss? Oh, it dates back to the Flood! It was at the time of Pamela, the girl of Château d'Eau. She did not do him any favours. With Pamela it is 'Money in hand, pants down.' Cyprien could afford to buy with her small pleasures from time to time. During his prestigious job as a snoop in Paris big offices, he was even able to buy himself a whole night of love. Pamela's last kiss was a missed opportunity. Cyprien was in debt to her. Not only was he unable to pay off his debt, but he was also asking to buy on credit.

"Let's not exaggerate, dear friend," Pamela had told him. "This is Paris. I didn't come here to listen to your 'I love you'. Is that clear?"

Their lips had hardly made contact. The magic effect that brings bodies together had not occurred. Pamela had turned on her heel and they had not seen each other since then. Cyprien tries to put an end to this daydreaming. He has to do something else to escape from it. Perhaps he needs a change of environment.

He stands up abruptly.

"Eh! buddies! Excuse me one moment, I'm going to get some tobacco."

"Hmmmm ..." comes the reply, without an uncoupling of mouths.

16

Yasmina returns with a start from wonderland, pulled away by the phone ringing. Jules licks his lips, trying to bring some order to his dishevelled hair. At the end of the line, an almost familiar voice asks for Cyprien.

"Who are you exactly?" Yasmina asks.

"Swear that you do not recognize me anymore, my Beauty! It's me, Jean. I'm calling from Benin. It's an emergency."

"Hey Jean! Did you try to reach him?"

"I can't reach him! His phone ain't working! Same for Jules."

"What do you have for him?"

"Please, run to Saint Ouen and tell him that he is extremely exposed. He must leave the pad in a hurry. Do you know the address? Seventeen, M ... Street."

"No, Jean! You are making a very serious mistake! You shouldn't have given the address. They are eavesdropping on us."

"I'm sorry, but I couldn't help it. How are you going to find your way around without address?"

"I'm currently in Saint Ouen, in this apartment you're talking about."

"Great! I think Cyprien is there with you. If yes, pass him over to me!"

"I'm here with Jules. Cyprien went to buy firecrackers at the *Chink's*. He will be back in a moment."

"No, do not wait. This moment can be fateful for him. Run to the store right away and convince him to leave without delay."

"Is there a bomb in the closet?" Jules asks, his mouth close to the microphone.

"Jules, it's nice to hear your voice. This is not a joke. You know me well enough. I'm not a municipal theatre goer. This is serious. *Nickers* are going to show up, and woe betide you if you wait another minute."

Cyprien arrives cheerfully, smoking."Hello lovers!" he calls out.

Yasmina holds out the phone to him. "Cyprien, Jean wants to talk to you. It's urgent."

"He took the risk of calling me?" He grabs the phone and sticks it to his ear.

"Ah! my little *bruh*! It's me, Jean. I'm glad to have you. You and your *droogs* have to leave my pad within the next two minutes."

"What? Within two hours, you mean!"

"No, I said two minutes. If not, there will be some trouble. Now you only have one minute and forty seconds left. Do you hear me? The gang bangers will be there any minute. And you know we don't play cowboys with them. I'm the one they're coming for. I've got some red mercury and some crack in my closet. I advise you not to touch them. Let the guys take it. I had a deal with a ball-less loser who betrayed me."

"Where are you now?"

"I am still in Benin, but I am updated on everything. I'm on the move! It's for you that I'm tripping, my boy. You are at the crossroads of two cases! You'd better do something about it!"

"Where can I go?"

There is not another word. Jean has hung up.

When Cyprien turns around, he sees Yasmina handing him a coat, her own down jacket with a furry edged hood.

"What should I do with a woman's coat?" he asks.

"You have to wear it. Wear it, go ahead! Here's my scarf too. Wrap your neck and mouth with it. Leave only your nose and eyes. Just to see and to breathe through! Do you understand? Jules, I need a stroller. Go up to the first floor and find me one that looks sturdy."

While Cyprien puts on the clothes, Jules climbs the stairs, two steps at a time, to find a stroller. Several remain permanently wedged under the stairs at the entrance to the building. Jules pulls one of them out.

"Take this," Yasmina says to Cyprien. "You're a good mom pushing her baby. Go and wait for us near the car at the mall square."

Yasmina removes the chip from her phone, throws it in her mouth and chews it. She spits out the debris. Jules closes Jean's door and puts the key in the garbage bin.

Walking up the slope, Cyprien comes face to face with a group of policemen who are moving fast. He stops to let them pass on both sides of the stroller.

"That's nice, ma'am," one of them says.

Cops invade the basement. Jean's door is closed.

The team leader of cops who are stationed between two buildings to keep watch asks: "What do you see?"

"Two young people kissing and a closed door."

"Hello," one of them says to Yasmina and Jules. "Excuse us for disturbing you. We just want some information. Do you live in the building?"

"Why do you want to know?" Jules asks. "Do I come to your house to ask you questions? Even when we want to be a bit cool in our suburbs, you guys always bring your big mouths to create a goddam mess."

"We are sorry for being spoilsports. Do you know who lives here in the basement?"

He points to Jean-le-Mec's apartment.

"What do I care? Just do your damn *gig* and leave us alone."

"Sir," Yasmina says, "the janitor Mister Chavez and his wife Esperanza live here. Are you looking for someone?"

"Of course! A black man in his forties."

"I have no clue," she says. "But one day, I saw a black man coming out of the sub-basement."

"Why did you tell him that?" Jules asks, looking fiercely at Yasmina. "Don't be that six-year-old ninny! They will go down and kill the poor nigger, and that will be your fault."

"What did he have in his hand?" the cop asks Yasmina.

"Nothing. He was only black!"

"Is that all?"

"That's all!"

"Thanks a lot!"

The invaders go down into the sub-basement and spread out across the hallways in small groups. They carry out a brutal search. One can hear the bangs of bolts being sprung. Tenants of the building have stored in cellars their old items they don't want to get rid of. Sewing machines, old guitars, paintings, inflatable dolls ... Another team, no less fierce, summons the janitor to open his door if he doesn't want to see them break it open.

Yasmina and Jules sneak out slowly. They go on tiptoe to the mall where Cyprien is waiting for them by the car. The Sedan starts in a hurry.

17

IN A WARM apartment in the Latin Quarter, Mrs. Benaoui is waiting for her daughter Yasmina. The latter left the apartment in a hurry earlier that morning, after receiving a beep on her phone. She left without writing a note for her mother as she usually did. She did not come back for lunch. Mrs. Benaoui is anxious and disgruntled. Does Yasmina know that her mother is waiting and even going without a meal because of her? *Does she even care?* Mrs. Benaoui says to herself. *What teenage girl considers such things?* She recalls how Yasmina had not hesitated to take away from her the spare key of her room on the evening of her eighteenth birthday. Mrs. Benaoui sighs. "Ah, things that happen to children when they think they are grown-ups!"

She tries unsuccessfully to reach her daughter by phone. She has the number of her boyfriend Jules, but she dares not call the boy, for fear of her daughter berating her later like a child. However, it is not yet time to worry. The girl is nineteen. She can go out at any time with whomever she wants, without seeking her mother's consent.

Puffs of steam escaping from the dishes have stopped clouding the kitchen. The meal is slowly cooling down. Mrs. Benaoui has her eyes fixed on the street.

She has positioned herself to have a good view of the bus stop outside. Her imagination is going wild. She hears her mind thinking of things that her mouth would have said to her daughter if she were here. Her phone lies on the pedestal table. She wishes it would ring. She wishes she would hear her daughter's voice saying, "Mom, it's me, don't worry. I'm out here with my friends. I'll be back soon. Big hug, Mom ..." But the voice remains locked in Mrs. Benaoui's imagination. The phone lies silently on the table.

At the same time, the Sedan occupied by three young people arrives in front of the Pantin-Bobigny cemetery, like a hearse. Cyprien gets out. He has a scarf around his neck and mouth. A long anorak wraps his body down to his shins, while a chapka covers his head, cheeks and ears. The gate of the cemetery is wide open. He raises two fingers to symbolically hug his friends.

"Be strong, we will be back for you at night," Yasmina says.

"Also be careful," Jules says. "If Fournier stalks even into the grave as they say, entering the cemetery would be a piece of cake for him."

Cyprien smiles as he walks toward the entrance. He steps through the wide iron gate. In mythology, this gate is said to be the door to the underworld. A two-meter-wide path leads straight to a central stele dedicated to two soldiers who fell during the Liberation. Rows of neatly arranged graves stretch out on either side. The dead watch him pass. Here and there are tombs that are akin to real villas. Duplexes perhaps?

He calls out: "O ye the dead! Greeting to all of you! My name is Cyprien Ghezo. Descended from Behanzin's bloodline, famous king of Dahomey, the eleventh of the Houegbadja dynasty. I need your hospitality and your cover."

The gravel crunches under his feet in response. In the middle of the cemetery, a giant bronze statue represents the archangel Michael holding his sword and scales. With his foot, he crushes the head of the devil. How awful!

❧ The car leaves. Far from the cemetery, Yasmina points to a free parking lot.

"Here, here!" she says.

"How come here?"

"Let's stop for a moment."

"As you wish," he says.

"The weather is inclement, and I do not have my coat anymore. Hold me in your arms, Jules."

He parks hurriedly, without even trying to fit the wheels inside the white frame drawn on the ground. The girl moves to sit on his lap. She rests her back against the steering wheel. He passes his fingers through her thick hair and caresses her lips with his mouth.

Yasmina murmurs, "Hmmm … I love you, Jules!"

"I love you too."

"Do you know that I want you?"

"Yes, I can see that. But what can we do here in the street?"

"Tell me that you love me."

"I love you; I love you; I love you, a thousand times!"

"You have exaggerated, Jules! You're going to ignite me instead of calming me down. You should have said it just once."

"I love you, baby."

"Is that all?"

"Yes, sweetie!"

"Say it again."

"I love you."

"This time you didn't say 'sweetie'."

"I love you, sweetie."

"Do you?"

"Yes!"

She feels a warmth coming over her. Her eyes soften and she looks weak. Her voice gets thinner.

"Jules, when we were in Saint Ouen, you said that you loved my beautiful secret flower."

"Yes, I do love it."

"Tell me that you will never leave me."

"I will never leave you."

"Tell me something that comes from you. I'm afraid to make you repeat words you don't mean."

"No, everything you make me say, we both mean it. Do I have to remind you that we have the same brain installed in two heads?"

"Wonderful! I believe you, my love. I adore you."

She smiles tenderly. They bite each other's lips again.

Outside, the windshield wiper is lifted. Underneath it, a hand slides a piece of paper and lets the blade back into place.

"See what that bitch is doing!" Jules says. "She's just jealous."

"It's the parking police. We got a violation ticket."

"The bitch is right. The parking lot is not a free one, but we didn't purchase a ticket."

"Your father will be furious. What will we tell him?"

"We won't tell him anything. He will receive his reminder letter in a month."

Yasmina returns to her seat.

"I'm a little hungry," she says. "Let's go have a bite."

Jules nods as he restarts the car.

18

LATIN QUARTER. FROM her third-floor apartment, Mrs. Benaoui has drawn aside the curtains at a window. She watches the agents leaving the building. A team of plainclothes cops has just paid her a visit. Her daughter is in the sights of the judicial police. They have intercepted the call that Jean-le-Mec made to Yasmina from Benin. The telephone operator made the call list available. Without delay, the investigators rushed to Mrs. Benaoui's home. She could not believe her eyes when she saw that the group was coming to her apartment. She thought she has heard wrong when she was told that her daughter was wanted.

"Is my daughter guilty of cheating on an assignment, or of free riding on the transport?" she asked. "Did she smoke in a closed space without remembering the new law? Tell me!"

"You're funny, ma'am," an investigator said. "Do you think your daughter is capable of nothing more than those little nonsenses?"

"So, tell me, please!"

"She is involved in drug trafficking and counterfeiting of banknotes. We will search her room."

They broke into every room in the house and ransacked everything. When they were done, she asked to know the outcome.

"What have you found, gentlemen?"

"Nothing, for the time being."

"I know my daughter!" she said. "I was sure she wouldn't know how to do such things. It's true that she's got a little crazy since she started going to casinos with her boyfriend from the same university. But to say she's a drug dealer, I think you're wrong."

"Her troubles have just begun, ma'am! There is another case that we are not responsible for investigating."

"This is pure fiction! Why do you want to demonize my daughter? If she didn't come home for lunch this afternoon, it's purely a family matter. What are you meddling with? Leave my house right now, please."

"We'll need to hear from her."

"As you wish! But I know she won't tell you anything, because she doesn't know anything."

"Have a good evening, Mrs. Benaoui. Thank you for having us."

From the window, Mrs. Benaoui watched the cops get into their car, drive around a traffic circle and exit into another boulevard.

Yasmina and Jules take turns behind the wheel. She is the one who drove to the street where she lives. Her mother hasn't left the window. She is keeping her eye on the street below. She almost collapses when she spots her daughter getting out of a rich person's car and passing the wheel to Jules. Unbelievable!

"That's my daughter! That's her!" the woman shouts, tapping her chest in consternation. "The accusations of the police are true! O Lord!"

She covers her mouth to stifle any screams that may burst out of her. Her eyes are red with tears. From the window, she goes back to the sofa. In the hallway, the door of the elevator opens, then the doorbell rings. She doesn't find the strength to get up and open the door. Finding her own keys, Yasmina unlocks and opens the door and comes in wearily. She stops at the sight of her mother on the sofa with tears in her eyes.

"Mom! Are you sick?"

Her mother remains silent.

"Speak, Mom! I'm calling the Medical Emergency for you!"

She rushes to the phone, repeating the number of the SAMU.

"No, Yasmina, I don't need an ambulance."

"But you have a problem, Mom!"

"No, the problem is you."

"Me! What do you mean?"

"Tell me that it is not true, Yasmina!"

"What are you talking about? Your psychic across the street has been telling you things about me again! Hasn't she? That I'm nine months pregnant! Right? And you, Mom, you believe every single lie she tells you!"

"Daughter, why did you do this? How did you get involved with forgers and drug dealers?"

"Who told you such crude lies? I can't believe it!"

"You want to fool me, Yasmina! Everything is true. The judicial police were here. They searched even in the toilets to see if you hid something there."

"Mom, the police really searched our house?"

"Yes, there is a day when Allah reveals every hidden thing. I found it out today. You're flourishing into shady businesses. I saw the car you banged. It looks like the property of an emir's wife. I saw you with my own eyes getting out of that car and handing over the wheel to your boyfriend. I understood everything. You couldn't leave that car in our building's parking lot for fear of being busted. That's the life of a faker. You're barking up the wrong tree, girl!"

"Mom, you're overwhelming me! You won't even let me defend myself. I know what the police came here for. It's not about counterfeit money or drugs."

"My daughter, they are not postmen who came to deliver greeting cards. They are agents of the Research and Investigation Brigade."

"It doesn't matter to me if they were Lucifer's agents. Don't be stupid, Mom! They've done a thorough search and found nothing. You should come to the right conclusion yourself."

"What could they find here, if you hide your products elsewhere like you hide your car?"

"That car is not mine!"

"You're a liar!"

"I am not lying to you. That car belongs to Jules' dad."

"And the drugs?"

"I've never done drugs. Trust me, Mom!"

"The criminal police have the wrong address and name, you want me to believe?"

"These stories of drugs and counterfeit money are only collateral affairs that do not concern me. The real problem is elsewhere."

"Tell me about it," her mother says, sitting back in her chair.

"The police are looking for documents that were stolen from the National Archives."

"Do they suspect you know the thief?"

"It's more than just a suspicion."

"So, you know the thief!"

"Not only do I know him, but I'm one of the group."

"I heard that the fire at the Archive Center caused the theft of many valuable documents. If you have a single document from the Center, please return it to them."

"I did not take advantage of the fire as you have heard. We were the ones who set the fire."

"*Ya Rabbi!* What's this I just heard?"

"They were fireworks, Mom."

"You surprise me, Yasmina! Why did you let yourself be deceived like that? Who is using you in this despicable way?"

"Mom, we are working for a just cause. My friends and I stole these documents to try to uncover a state crime committed under Louis XIV."

"You are risking your life in a case that doesn't pay you anything. There have always been state crimes. What have you done with the crimes of the 20th century?"

"It's important!"

"What crime is it?"

"That's the only good question you've asked, since you started to hold my feet to the fire as soon as I came in. I'm happy to answer you. This is the thing: On November 26, 1664, Her Majesty the Queen, Marie-Thérèse of Austria, Louis XIV's wife, gave birth to a mixed-race child resulting from her clandestine love affair with her black slave. Did you know that?"

"You are delirious!"

"It is true!"

"True, in the Court of this France?"

"Yes. The child was hidden, or even killed. Her name was Louise-Marie. Her traces were lost. No history book talks about her."

"If historians do not mention her name, it is for a simple reason. Louise-Marie never existed."

"She did exist, since an engraving discovered in a jail in the Versailles Palace gives account of her."

"Who found the engraving?"

"Cyprien, Jules' friend."

"Archaeologist?"

"Student in *mol bio*."

"That's crazy! Tell me who brought that nonsense to your mind. That's why you put your life in danger?"

"Mom, it's not crazy to fight against racial discrimination and infanticide."

"You don't have weapons to wage war against the State. They'll blow you away like dust. I don't want to lose you, my girl! I have already lost too much in political struggles."

"Our struggle is not political. It is social."

"Ah! What shall I tell you! Social struggles are not the most peaceful ones. Nobody foresaw in 1961 that the events in Saint Denis would degenerate into a massacre. Yet I lost my father in there."

"It was under the Vichy Government. Those days are gone."

"It doesn't matter! The adversary remains the same. Law enforcement officers don't care about the rightness of the cause they are defending. They go where they're told to go and arrest whoever they're told to arrest. They have never changed, from King Clovis to the present day. Go and see what a mess they made of your room."

Yasmina turns around while smoothing her hair. Small white grains fall out.

"Did you fall headfirst in a bag of rice, my little baby?"

She gives no answer. Her mother looks at her, shaking her head.

19

THE BAD WEATHER has not offered a truce. In this winter season, the night is already deep at five in the evening. Mrs. Benaoui puts dishes into the microwave oven one after another. Afterwards, she knocks on her daughter's door.

"I warmed up your meal, sweetheart."

Yasmina has locked herself in her room for a while, rescuing it from the mess left from the police search.

"I'm not hungry, Mom!" she says from behind the door.

"What do you mean you're not hungry?"

"I already had lunch."

"Come and have a glass of juice."

"I'm not thirsty!"

The mother withdraws. She turns on the ceiling light and goes to the window again. Before she draws the curtains, she glances out at the street one last time. What she sees turns her stomach. A troop of policemen, this time in uniform, are getting out of a vehicle.

"Yasmina! Yasmina!" she shouts.

"Leave me alone, mom! I don't want to eat!"

"They're here again! Come! It's another team!"

Yasmina quickly comes out and looks at the scene below. The police have crossed the street and are heading toward the entrance of their building.

The interphone rings.

"They are coming for me, Mom!"

"I suspected it. Go and hide quickly. I don't even know where! Behind the hot water tank, maybe?"

"You're so stupid, Mom!"

"In the closet?"

"No, I know what to do."

"Then I won't answer. Okay?"

"You'd only make things worse by staying silent. They may have seen the open curtains and the ceiling lights. Answer them and send them upstairs. I'll hide on the sixth floor. Be quiet, Mom!"

"All right! Hurry up! Hurry up! Hurry up!"

Yasmina goes up to the sixth floor, opens the emergency door and sits on the dimly lit stairs. The cops arrive on the third floor. Lieutenant Toulon introduces himself.

"Is this where Miss Yasmina lives?"

"You are at the right address," Mrs. Benaoui replies. "But what do you guys have against her?"

"We want to question her. She's involved in a case of aggravated delinquency."

"She has been out since this morning. I haven't heard from her."

"Are you her mother?"

"Yes, I am."

"Do you know a resident of the sixth floor of your building?"

"No, not a single one. I don't have to memorize the list of all the occupants of the building! Why are you asking me this question?"

"A routine question. We ask it every time we visit the third floor."

"What if I lived on the fourth floor?"

"We would ask you about the seventh."

"That is, your suspicion is on the third floor above the home you visit."

"Yes, that's about right. That's where many people who sense danger go to hide and wait for the storm to pass."

"I'm not sure if my daughter has ever been more than a foot above our floor . But let's get back to the facts. What exactly are you accusing her of?"

"We'll be back. Thank you for talking to us, ma'am."

Toulon and his men leave.

Mrs. Benaoui watches them from the window as they drive away in the opposite direction to the one the Research Brigade took earlier. Obviously, two different police teams operating! *What is my daughter steeped in?* she wonders.

Yasmina comes down shortly from her hideout. Mrs. Benaoui is still in shock as she speaks.

"They've left! How scared I was!" she says.

"Don't be afraid, mom!"

"No, my daughter, don't tell me that! You have to listen to me. Forget everything you're planning and surrender to the police. They will see that you don't want to hurt anyone, and they will clear you."

"No, you don't understand. It's not about feelings. I was involved in a criminal act. I have to take responsibility. The police won't give up until they arrest us. Now we are running against the clock. We need the stolen documents to help us get to the bottom of Louise-Marie's disappearance before we're arrested. That's what's at stake."

"What benefit can you get from that madness?"

"I have to help Jules to help his friend Cyprien."

"You are helping Jules to help Cyprien ... You and Jules are both crazy!"

"Mom, I don't want you to talk about my boyfriend in those terms."

"Excuse me, darling."

"I'm working on it because I want to be useful. I want to honour my sensibility. You know what association I belong to."

"What do you think of associations? I also belonged to a few of them when I was your age. Then, one day, I became wise. So, I slammed the doors. It's your turn to be wise! Associations squeeze you and extract all the juice out of your youth. When you become useless, they drop you like those umbrellas that are left on street corners when the rain has stopped."

"I respect your idea, but we have a meeting, the three of us."

"Does that mean you're going out again?"

"Yes, it does. I can't betray my friends. Jules and I have to help Cyprien find the traces of his ancestress. Doesn't that seem like something big to you?"

"What do you mean, his ancestress?"

Yasmina tells her the story.

"Do you understand me a little?"

The mother doesn't answer. *My daughter has lost her mind*, she thinks. *Who put this kind of madness in her brain?* After a moment, the mother asks: "Can I get you a coffee?"

"No, thanks. I've to go out again right away."

She returns to her room. Her mother follows her to the door. In her backpack, she puts her laptop, two Wi-Fi adapters for wireless Internet connection, and a minicomputer the size of a calculator.

"Where are you going, equipped like a soldier fighting in future wars?"

"I'm going to meet with my friends," she says, walking toward the door.

"Don't go to them again, please."

Her mother tries to block her with her massive body.

"Get out of the way, mom!"

"No, my daughter, stay with me. You are too precious for me to lose you."

She grabs her by the forearm.

"Let me go! I am of age so I will do what I want."

"Stay with me, Yasmina. My dear daughter!"

"I am not your daughter, just let me go."

"No, you're not going out. I know you won't dare call the police on me because you're wanted."

"So that's your plan? It's inane! Aren't you ashamed to call me your darling daughter today? I know you didn't want me to be born. I narrowly missed an abortion. It's pure exaggeration for me to call you mom."

"Who told you that nonsense?"

"You're now forcing me to spit everything out. I saw the medical report. You wanted to deny me life. Are you going to tell me otherwise?"

"You've definitely got your eye on everything. Finding out what people are hiding will bring you nothing but misfortune. Beware of the consequences. I have to admit it to you today. It's true that I tried to do that, but it was for a good reason."

"You wanted to make yourself feel better, didn't you?"

"Girl … I'll explain. Things were more complicated than you think."

"I don't expect anything from you! Besides, you always hid my father from me."

"Your father, he's dead!"

"I don't believe you. You were separated from him at the time I was conceived. To erase traces of my father from your life, you sought to have an abortion, which doctors denied you. Your pregnancy had grown pass the stage where you could lawfully have an abortion. Isn't that true, bad mom?"

Her mother covers her face with her hands, shouting, "Ouch! … Ouch! …"

"Let me go, mom. This is a duty I have to fulfill, out of solidarity. Louise-Marie is my twin sister. The difference is that I have an identity card that she didn't have. I also have, unlike her, a hypocritical mother who pretends to love me whereas she had never had a crib in her house to welcome me. My life has always been a struggle at all stages. It is my nature. I don't have to stop tonight because you're cluttering the door with your bulk. Let me go to those who have a similar fate to mine, those for whom the earth is too precious to accept their miserable feet."

This last statement is particularly bitter. Mrs. Benaoui has often been told that she has a few curves. Fair enough. She doesn't mind the observation. It's therapeutic poetry to her. But this bulk thing that her daughter just came up with to describe her never crossed her mind.

She touches her thighs, thinking A*m I a bulk after all?* She steps away from the door. Her eyes are wet. Yasmina leaves the apartment.

20

CYPRIEN HAS NOT yet seen the flashing headlights he was told to expect. He is worried. If the team breaks up for some reason, their quest cannot continue. He comforts himself with the conviction that his friends will do anything to help him. Yasmina is an active member of the association *Naître et Vivre* (Living Babies) dedicated to the protection of children. Louise-Marie's case is of personal concern to her. As for Jules, he cannot defect at such a critical moment because he has a very noble idea of friendship.

Cyprien is right to be concerned, although the absence of his friends is not a sign of abandonment. While he is waiting for them at the cemetery, Jules and Yasmina are instead engaged in a surprising operation. They are scouring the streets in search of Internet cafés. Each time they find one, they park in the vicinity, some fifteen meters from the establishment. They plug in their laptop and insert a Wi-Fi adapter into a USB port. If the connection to the Internet is made, they declare the server unencrypted. They have identified several of these free server cybercafés in several neighbourhoods and grouped them by zones.

Now they are going down to the Pantin cemetery. The night is dark. Young trees share space with streetlights. Their branches, moving with the breeze, project zebra shadows on the sidewalk. Jules switches on the full beam. The headlights flash. Nobody reacts. They drive around again, making a big loop and coming back to the same spot. Before Jules can do the signal again, the rear door opens. It's Cyprien. He leaps into the vehicle. Jules and Yasmina jump.

"You scared the hell out of us!" they say in chorus.

"We thought you would come out from the cemetery," Yasmina says.

"Aren't you afraid of ghosts?"

"You don't look like a ghost. You're Cyprien."

"I am a ghost who has taken on Cyprien's features," he says, altering his voice.

He speaks in a nasal voice, effortlessly, as if he really belonged to another realm. He shows his friends blurred photos.

"Look at these photos. These people you see in them are morticians. They're our friends, our drivers. They are getting married tonight."

Looking at the photos, they can't decipher a single line out of them.

"You're making me sweat, my friend," Jules says, who starts the car trembling. He casts a quick glance at Cyprien to reassure himself. Far from the cemetery, the car stops. Yasmina takes out the computer equipment and hands Cyprien a minicomputer and a Wi-Fi adapter.

"You're now equipped. The battery is full but think of the energy saving options."

"What's this box for?" he asks, nasally.

"Stop scaring us, Cyprien. You're not a ghost," Yasmina says. "What I just gave you is a minicomputer to communicate with us."

"Thank you!" he says. "Let's keep in touch. Don't miss any of the tunes from tonight's concert."

Jules gives him the list of cybercafés that have not coded their servers.

"These are anchor points," Jules says. "Welcome to our little cyberworld."

He also gives Cyprien one of the pizza slices and some crunches that he and Yasmina have bought.

"What are these?" the so-called ghost asks.

"These are cakes," Jules says.

"Ah, thank you. My friends will love it! I have to go back to my house right away."

The three friends give each other hugs.

"Go back where?" Yasmina asks.

"To the cemetery!"

"Cyprien," Jules says, "don't try to be that prankster. You know we don't joke about ghost stories."

"I know, I know," Cyprien replies in a very strange voice.

"The three of us have to go to the night club. The best way to hide is to blend in with the crowd. We'll have fun until daybreak. Our homes smell of insecurity. Yasmina is okay with the plan. How about you?"

"Oh! Not bad, go ahead, young people, have fun. I will report to your friend Cyprien how well you treated me. Tell me, this box of matches that you gave me, girl, is it to warm up one's hands?"

"No, I already told you that it is a minicomputer."

"What is it for?"

"It's to communicate."

"Oh! Yes … with the beyond! Isn't it?" he says with a sepulchral voice.

"No, with us."

"Young people, I will tell him that you are very kind. Enjoy your time."

He slams the car door and starts running backwards towards the cemetery. In a few seconds, he disappears into the night.

"I'm so scared," Jules says.

"It sounds serious," his companion remarks.

"But we're not going to overthink it. I know it's not a ghost that has just visited us. It's Cyprien. He's going through a drama right now. You know, in order to overcome certain situations, you need humour and comicality."

"Ghost or Cyprien?"

"Cyprien turned into a ghost?"

They laugh out loud to raise their spirits.

At that same hour, Mrs. Benaoui is daydreaming. She is reviewing forty-one years of history. It is her age. She was born in Algiers, fatherless. Her father had died in the riots in Saint Denis in 1961. That year, Algerians were massacred and thrown into the Seine, while they were demonstrating and singing their Kassaman. Her mother was pregnant at the time. It was in this mourning atmosphere that the widow went to give birth in Algiers, where she settled down for good. Benaoui returned to Paris as a teenager, where fate led her to a man who would leave her during an unwanted pregnancy.

She thought abortion would be the way out. But the doctors were against it.

Benaoui would have liked to tell all these things to her daughter, to confess to her, to ask her forgiveness, if necessary to throw herself at her feet. She would have liked to explain to her daughter that she wanted to spare her the suffering of growing up without knowing her father. Because that was her own drama. She remembered how she would burst into tears every time her little friends at school would tell her about the delights of their weekends with mom and dad. She didn't want her child to experience that. But nature had decided otherwise. Through a forced birth, Yasmina was plucked out of her mother's womb. Mrs. Benaoui sighs. What can she do! The girl is not in a conciliatory mood. She left without even giving her mother the time to try an apology.

21

THE NIGHT WAS long and unsettled. Someone has reported to the hotline of the municipal police of Bobigny that a desecration of the local cemetery was about to take place. Several residents off Jean Jaures Avenue testified that they saw suspicious movements around the necropolis at the stroke of 9 pm. A small patrol was sent to check out the scene. Young policemen raided the area, armed with Sig-Sauer pistols and flashlights, and accompanied by dogs with raised ears. As soon as they passed the first graves, the dogs began to bark in an astonishing manner, as if suddenly enraged. Two policemen wondered what was going on.

"Tell me, do you think the dogs felt a human presence?"

"Yes, I am sure of it! The dead! There are plenty of them. There are lots of spirits floating around here. The dogs don't like to scent them. You see, our presence disturbs the peace of the cemetery."

"Do you think we are taking a risk?"

"You dare think of risk! You must rather say retaliation! Besides, we are not armed enough to enter this place at night."

"Don't you have your gun?"

"My poor man! Cemetery wars can never be won with guns. We need something decisive. You don't chase ghosts with a baton or a Sig-Sauer gadget."

"So, what do we need?"

"A crucifix."

"I was thinking of wood."

"Well, you're on the right track. A wooden crucifix would be ideal. Do you know why there's no longer a janitor in this cemetery?"

"No, tell me!"

"It's been on the news that there is smoke coming out of some graves at specific times at night, orchestras giving concerts, invisible horses neighing, iron blades clashing and breaking in a duel with swords that you can hear but cannot see. If there were only jokes in these unusual things, tell me why the cemetery has no guard. Tell me why the dogs go crazy."

"O God! Protect us!"

They made a fleeting turn around, skimming the perimeter wall, then went back out. Their report mentioned no evidence of profanation. Nothing suspicious. A simple black cat sitting on a grave, its eyes glowing under the light. This cat was well known. It was said to embody the spirit of the grave's occupant, because for sixteen years it had come to keep watch every night, only to fade away at dawn. The next day, a cemetery patrol found a pizza wrapper and a leftover cake behind a grave. The conclusion was clear: whoever left this waste behind was not a desecrator. He was a nutcase or a fugitive who needed shelter.

✑ As the first cybercafés are opened, Cyprien sends a cryptic email to his friend inviting him to a secret location. The response is swift: a rush of police officers to the place where the email originated. While the cybercafé is searched and the manager is subjected to a battery of questions, the fugitive continues on his way. The retrieval of the message in another district further away provokes the same movements. Jules, equipped with his laptop, does not need to leave the driver's seat to get his email. He easily connects using the wireless process that our century offers, keeping one foot on the pedal. In the following minute, the network provider has forwarded the IP address of the computer used. The cybercafé is located on the city map, as well as the Internet user. The General Intelligence forwards the piece of information to Laurent Fournier, who hurriedly sends his men to the scene. Unfortunately, the hunt is fruitless. Again! On the opposite side, the encrypted message has easily brought together the three acolytes. Cyprien, the victor of the storms, talks about his brief stay at Pantin-Bobigny cemetery: "I had a lot of talks with the dead last night."

"We have no doubt about that," Yasmina says.

"The cemetery is a violent place," Cyprien says. "The dead set traps for one another, step on one another, ride on one another's back, break one another's faces ..."

"I used to believe that it is the temple of peaceful rest," Yasmina says.

"Never mind! Our earth is more peaceful."

"Did you have nightmares?"

"No nightmares."

"So, you imagine the dead doing everything you just described!"

"It's not imagination, I saw them."

"How did they welcome you?"

"They have many things to confide to us, but we neglect them."

"By the way, I have a concern. Tell me sincerely if you were the one hidden in the so-called ghost of last night."

"What! Did you see a ghost?"

"I'm not sure. When Jules and I handed you the computer material last night, you seemed strange. As we were leaving, you didn't look like Cyprien anymore. Tell me if you were playing a joke."

"Ah, what shall I tell you, dear friend? In every being there is a bit of a human and a bit of a ghost. To be human or ghost depends which side of this duality is more dominant. But remember that what happened to you is your fault. You should never talk about ghosts without touching wood."

"You seem to have mastered the world of the dead."

"I certainly have!"

"Do you hear them?"

"Of course! They're here, close to me, talking to me!"

"You should pay attention to Louise-Marie's voice."

"Louise-Marie is not in Pantin cemetery. I had an idea that could bring us luck. As you know, night brings advice, as does the cemetery. So, a night in the cemetery results in advice given twice. This night inspired me to go and check the Bourbon vault in Saint Denis. That's where the illustrious kings of France and their families are buried."

Jules sounds doubtful. "We have already confirmed in books that there was never a funeral procession accompanying Louise-Marie to Saint Denis."

"We are going there in search of hidden clues," Cyprien says. "Everything is codified in this life. Decode, and you will understand. Such is the principle."

"You're a coward, Jules!" Yasmina says. "You're bringing that up because you're afraid to go down the underground crypt of Saint Denis. Ain't you?"

"There is some truth in what you say, my dear. I hope you will give me courage."

"And some milk from my breast too, my little baby."

Soon after they have had the idea, they head north to Saint Denis. They enter the city using a detour leading to the Stadium of France. As they walk down the Port Street, Yasmina recognizes the Pleyel Tower, which they see rising 140 meters above ground in the distance. She had come to Saint Denis before with her mother when she was just a child. It was for the commemoration of October 17th. They stopped on the train station bridge laid over the canal. Yasmina was enjoying the frenetic gliding of the trains on the rails while her mother was focusing her attention on the waters soiled with alluvium and greened by the reflection of the littoral moss. The child could not contain her surprise when her mother murmured words in Arabic, meaningless to her, before throwing into the water a poem she had composed the day before with tears in her eyes. Around her elegy, she had drawn green plants that formed a beautiful frame.

"Why are you throwing that letter in the water, Mom? It has beautiful drawings on it!"

"It's for your grandfather."

"My grandfather!"

She kept her astonishment to herself. Short after, not looking at the trains anymore, she asked: "Is my grandpa a crocodile, Mom?"

"No, he is a person like all of us."

"Does Grandpa live in water, Mom?"

"No, he doesn't. He drowned here long time ago, and he died. He was never found."

Yasmina asked no more questions, satisfied with her mom's little explanation and resigned to the fact that her genealogy would be limited to her mother. She had never known her father, and now she had learned her Grandpa was living in a canal, under the bridge of Saint Denis train station. As her mother was giving alms to beggars who were sitting on mats, the child turned her curiosity elsewhere, to the Pleyel Tower. She could see the huge advertising sign perched at the top of the tower, visible throughout Saint Denis Plain. Nowadays, this rotating ellipse with a thirty-five meter span holds the world record for the largest advertising signs. Her mother could not dare to tell her about the sinister events of October 17th. How could she tell the four-year-old that humans are capable of killing and drowning others right in the heart of the civilized world? And yet, the Seine and the canals had swallowed those bodies. A collective tombstone executed by the City of Saint Denis remains fixed to the railing of the station bridge. It bears an epitaph that cries out to all and sundry: "LET'S NOT FORGET THE ALGERIAN DEMONSTRATORS KILLED BY THE VICHY POLICE AND THROWN INTO THE SEINE ON

OCTOBER 17, 1961." The epitaph is there, clear, visible, eternal, so that no one pretends to ignore it, so that the negationists learn from it.

Now Yasmina sees the tombstone again as she crosses the bridge. She only has time to glance at it. She draws Jules' and Cyprien's attention to its presence, but the three friends don't get out of the car to pay respect to the tombstone. They have an urgent mission at the basilica.

Jules, who plays the connoisseur on the street and calls himself GPS, has just made a shameful mistake. After driving the wrong-way and narrowly escaping a collision with the surface train, he comes up onto Paul Eluard Street. Driving along randomly, he ends up in front of Gerard Philippe Theater, from where, fortunately, they can see the bell tower of the basilica.

22

In his Paris office located on the second floor of the police station, Commissioner Laurent Fournier has gathered his men to take stock. All the participants in the operations are there; from the teams assigned to the field operations to the switchboard operator receiving and dispatching communications. Around the table, they are listening to the chief's sermon. Fournier is not cuddly by nature. This morning, all circumstances have conspired to make him even less so.

Walls are covered with maps. He is standing next to a gigantic one, the map of the Paris region. In his right hand, he holds a pointer. His dissatisfied look infuriates the agents who think they have given their all to accomplish their mission. Fortunately, he acknowledges that failure is not always the result of incompetence.

"It's not easy being a cop in these snowy times," he says. "But let's not attribute all our failures to the road conditions and fugitives being hooded. We have a big challenge ahead. Need I remind you again, we are only some fourteen hours away from the deadline! By midnight tonight, we will have failed in our mission if we have not returned the stolen documents to the National Archives Center. After that time, anyone can publish the contents without penalty. You understand what is at stake. It is true that we can always prosecute the criminals for theft and vandalization of public property, but what the State wants to protect would have been revealed. This would be the most bitter outcome."

"What are they protecting in those papers, Commissioner?" an officer asks.

"I can't tell you. It is a three-and-a-half-century-old state secret. It dates back to Louis XIV. It has been protected from reign to reign, from government to government, until the Fifth Republic. Are we to suffer the legendary shame of not being able to maintain it in our turn? If we were, I assume you can imagine what the consequences might be for your careers."

A*nd yours too, Commissioner,* an officer thinks.

"Time is running out," the Commissioner says. "Be more vigilant, more pugnacious in questioning, more intuitive. The first tool of an investigator is his intuition, his flair. Go for everything that seems suspicious."

Are we going to strip people on the streets to identify them? another officer thinks.

"Look at this map," the chief says. "This is the Île-de-France Region. Here is Paris in the middle, like an egg yolk. Try to study Ghezo's movement on the ground. He was reported to be hiding in Saint Ouen, which is here." He points at an area in the northern suburbs. "Then in Saint Denis Plain, in Bobigny, and this morning in Bagnolet. He even offered you a gift that you refused to take. I am not happy that a fugitive comes to a cybercafé and leaves peacefully after using the Internet network that we are monitoring."

One of the members of the team is thinking: *You just have to put a policeman in front of every cybercafé.*

Ghezo and his friends are pros, another says to himself.

"As we speak," the Commissioner says, "the managers of those businesses are being questioned to determine their degree of complicity in the case. What do we find out from this itinerary? As you see, it is easy to notice that the man is moving around Paris in a clockwise direction. Look at these points, here, here, here, and here. He does not dare to cross the Ring Road. What conclusion do you think we can draw from it?"

A young man raises his hand. The Commissioner gives him the floor.

"I can conclude that he has respect for Paris, my Commissioner."

Everyone bursts out laughing.

"He has respect for Paris, yes," the Commissioner says, "but still, he was able to commit acts of vandalism in the Third District. In the heart of our capital. I mean just a stone's throw from our City Hall. You're kidding, dear sir! Do you want to be on guard for two weeks by yourself?"

"No, Commissioner."

Others who were about to speak think twice and don't.

"Anybody else?"

Someone raises a hand. "I see that he chooses low traffic areas."

"Well," the Commissioner say. "He avoids populated areas, hence his passage through a cemetery. Giving credence to your idea, assuming he moves in the same direction around Paris, what do you think is his next likely stop?"

"Bois de Vincennes!" three or four people say at once.

"Good point!" the Commissioner says. "And then?"

"Bagneux Cemetery!"

"Good!"

"Saint Cloud Park!"

"Good!"

"Bois de Boulogne!"

"Very good! Your anticipation of his movements represents a great leap for our task. We must position plain-clothes officers in all these places that you have mentioned. Before you go back to work, I would like to announce that I too have decided to move up a gear. In addition to the call for witnesses launched yesterday, here are the three photos that I will get published on the 1 pm news."

"Commissioner," Toulon says. "Don't you think that this publication would be detrimental to the discretion of our investigations, which is moreover the will of the Head of State?"

"Lieutenant Toulon, we have been given a job and it is up to us to define the method. Success has several fathers, but failure has only one. The discretion approach is over! We'll now put the steam roller in motion, and you'll see the result. Let's get going."

He adjourns the meeting.

While he remains to examine other aspects of the problem with Toulon, the men go out and rush into the vehicles. A policeman notices something unusual about one of their cars parked in the street, an object on its roof.

"It looks like another banana peel," his partner remarks.

The police break into an excited babble.

"Yes, it is a shit peel."

"Unbelievable! They are teasing us even in front of our premises!"

"And what is there on the hood?"

"It's a dog turd!"

"Let's take note of it. This is declared war. On your guns, guys!"

23

SAINT DENIS BASILICA is a semi-Gothic monument with a heterogeneous architectural composition that testifies to the great adventures it has gone through over the ages. Its rose window stands like a huge eye opened out onto the city. From Republic Avenue, the monument can be seen from the front as a gigantic one-piece square topped by a bell tower. It is accessed through three large oak wood doors. These are surmounted by arcades made up of a cluster of concentric semicircles. On its left, a stone indicates the location of the former Charlemagne's Palace. The basilica was originally nothing more than a tomb. It is only in recent times that a chancel was added to it to change it into a place of worship.

According to legend, it was built on the very spot where Denis, the eponymous saint, died in the third century. Denis was the first bishop of Paris and died as a martyr, beheaded on Montmartre Hill. After the deadly blade had separated his head from his body, he heroically picked up his head in both hands, stood up and began to walk northbound. At this place, which would bear his name centuries later, he entrusted his head to a young nun and died. Inspired by this miracle,

King Dagobert I got an abbey built there in the 7th century in honour of the martyred saint. This shuddering story is told in images on the underground walls of Saint Denis Basilica subway station, where you can see the martyr proudly holding up his head to the passengers sitting on the train.

It is into this unusual universe that Cyprien Ghezo, Jules Bartoli and Yasmina are about to set foot for a cause they consider just. It is a dull snowless day. Jules pushes open the metal gate of the fence that surrounds the monument. His two friends follow him. An arrow planted on the lawn shows visitors to the crypt the direction to the reception. The three young people turn to their right, walking along an alley soberly lined with plants. At the level of the right nave, a wooden kiosk awaits them. Nobody is there, curiously! This is the ticket booth. On the opposite way, another arrow leads them to the side entrance of the basilica. There, two female attendants, pinned down by the cold, have taken shelter behind the door, to work the booth. One of them is Loukia, a young woman, the other Amelie, an older colleague. The friends push the heavy panel and enter one after another, Jules leading the way. The girl greets them, mistaking Cyprien for a lady. "Good morning, ladies and a gentleman."

"Good morning," Jules replies.

"You have come to visit the crypt?"

"Exactly!"

"Do you have passes to the museums of Paris?"

"No, we do not."

"Do you have any discount cards?"

"No, we don't have them either."

"Then you're going to pay three times six euros."

"That makes it six hundred and sixty-six!" Cyprien says ironically.

"No, wrong calculation! That's six plus six plus six equals eighteen. You pay eighteen euros, ladies and a gentleman."

"Fortunately!" Yasmina says.

The girl gives them tickets, then directions: "To reach the crypt, take the stairs on the right that go underground."

They move on. Starting from the top of the stairs going down, a yellowish kind of lighting is struggling to overcome the darkness. Behind, at the booth, Amelie says to her young colleague Loukia: "You see, my dear, the joke this black girl just made did not please me. How can one imagine 6 × 3 to make 666?"

"Don't see the devil everywhere," Loukia says. "These are young people's antics."

"No. There are some things you shouldn't bring up in certain places. We are in the crypt of a basilica. I have always heard that around the necropolis lurk evil spirits."

"Damn! Forget about it! The dead don't scare me. My house in Greece rests on an old necropolis. Don't think that all the demons of our mythology that have passed through there are keeping me awake." Loukia is a young Greek student on an internship in Paris. She has been around all the monsters featured in their national mythology and yet, she has never found one that has scared her. For her, a mythological story is the best one to tell at night to put children to bed.

"You haven't been paying attention, Loukia. Haven't you noticed that this black girl is a bit strange? Her voice almost sounds like that of a man. And she's the one who came up with 666. Go figure what her intentions are!"

"Whatever you want, Amelie! We would have followed them if the video surveillance were working."

"It is working, but the receiver is in the sexton's office. He just left, so what can we do? We don't have his keys!"

"Well, that's it then!" Loukia says to dismiss the subject.

The three visitors move towards the choir of the church. Spread out in front of them are white marble and stone recumbents. To their left, the imposing tomb of Francis I elevates the monarch, shown standing with his entire royal family around him. He appears in his resurrection clothes, without the throne, crown, or scepter. Look! The King is king on earth only, it seems to mean. Heart recumbents and guts recumbents are scattered here and there below the altar. All of them have dogs sitting at their feet, symbols of fidelity and hope in the resurrection. It is as if the Sunday masses at Saint Denis Basilica are said only to the dead. Signs of life are scarce in this place. They are down to a few birds flying to their nests. The three pilgrims see the staircase on their right. They walk to it. This is a fateful moment. As in almost all crypts, the staircase reveals stonework that has been polished by the scuffle from people's steps through the centuries. They descend under the ground. The lighting is dim, the temperature lukewarm. It is a pleasant dampness, resulting from the natural heat of the crypt merging with the cold of a church at the mercy of winter. Just beyond the entrance to their right, stands a door that is protected by rusty bars. Two bronze angels supporting a shield topped with a crown are embossed on the gate, with the words: "Princes' Vault." Through the bars, one can see a few coffins made of oak, roughly carved, resting on trestles. It is impossible to approach them. The door remains closed. So, they move on.

To their left, a large room spreads out its great dead. Under marble slabs lie Louis XVI and Marie Antoinette, their necks still dripping with fresh blood resulting from their guillotine execution on the Revolution Square. The tomb of the young Louis XVII stands next to it, with the question, "Is there anyone in it?" To get to the surrounding wall, visitors must walk on the bare ground around heaps of rubble. There are so many holes! Holes here, holes there, holes everywhere! Archaeologists have excavated the ground in several places, looking for old bones.

Jules experiences some chills, but he holds on. It seems to him that, for the first time, he is not all that afraid of the dead. He is quite right. The dead are never more than paper tigers. It is of the living that one should be fearful.

Behind them, a deep female voice asks: "Can we help you?"

It is the ticket seller, Amelie, who has come down to the crypt.

"Yes, Madam! What is this huge stone?" Yasmina asks.

"It is a sarcophagus. An old-fashioned coffin, carved in the rock."

"Is there someone inside?"

"Of course, there is! It is the sarcophagus of Queen Aregonda. But many of these coffins and tombs you see here were emptied of their corpses during the Revolution.

The insurgents were enraged against the monarchy. The living kings were guillotined, the dead ones exhumed and thrown into a mass grave. Only a few, like Francis I, were able to escape this pit of shame."

"And why him?"

"Francis I was the idol of his people. In his time, he governed France with love and wisdom. It is to him that France owes the success of the Renaissance movement. The opening of our borders to new ideas. If the Mona Lisa stands today in pride of place in our Louvre Museum, it is because Francis I had the painter Da Vinci brought from Italy. Perhaps we would be obliged to speak Latin in France today, if the King had not decided, against the Pope's wishes, to make French our official language."

"Is it in his honour that the official language is called French?"

"Good deduction! Our language was even first called François before becoming French. I think this confusion is just a happy coincidence. Before Francis I, people already spoke François in the Paris region."

"And the mass grave, where is it?"

"It was on the site of the current garden, on the north side of the monument, facing Quatre Chapelles Street."

"Are the Kings still lying there?"

"Of course not! The excavations were made during the Bourbon Restoration. Some bodies were recovered and brought back to the vault. But who knows exactly which ones? It was all politics. Louis XVIII had the obligation to find the bodies of the previous kings to justify his own presence. Do you understand? A king can only succeed another. He had to restore the chain."

"We want to visit the vault," Cyprien says.

Ouch! This male voice does not reassure me, Amelie thinks. *This girl must not be the Blessed Virgin.*

"You want to visit the Bourbons!" Amelie says. "They are just behind you. There's the door to the vault." She gives Cyprien an oblique glance as the group moves away.

In front of them, the door shows a large image of crucified Christ in bronze. They cross the doorstep and access the arch-topped vaults. The ceiling light spreads a yellowish light. The first funerary medallions indicate the tombs of the dauphins of France. The side aisles are occupied by the dead—lots of them! With each step forward, the tombs increase in size, becoming more and more enormous. The biggest one is that of Louis XIV, the sun star that shines throughout the vault. His funeral medallion is surrounded by two mourners in tears and features an angel carrying the King's heart in his hand. Amelie, the ticket seller, is still there, trailing them.

Jules points at the angel. "What does this representation mean?"

"It means that we are in front of a heart sepulcher," she says.

"And where is the body of the King?"

"In the mass grave. It was destroyed with lime like all the other bodies that had occupied thrones when alive. Long afterwards, the King's heart was brought back here."

"Let me get this straight," Yasmina says. "If I understand correctly, the revolutionaries took the time to dismember the bodies to keep a part of them as a souvenir?"

"Oh, no! You are mistaken. The dissection was done before the burial. Before a body was embalmed, the heart and guts were taken out of it. A single person could be buried in three separate places. There have been cases of monarchs being buried in three countries at a time to honour three different nations. This separation was the best solution found by the English to preserve their dead, since the guts inside the body did not stand the test of time. Didn't you see up there, recumbents of body, heart, and guts?"

"I only noticed recumbents of body and heart," Yasmina says.

"You missed the ones with their guts out," Cyprien says. "They carry small baskets or saddlebags, containing, of course, their guts."

The woman regards Cyprien with a mix of admiration and suspicion. "That's it! You are vigilant, young lady!"

To the left of the sovereign, some famous names lie under not very imposing tombs. The only monument of equal size is the one housing the remains of his wife, Marie-Thérèse of Austria.

Yasmina points. "We are in front of Louise-Marie's mother."

"This is an unforgettable moment!" Jules whispers. "I feel myself being transported to the beyond."

Cyprien is surprisingly quiet. He examines the medallion of the Queen overhung by two cherubs in tears. Between them they keep a black urn which must contain the heart of the sovereign. The tombstone bears the following epitaph:

> HERE IS THE BODY
> OF THE VERY GREAT AND VERY POWERFUL
> AND VIRTUOUS PRINCESS

MARIE-THÉRÈSE OF AUSTRIA
SPOUSE OF KING LOUIS XIV
DECEASED AT THE VERSAILLES CASTLE
ON JULY 30, 1683.
REQYIESCAT IN PACE.

"This string of praises doesn't get us any far," Jules says.

"Are you looking for something specific?" Amelie asks.

"No, madam, we can manage on our own. Thank you."

"Can you tell us about Louise-Marie, the daughter of this sovereign?" Yasmina asks.

"Who am I to explain it to you? It is a taboo subject covered with a leaden screed in the history of France. She was called the Mooress—"

"What does this name mean?"

Amelie smiles. "Now you are dragging me into the history of the great conquest. But I'm happy to explain: In Mauritania, a region located in the west of the Maghreb and encompassing, among other lands, present-day Morocco, their inhabitants, who were of strongly mixed race, were called Moors. It was from that region of Africa that the Arabs attacked southern Europe in 711, crossing the Strait of Gibraltar. If you consider that this strait is only seventeen kilometers wide, you can understand how easy it was for them to invade. As a result, the name 'Moor' remained in European society as a preferred term for 'African'. Mooress simply means Black woman, and we close the parenthesis. Some historical elements that we have of this daughter born out of adultery have been transformed into legend. You see how human mischief works! History is transformed into legend and legend into history. Consider how much weight is given to the story of a decapitated man who picks up his head and starts walking. To me, this is less real than the birth of this mixed-race girl who was seen and touched by all the King's doctors and the Queen's maids. Many other courtiers had seen her."

"Was she never buried here?"

"Never! Read the epitaphs for yourself. It is her absence from the Bourbon Vault that turns her whole story into a legend. She was declared dead after her birth, but nothing is less sure. Why don't you go to the National Archives if you are so interested in the subject?"

"No, ma'am, it was just a matter of curiosity."

"Anything else?"

"Nothing for the moment."

"Please let me know if you have any concerns."

"Thank you very much, that's very kind of you, ma'am."

Amelie walks back to the stairs and starts moving up, leaving the trio more confused than satisfied.

To the left of the Queen, a large stained-glass window displays three lily flowers that symbolize the crown of France. In the middle of the lilies, one of the nails that were used to crucify Christ, can be seen sticking out. This old metal from the first century, well protected against the assault of rust, is a reliquary treasure carefully preserved by Saint Denis Basilica. The Papacy wanted to reward France for its outstanding commitment to the spread of Christianity.

The crypt is silent. The three friends look at each other, contemplating their failure.

"We're not out of the woods yet," Cyprien says. "We have to rethink our plan."

"The crypt has not given us any useful information," Jules says. "Can we still have hope of finding something?"

"The main protagonists are present," Yasmina says. "The victim's mother and her adoptive father. The very one who had ordered the murder. The only missing character is the victim herself. Perhaps under these graves there are other unsuspected people who took part in the crime, or who knew a lot about it. You know, the dead are in all corners of the basilica! Some can be found outside too. They are everywhere! One cannot excavate Victor Hugo Square without dislodging them. The marketplace itself is a necropolis. People step on them as they buy and sell."

"Unfortunately, the dead don't talk," Jules says.

"Jules, we are going to make the dead speak," Cyprien says. "That's where our hope lies."

"Are you going to descend into the underworld to record them with a mic?"

"They will come up from the underworld and tell us what they know. We're going to use spiritism."

"SPI-RI-TI-SM!" Jules says, frightened.

"It seems to me that it's dangerous to communicate with the hereafter," Yasmina says.

"That's what they say," Cyprien replies. "But we have no choice. Look around you. It's a vast and macabre mass killing site, pits of dissected bodies, hearts, guts ... We are already too far gone to back down. I hope that here, six meters under the ground, you guys understand that you have crossed more than a surrounding city border. These are no longer the northern suburbs of Paris. This is a crossroads of several worlds."

For the first time, Jules asks for a cigarette.

"Smoke, smoke, my boy," Cyprien says. "But don't get caught by that snooper! Smoke. It will repair your morale."

24

THEY RESURFACE ON Victor Hugo Square. A chilling wind is shaking canopies over stores. People rush into the subway mouth to take shelter. The Sedan is waiting there, faithful and impassive, like a good dog. Jules pulls out the car keys as the trio approaches it. He suddenly stops, sees something under the windshield wiper.

"They gave us another ticket; I don't know what for!"

"It's so stupid!" Yasmina says.

Cyprien pulls the paper out. "It's not a ticket. It's a handwritten note!"

"Who from?" Jules asks.

"Ah, it's James Bonnot! Our invisible teammate."

"What a curious encounter!" Yasmina says. "How did he know that we are here?"

In his letter, Bonnot invites Cyprien to join him at Le Khedive café, located right in front of the basilica. It is far from an anonymous letter. He has signed it and refers to Cyprien as "Dear friend."

"What are you going to do?" Jules asks.

"I'm going to meet him, but I beg you to stay away. If this invitation is a trap, let's not all three fall into it. The search must go on, even if one of us disappears. You know what to do now. Start searching on the Internet for the address of a spiritualist who can help us make the dead talk. If it is really Bonnot who is inviting me, I can't determine where chance will lead us. He is a very resourceful man. Be brave, friends. I have confidence in you."

He gives Yasmina a hug and bumps his fist with Jules'.

"Good luck, be careful," Yasmina says.

At the same time, inspectors of the GI are engaged in a vast recce operation while Commissioner Fournier is in the field lending a hand. The photos published on the 1 pm TV news have had an effect. The Commissioner had made it a point of honour, and now, in the eyes of all, he has won the bet. Just after the broadcast, he receives a phone call on the green line open to the public. In a quavering voice, a woman, probably in her forties, gives him some clues about the wanted young people. She begs the Commissioner not to reveal her identity. She would commit suicide if he did, she tells him.

"They are driving a black sedan, Commissioner."

"Which way did they go, ma'am?"

"I don't know. Look for them in Paris. I don't think one can be dragging a car like that in the suburbs."

"Do you have any more details, ma'am?"

She doesn't answer. She bursts out into subs, then into tears.

"I'm sorry, ma'am. Don't feel bad. You have just done your service to the State. Your gesture is patriotic. I thank you on behalf of the National Police."

Suddenly the Commissioner realizes he is only talking to himself. He has heard the woman hang up. He hangs up too and immediately asks Toulon to come and pick him up at the police station. Soon after, both leave under the snow floating down.

Le Khedive café is a small boiler. Cyprien sits opposite James Bonnot. He is still amazed that his accomplice was able to locate him so easily.

"I did it by intuition, dear friend," Bonnot says. "Just like a river always ends up in the sea, one cannot investigate the Bourbon dynasty of France without passing through the Vault. Now that I've caught you red-handed, tell me what you got out of there."

"Nothing new. My buddies and I went through all the dead in the crypt without getting a single word out of their mouths. But we will not digest this failure. We are determined to keep grinding on. The dead must speak. My two friends have taken it upon themselves to find a medium who will put us in touch with the hereafter."

"Are you really going to do that?"

Cyprien looks at him blankly, then gives a firm "yes". Bonnot makes no comment. Instead, he recounts his own epic journey to trace the Queen's lover.

"You know, Nabo's case is not a small one. Yesterday, I impulsively went to the Bastille Square."

Cyprien laughs. "What for? What is this Nabo you're going to look for in the Opera backstage? You're going back more than two hundred years, dear friend!"

"I'm telling you the truth, at the risk of being accused of anachronism. You know, when you can't find a way out, you shouldn't give up. You have to seek another door. A hidden door can always open up to a blind person groping the wall for it."

"I guess you were quite disappointed."

"Think again! I was rather well received by the statue that dominates the square. In the very place where thousands of lives were buried for centuries for the pleasure of various kings, today a giant stele supports a golden angel wielding a torch."

"You did not go there to become a poet!"

"That's right! I went there more to get ideas than to find Nabo. A door can open from anywhere. You just have to move. I know that from the bowels of that ground covered by the present tar, the muffled cries and voices of ancient prisoners are still rising. The 'Iron Mask' lived there. The mystery around that political prisoner has not been solved yet."

"It is said that he was the twin brother of King Louis XIV, that the monarch was afraid he would usurp the throne. To protect himself from that threat, King Louis XIV sent him to prison, with an iron mask around his face."

"Wrong! It is not said in any biography that Louis XIV's mother, Queen Anne of Austria, had twins."

"Voltaire says that the 'Iron Mask' was a person of average height. However, Nabo was always depicted as a dwarf."

"Wrong! Voltaire is the master of irony. I don't believe Voltaire at face value. His own friend and confidante Catherine II of Russia hid a lot of things from him to avoid being mocked."

"Do you mean that the 'Iron Mask' is our Nabo?"

"It is one possibility among many others."

Cyprien in turn is flabbergasted by this assumption.

"I also went to the Louvre Castle this morning," Bonnot says.

"You mean the Louvre Museum?"

"No, I said castle! The remains of the royal castle of the Louvre if you like. Access is through the museum, so you're not wrong at all on that account. Behind the Sully wing lies the ancient dungeon surrounded by a moat in the underground rubble. The curators have called this part the 'Medieval Louvre'. Many visitors forget to make a detour there. They prefer to stop in Denon galleries to stare at Venus' genitals. But it is in this old rubble that the rich history of the castle is hidden. It was not originally a royal residence, let alone a museum. It was a simple watchtower set up on the banks of the Seine to keep an eye on the Vikings arriving. The Vikings used to invade Paris through this river gateway, paddling their very fast *drakkars*."

"Where did you find all that information?"

James Bonnot smiles and puffs himself up. "I did some research this morning."

"Not in a library, I hope!"

"Don't worry, I've been warned. I used the Internet to remain anonymous."

"I don't understand your purpose in going to the Louvre."

"Ah, here we are! You know that Louis XIV was an itinerant king who never spent two nights in the same castle. Before settling in Versailles, he took his family to Vincennes, Fontainebleau, Saint Germain, and the Louvre. It was from the latter that he had moved to Versailles. In this castle of the Louvre was an abandoned well that had been transformed into an execution pit for some category of prisoners."

"Could Nabo have been one of them?"

"Who knows! The pit still exists, I saw it! But it has been filled up to four meters deep only, and it is now fenced off for the safety of visitors. The Medieval Louvre is a mysterious place. When you are there, you can hear past whisperings through these walls of large stones laid more than thirteen centuries ago."

"I didn't know that beyond the Sully wing there was another site of interest."

"When we're done with these investigations, you can take some time to visit the place. Don't look at it with the eyes of a tourist like everyone else. Look at it with the judgment of someone who is trying to solve a mystery. Perhaps you will ask yourself the same question I did: 'What are the monuments of Paris hiding?' The monuments of Paris, ancient as well as modern, have not been placed randomly on the ground. From the apartments of Napoleon III, you can see the ultramodern business center of The Defense in the distance. Its Great Arche is aligned with the Triumphal Arche. The Triumphal Arche aligned with the Obelisk of the Concorde Square through the Champs Elysees Avenue. The Obelisk is aligned with the Triumphal Arche of Carousel. The Triumphal Arche of Carousel points to the tip of the Louvre Museum's pyramid. The pyramid in turn is aligned with the keep of the Medieval Louvre. If you extend the line, you end up at the Bastille! From the past to the future, or in the opposite direction, the history of Paris is written in a single straight line. What do the monuments of Paris hide? It is not trivial, if someone has recently unearthed the remains of a woman, a biblical character who knew Christ closely, hidden in one of these places under the magic line, and which has henceforth become a place of worship for a certain order of believers. What do the monuments of Paris hide? Dear friend, this century will not end until all veils are lifted on the great mysteries of humanity."

"James, you have stuffed me with too much information. If I keep listening to you, we will never move from here."

"And you, you did well to come to this meetup. We'll keep in touch. While you're looking for your medium, I'll be exploring a third lead on Nabo's track. Another theory is that he was sold into slavery in Nantes and was taken to the Americas. The lead is open, and I'm going for it. You have my address. Ring my doorbell any time you want, you'll be welcome. But then, only as long as they don't call me back tomorrow to work on another site."

They get up and leave separately. Each one goes his own way, as if they haven't seen each other.

25

LAURENT FOURNIER IS about to make a career move. Assisted by the experts of the GI and latest recon technology, he was able to locate a black 6-door sedan with two occupants on board. From a military recon satellite, technicians were able to zoom in and film several streets in Paris, to find the precise shape of the vehicle. All technical tricks are possible in this century, with these artificial eyes looking down on us from above. This success came on the heels of a failed attempt. At first, Fournier followed a vehicle several miles south, only to discover that it was the wrong target. The moment he was about to point his gun at the driver and order him to stop, Fournier realized his own mistake. The driver was a harmless gray-haired citizen in his fifties with a coquettish pipe wedged in the corner of his mouth. The Commissioner let him peacefully disappear into the mouth of the tunnel. Then Fournier had turned to head back to Paris. Now, this other vehicle in the east, the right one, is in the crosshairs.

He and his henchman are now in the Grands Moulins neighbourhood. This time, things seem much more precise. To top it all off, the car's registration number sent to police headquarters for verification shows the car to belong to a certain Bartoli. Upon reception of this detail, Fournier gives Toulon a look, shaking his head.

"It's Jules' father," the Commissioner says.

"There's no doubt about it," the Lieutenant replies.

The two cops have refrained from making any sudden moves. They decide they will first just follow the fugitives to discover their hide-out.

"We have them all in the trap. But tell me, how can a respectable father support his son in such stupidity?"

"Commissioner, we only criticize what we don't know. You don't know what he, the father, is getting out of this."

"That's what we're going to find out. The end is near. Since Syracuse III satellite was launched five years ago, it has worked only in remote areas. Now, for the first time, it is providing us with real service on French territory, in the capital itself. Thanks to this device, both our suspects are in the net. I'd like to see them paraded in the 8 pm news. You see, Lieutenant, I'm thinking right now that this Mr. Bartoli is not just trying to keep his son out of trouble. He must be involved at the highest level in this case."

"For what reason, Commissioner?"

"To harm the Republic, for example. You'll say I'm suspicious, but ... Don't you know his origins? Don't you know the association he has always belonged to as member? Don't you know that his peers have just entrusted him with the presidency of the organization? Are you telling me that the Association of Corsicans in Paris is an association without tendencies? Worrying things are happening these days. Statesmen have been taking turns receiving anonymous letters containing bullets. Who is behind this threat?"

"It's strange, Commissioner, but we are only at the stage of suspicion."

"You know, our actions always start with suspicions. If Mr. Bartoli has been involved, I wouldn't be surprised. It would just be following a classic pattern."

The Sedan turns right. Since it has been drizzling for a few minutes, the condensation on the side windows distorts the silhouettes of those in the car. As a result, the cops have not been able to identify the suspects. But the fugitives have noticed the disturbing presence. The rear window wiper clears a portion of the windshield. In the front mirror, a white vehicle equipped with flashing lights springs into view, like a tiger who has been lying in wait for a hiker on a trail. "We are being followed!" Yasmina exclaims.

"I can see that, my chick," Jules says. "I noticed it long time ago, but I didn't want to tell you. Don't panic. We'll get through this. Trust me."

"Let's stop for a moment to see how they behave."

Jules signals and slows down.

"They're stopping," the Commissioner says. "This moment will have cost us a total of four days of steady effort. Now comes the apotheosis."

Toulon, with a fixed look, doesn't answer. He taps his thigh, feeling the outline of his gun. The Commissioner checks his watch, as a referee does in order to blow the final whistle to end a match. They arrive on the spot and block the Sedan on the left. The Commissioner gets out first. He walks on the tarmac with his slightly duck-shaped feet. His navy-blue coat is beaded with small snowflakes melting away as quickly as they fall. He begins to spew orders.

"Young man, police! This is the National Police, if we need to introduce ourselves for the umpteenth time! Turn off the engine and get out of your vehicle! You too, young lady, I want both of you out of the car."

Jules ignores the Commissioner, who shouts again: "Shut this engine off. That's an order!"

Nevertheless, he has a twinge in the heart when he notices the big game is not on board. It is an ordinary girl with soft eyes, not the elusive fugitive, who is occupying the passenger seat. Does he have the power to transform into a woman, or power for other similar feats? The big cop is a bit confused. Capturing Ghezo has become a personal challenge beyond simple professional duty for him. He realizes at this moment that nothing is played out, not by a long way! Jules shifts into reverse and does a pirouette that surprises the policemen. Before the Commissioner has had time to get in his car, the Sedan has made a U-turn. Jules merges into the main boulevard that leads to Denis Diderot University where he and his girlfriend are students. In his haste, he disregards all road signs.

"Commissioner!" Toulon says. "He is playing into our field of competence: car chasing. I can assure you he will not get past the first intersection before we've got him."

The Commissioner calls for reinforcements, something he has not thought to do before. Ever since he has been on the tail of the Sedan, he has imagined a simple scenario in which he would unglue a bewildered young kid from the steering wheel, put a hand on his shoulder and say: "My little boy, everything will be okay. We know you were set up. Come with us to the station to answer just a few questions, after which you'll rejoin your family. Do you have Dad's number?"

But now, the scenario that plays out before his eyes is quite different. Jules has taken off like a bullet, shifting gears relentlessly, driving with the audacity of a superman that has been dormant inside him through his years at university. The siren behind him is screaming loudly. He gets off the road as soon as he catches sight of the first of the campus buildings. He takes a street that winds around the campus, serving several faculties. Toulon does not let his quarry lose him that easily. He uses the blast of his siren to open his way. With fierce impetus, he takes an unconventional way towards his prey. In no time, the Sedan is cornered.

Jules doesn't know how he got there, to a sudden and shattering stop. He only remembers his car being forced onto the sidewalk without any way to bounce back. He can still hear the bang from his bumper uprooting a parking meter. The two policemen get out the van and slam the doors. Game over!

Just when Toulon has become master of the situation, reinforcements arrive. He is deflated and feels robbed of the glory of having caught the fugitives all by himself. Why did they arrive so promptly, just when he had things under control? But then he is saying to himself: *Well, what does it matter! The Commissioner has witnessed everything. He now knows to whom he would entrust critical missions.*

The police unhook an agitated Jules from the wheel. One of the policemen throws him onto the ground. Yasmina yells at him in protest. To immobilize him, the policeman puts a foot on the boy's throat. Yasmina slaps the man, and she is grabbed in turn. She and her boyfriend are handcuffed. Students have gathered to watch. Among them, some classmates recognize Jules.

"Hey, Jules! What happened?"

"Guys, I am dealing with savages. I was late for class, and I refused to stop."

"Is that all?"

He doesn't have time to answer. The police take him into the van and throw him onto a seat. Yasmina suffers the same fate.

"All this violence on young people for a refusal to stop?"

The horrified crowd moves into action. They whistle, throw stones. The Commissioner orders his men to leave immediately. The last vehicle to leave the scene is heartily stoned. Smell of gunpowder pervades the campus.

26

IN A LITTLE busy street of the northern suburbs, a person walks towards a telephone booth. She is wearing a black down jacket with a fur-edged hood. Her gait is impeccably undulating. A handbag tucked under her arm. She pulls open the door of the booth and gets inside. Then, she rubs her hands energetically to fight the cold. From her purse, she pulls out a card and dials a number. A phone rings in an office in Paris. As no one has picked up, the answering system starts. A recorded voice gives the hours of operation and the days when visitors are received. It also gives an alternative number to whoever wants to contact the duty service. The caller dials this alternative number right away. This time, the number rings in Lyon. A man picks up the phone and introduces himself. He is the receptionist at the Spiritualist Studies Center in Lyon. The caller introduces herself too. She is none other but Cyprien Ghezo in drag.

"How can I help you, sir?" the receptionist asks.

"I'm calling to know if you can help me get in touch with a relative of mine who has died."

"For what purpose do you intend to communicate with your deceased?"

"I am waiting for some important information from him. Very important."

"Oh, I am afraid our Center cannot help you. We are Kardecist spiritualists."

"What do you mean by Kardecists?"

"This means our spiritualist branch was inspired by Allan Kardec. We have our principles and our rules which differ from those of others."

"Don't you have any mediums at the Center?"

"Of course, we do. In fact, we are all mediums, each in his or her own field and specialty. But we don't do summoning for entertainment purposes, sir!"

"I don't believe that having a dead person testify on an important issue is entertainment. Unless you declare it as such."

"Absolutely! The *Gospel According to Spiritualism* allows us to contact the dead for the sole purpose of helping grieving souls and lost souls find their way. The only thing I recommend is that you enter into prayer. Pray, pray very hard. Christ will answer your questioning and spare you a cumbersome and potentially dangerous communication."

"Do you have anything else to offer me?"

"No, I'm sorry I can't help you further. If you would like us to pray for the repose of the soul of your deceased, we are willing to do so."

"Thank you for having me."

"You're welcome, sir!"

Cyprien hits the pound sign twice and dials a second number on his list. It's a cell phone number. At the end of the line, Sahid picks up. He introduces himself as a medium, without any diplomacy. He works every day, at any time and wherever he is invited. He makes a living mainly from his spiritual work, in addition to curing illnesses and other psychic affections. Many Parisians know him from leaflets he mails out from his office. His website is a magnificent constellation of stars twinkling on a dark blue background streaked with meteors and supernovae. Everything to help transport you to the clouds. A phenomenon! It was on this site that Cyprien got his contact. He then sent an email to his friends to inform them, but they have not yet responded.

Sahid is relaxed and open. "I can help you get in touch with your deceased," he says, "with no strings attached. All I expect from you is that you participate in the seance so you can ask the dead your own questions."

"It's a deal, Mr. Sahid!"

"Tell me, how long ago did he die?"

"Oh ... he died years ago!"

"About how many years ago?"

"I can't tell you exactly. At the time, I was very small."

"Did you know him?"

"Mmmm ... yes!"

"Perfect!"

"His first name?"

"Louis."

"That's perfect! According to my schedule, I have time for you tomorrow night. For Louis, tomorrow will be a very good day for his descent. Does that suit you?"

"Oh no! Too late! I need your help now!"

The spiritualist laughs.

"Is it that urgent, sir? Don't tell me it's a treasure hunt. I have often seen such haste in inheritance disputes." He laughs again. Is this a man or a spirit laughter? Hard to tell!

"It is quite different, Mr. Sahid! I have no materialistic purpose hidden behind my request."

"It would not have bothered me if you did. My role is limited to bringing you in contact with your deceased one. I don't worry about the rest. But, as for your demand that I act immediately, be advised that I do not summon spirits in broad daylight."

But why? Cyprien asks himself. *Would the Sun King hate the day, as long as he is the star of it?* "I beg you to receive me this evening, Mr. Sahid," he says.

"Well, I'll do you that favour but know that an emergency job will cost you a different rate."

"The rate is the least of my worries. Tell me if I can bring some friends."

"Yes, I recommend that you do. But choose serious friends, not curious ones. If they really want to support you morally and spiritually, they are welcome to my office."

"Thank you in advance, Mr. Sahid. You are removing a thorn from my side."

"I hope so. Be spiritually prepared, because talking to the dead is not without its risks. I will be waiting for you and your friends in my office. You should all dress in black."

"We will do. I can't thank you enough!"

"You are welcome."

27

THE CAMPUS OF Denis Diderot University has gradually become an inferno. In their discontent, students have set fires everywhere. Classrooms remain empty, while barricades guarded by strongmen screen the campus entrances. Banners, hastily made and hoisted high, demand: "We want our mates back!"

At the police station, the scene is quite different. In his cozy office on the second floor, Commissioner Fournier is doing the questioning, his favourite exercise. He has started with Jules Bartoli who invariably uses his alibis and insinuations to confuse him. The young man has denied all the accusations about his complicity with Ghezo, before adding that the police are against him for the simple reason that he is Corsican. The Commissioner, aware of the direction the young man is trying to drag him into, has stopped hearing him. Phone calls and a flow of faxes sent from the Ministry of Homeland Security punctuate the pause to the questioning; after which the Commissioner gets back to the young people. He is suddenly less pugnacious and is now more open to listening to what they have to say.

It is Yasmina's turn to face this questioning machine called Fournier. He never missed any opportunity to strengthen his reputation in the annals of the Investigative Police. It is undoubtedly in view of his past prowess in this area that the authorities invested him with the present mission. He was born in the Sixth District fifty-two years ago, and he knows Paris like the back of his hand.

Visibly annoyed by her new environment, Yasmina does not hide her feeling.

"I'm tired of being held here, Commissioner," she says.

"You know, young lady, a custody lasts forty-eight hours and can even be extended."

"I've already told you everything I know. Don't think that you will use me as a mill to grind out answers to your questions. I want to get out of here. Can you believe it? I even came close to doing something despicable just now."

"What do you mean?"

"Forget it, Commissioner. If I had taken the step, we wouldn't be here killing time."

The Commissioner twirls his moustache, as thick as a broom brush.

"What are you talking about, miss? Don't tell me that you intended to kill yourself in the cell!"

"No, you're way off base."

"Tell me what then."

"I almost killed you."

"Killed me?!"

"Yes, Commissioner! You humiliated me in front of my friends, and I won't stand for it. I'm guessing Jules is holding the same grudge."

"Are you carrying a concealed weapon?"

"No, your men searched me like savages, taking away all my belongings. It's a wonder they left me clothed."

"How can you think of killing me without a weapon?"

"Do you think you need Hi-Tech to kill a person? I have my archaic methods that work just as well as a gunshot."

"Who are your hidden accomplices? Which secret organizations are supporting you?"

She does not answer. The man glances around the room in vain for a sharp or pointed object.

"I find it hard to believe you. You can't kill me without a weapon. Perhaps you thought of poisoning my coffee?"

"Poison is the weapon of cowards. A worthy enemy reveals their face."

He looks at this little slim girl, a killer by pretense. His gaze still circles the room.

"I guess the weapon is what you're looking for," she says. "Turn around and look at what's in the wall, right behind your head."

He turns and looks at the wall, noticing nothing. "I don't see anything," he says.

"It's not an object, it's a drawing."

He turns again, scanning the wall. "It seems that I have suddenly lost my sight with my eyes open!"

"Turn around and look at me now, Commissioner."

"Ouch!" he shouts as he faces the girl.

She is now standing, with glowing eyes, gripping the metal chair she has been sitting in. She holds the chair, like the sword of Damocles, over the Commissioner's skull.

"You see, it's that simple," she says. "I would have bashed your brains out if I had wanted to, when you had your back to me." She puts down the chair.

The Commissioner sighs with relief. "Why did you spare me?"

"I don't like loose blows. I like to give and receive all my blows in the face."

"Have you ever killed a man?"

"No, not yet. You would have been my first."

"You're off to a bad start, young lady. Real killers don't hesitate."

"A day will come, Commissioner. I'm giving you a reprieve. You're safe for now."

He looks at her with moving lips, thinking. *And me, what am I going to do with you and the other asshole who just told me about his Corsican origin?*

On the campus, banners of all kinds rule the day. At the ministry of Higher Education, officials lean towards favouring measures to appease the students. They calculate that it would be better to seize an opportunity to deal with the students' demands at this early stage while they are still modest. It would be unwise to wait for the demands to turn into political grievances. The Minister of Homeland Security is leading in the polls for the presidential elections. He doesn't want to risk this political edge he is enjoying a few months before the vote. At this strategic moment in the campaign, he doesn't want people to accuse the police of using disproportionate force against students. But it seems too late for him to avoid blame. On the campus already, someone has made a puppet-minister that is swinging pitifully atop a stick in the demonstration. The contents of a burst egg are pouring down the chest of the puppet.

In a restricted Council of Ministers session, the Head of State urges that, for the sake of appeasement, the detained students should be released under certain conditions. Recalling, he says, "Many of our colleagues have not yet recovered from the CPE crisis." This is a reference to the huge protest that had broken out around the program called 'first job contract' tailored for young graduates involving the Government and business owners. "Remember the hordes of young people in the streets of France. Do not throw another stone into the pond. A rebellious student is poison."

With the session adjourned, Commissioner Fournier is summoned by his supervisory minister. He is asked to release the students and make Cyprien Ghezo his main target. Ghezo is the one holding the box containing the Old Regime archives.

"Bitter pill, Mr. Minister!" Fournier says. "I need these two young people to find the trail of the main culprit."

"I understand your disappointment, Commissioner. But, in my opinion, nothing prevents you from interrogating them whenever you want. Put them under surveillance, not under arrest. Our goal is to prevent any unrest on the campus."

As soon as he leaves the ministry, the Commissioner gets a call forwarded to his cell phone from Police Headquarters. A woman is at the other end of the line. She does not introduce herself. She says she knows where Ghezo is hiding. The news buoys up the Commissioner, who says to himself: *That's life. You lose here, you win there ... One lead fades, another shows up. What a job!*

"That's great!" he says to the woman. "If you wish to remain anonymous, I assure you that no one, not even myself, will seek to know your identity."

"I am not afraid of being recognized, Commissioner. My name is Pamela, and I live in Château d'Eau."

"Tell me everything, Pamela. Where is he?"

"I have nothing to tell you, Commissioner. It's a deal. You placed an order, don't ask to get it delivered without paying a penny."

"I'm not sure I understand you, ma'am. Can you please tell me what you mean?"

"If you want to be clever, Commissioner, let's say goodbye."

"No! No, ma'am. Don't hang up! You want to talk about the promised reward, you'll get it! You'll get everything you want."

Pamela hangs up. To the Commissioner's disappointment, he can only hear beeps from the other end of the line.

28

At Sahid's place, the decor of the great seance evenings is slowly being set up. A round table, a black throw, red candles, incense, oriental perfumes and so on. The Ouija board is in place, with its planchette placed among the tokens. The practitioner is waiting for his customers.

While efforts to make the dead testify are taking place here, Laurent Fournier is waiting for his testimony from the mouth of a living person, Pamela. The Commissioner is bent on not wasting this unique opportunity the unknown woman is offering. At Fournier's request, a telephone operator has provided the address associated with Pamela's number. The Commissioner is now on his way to Château d'Eau, with some men following him at a discreet distance.

"I'm guessing this woman is not a prankster," he says to Toulon. "If she is serious like she seems to be, we'll have our game before nightfall. I want him featured on the 8 pm news. Tonight! Don't forget, Lieutenant, we're running against the clock. Tomorrow is not today. If we arrest him tomorrow instead of tonight, we'll have missed the deadline. Our pride as cops will suffer a hit. We will have failed to protect an age-old secret, to our shame. Not to mention the political fallout for which the State will hold us responsible."

"These politicians want to have their cake and eat it too," Toulon says. "How do you hold us to the rule that requires us to release accomplices?"

They find the street the operator identified without much effort. The entrance of the building is secured with an electronic lock-fitted door. The Commissioner rings Pamela's doorbell. She does not answer. When she hears the second chime, she asks the visitor to identify himself.

"Hello Pamela, it's your neighbour. I forgot my fob on my way out. Could you please open the door for me?"

"With pleasure, Commissioner!"

"She saw us!" Toulon says, looking in vain for a surveillance camera.

Pamela unlocks the door. The two men get in. Pamela is waiting for them at the entrance of her apartment, with hands on her hips, like a belligerent person.

The Commissioner hails her. "Hello again, ma'am! We have no need to introduce ourselves to you. Our apologies for the detours we had to take to get here. We wanted to spare you the big surprise of our presence."

Pamela waves off the apology. "You don't want your presence to surprise me. Yet you are here anyway! No need to justify yourself, Commissioner. You have forgotten these glass panels are transparent. Let's deal with the real issue. If you've come for the business, let's make a deal."

"You guessed right, ma'am."

"But I'll only do business with you privately."

The Commissioner turns to Toulon. "Wait for me downstairs, Lieutenant."

As soon as they are alone, Pamela says to the Commissioner, "Now, I'm all yours."

"We're not going to talk in the hallway, I hope."

"Okay, come on in, Commissioner."

Pamela's living room is soberly furnished. A simple fabric sofa and a dining table. In the corner, a television set rests on its cardboard box. It is this only visible device in the living room that allowed her to hear the police announcement. Posters of naked women line the walls. Through the half-open bedroom door, other more provocative posters can be seen.

"Look, Commissioner, have you thought this through? You pay me and I'll take you to Cyprien Ghezo. Do we agree?"

"Your methods are rather expeditious."

"You're the one going after him, not me. I know where to find him if I need him."

"Has he visited you in the last few days?"

"What good is that to you? But I'll tell you anyway. He slept with me last night."

"Unbelievable ... I'm stunned! But, ma'am, one can't pay a reward before getting served."

"I don't care. I have no proof that I'll get paid after handing over the one you're seeking."

"Do you take me for a rascal, ma'am?"

"Yes! You're trying to fool me. You're trying to put Ghezo's blood on my conscience for free. See how you lie. You told me on the phone that you would not seek to know my identity."

"I found myself obliged to do so. I doubted you would contact me again after hanging up."

"I have the same doubt when I think about your promise. Just see how you tried to pass yourself off as a neighbour to access the building. Besides, I've been watching you. Ever since you sat down, you've been looking into my bedroom. Do you think he's hiding here?"

"No, I don't. You're not lacking in wisdom to that extend. It's your posters that catch my eye. What good are they to you, all this?"

"Do you really need to know? They are sexual boosters. I hope that, after the war you are conducting with drugs and counterfeit money, you are not at war now with posters!"

"No, you can rest easy ... Well! Okay, that's your private life. Let's get back to the point. I want to work out a fair deal with you. The cheque will be handed to you when you tell us the location of the hideout. Whether we arrest the fugitive or not, that will be our business."

"When will you do it?"

"Right now! Do us a favour before it gets dark. I want you to understand the urgency of the situation."

Pamela thinks about it, nods. "Okay. I want you to provide a cab for me," she says. "I can't bear to be in your vehicle like a prisoner being led to a cell."

While she is getting ready, the Commissioner brings Toulon up to speed.

"Can you imagine, Lieutenant, that while we were scouring caves and cemeteries, the guy was getting his leg over with this chick?"

"His time in paradise is over, Commissioner. We have him in the net."

Pamela comes down. Her gray coat has a furry hood pulled down her back. A small black handbag is tucked under her armpit.

"Your cab is here, ma'am!"

"Don't leave me alone. Come with me, Commissioner."

The Commissioner instructs Toulon. "Lieutenant, follow us tactfully." He slips into the back seat of the cab, next to Pamela.

"Where are we going, ma'am?" he asks.

"Don't be so impatient, Commissioner. I'm all yours."

"That's nice, ma'am!"

"Call me Pamela. I'm not a lady yet."

29

THEY ARE IN the east of Paris, Guyana Boulevard. The cab moves very close to the ring road. For Laurent Fournier, this proximity is not insignificant. It makes sense when, further down the road, Pamela asks the driver to take the road to Daumesnil Lake. The lake is located in the heart of Bois de Vincennes. Once again, this is not trivial!

The driver refuses to take it, explaining: "It is a pedestrian road, madam, we cannot drive there."

"All right, good job!" the Commissioner says to the driver. Then to Pamela: "Let's continue on foot."

She agrees. From the cab, they begin to move at a slow pace. Some tourists, wholehearted lovers of nature, are wearing themselves out taking photos of the dead landscape.

"Is it still far?" the Commissioner asks. His patience is wearing thin.

"Yes, it is," Pamela replies. "I'm afraid you won't be able to keep up."

"We would have continued by car if the Lieutenant were driving us."

"I know that, Commissioner. You're free to drive on restricted roads without being held accountable."

The Commissioner smiles. He is getting into the mood of resuming the thread of his questioning.

"Excuse me, Pamela, you forgot to answer my last question."

"Remind me what it was, and I'll answer it."

"Why did you decide to hand your boyfriend over to the police?"

"He's not my boyfriend. I don't have a boyfriend! He is a friend, or an irregular customer, if I may say so."

"Does he know that you have no feelings for him?"

"He is grown up enough to know we don't see ourselves as Romeo and Juliet."

"What did he do to you that was so nasty that you wanted to get rid of him?"

"He did nothing, nothing at all!"

"Then, your action makes little sense."

"How many times need I tell you that I don't blame him for anything? I only need the money you promised. I want to furnish my apartment, renew my wardrobe into a fashionable one, and take a trip to Monaco when the summer comes. And if you want, you can stop tailing people for a while so we can both go on photo safaris in Kenya. Doesn't that sound good to you?"

"Now is not a good time to think about it, Pamela."

"What's the best time for you, Commissioner? I have already found you to be the perfect companion for this upcoming trip. I have enjoyed your company. I love your thick mustache above all. It looks like a feather duster." She makes eyes at him.

"Are we close to our goal, Pamela?"

"We are, Commissioner. I'm all yours. Take me right now in whatever position suits you and wherever you want it to happen!"

"What are you talking about? Tell me, are we close to Ghezo's hiding place?"

"I'm afraid not, Commissioner! Hold on. We're half-way there."

"Do you often visit these woods?"

"I come here as often as a bird goes to its nest."

"In winter too?"

"In winter! What do you mean? There is no bad season when it comes to relaxation. Look at all those tourists walking around. Do you think they're wasting their time? In my opinion, winter does not lack charm. Its pleasures are only different from those of summer."

"Oh well! You have a lot of sensitivity!"

"Thank you! May I ask you a question in turn?"

"Please do."

"Are you carrying a tape recorder, a camera or any other tracking device that might show that I brought you here?"

"No, just my cell phone."

"Could you turn it off to reassure me?"

"Yes, if you wish. Now, tell me why you are taking these precautions?"

"I don't want you to provide Cyprien with proof that it was me—"

"Don't worry, he'll never know. He won't even have time to think about it."

"What will you do with him?"

"He will go to jail for destruction of public property and vandalism."

"Who knows, one can't swear on your word."

"Yes, I see. You keep reminding me of that. If you are talking about my visit to your house tonight, you should know that one cannot remain anonymous using a home phone as you did. The next time you want to protect your identity for more than half an hour, use a pay phone."

"Here we are, Commissioner."

"Oh good! Here we are at last! Which way is it?"

The two are standing in the heart of Bois de Vincennes, which stretches out like a monochrome canvas.

"I'm not good at locating the cardinal points."

"Has he pitched a tent?"

"He's no fool to do so. He lives in an igloo. That's good camouflage, right?"

"Not a bad idea! Let's be discreet too, Pamela. Let's not both go to him, since you don't want to reveal yourself. Walk to the igloo and turn back, so my team and I can follow your footsteps in the snow." He turns around to see how close Toulon is. The Lieutenant, at this point, is in communication with his men who are on alert in a vehicle.

Pamela approves the plan, to the Commissioner's satisfaction.

"I need to be reassured, Commissioner. You know, I'm a little chilly. Give me a hug to boost my courage."

He does not hesitate. He holds her close. "It's not a big deal," he whispers. "It's nothing! Do not feel guilty. He's a criminal. Come on, be brave!" He gives her a pat on the back, the kind of pat all trainers give their foals when they throw them on the pitch.

She starts to wade through the deep snow. Her boots disappear up to her calves. She lifts her foot high to keep clear of the snow. But she has hardly moved six steps forward, when she stops abruptly, petrified. Standing on the roadside, the Commissioner watches her.

"Something wrong?" he asks, surprised and disappointed by her U-turn.

"I cannot, I feel that I cannot!" she says, gasping.

"Ah! I can read your mind," the Commissioner replies. "You are always suspicious of me. I'll write you a cheque, right away!"

"No, Commissioner, I feel I'm not up to this mission."

"What's the matter? You've made a good start. Stay on your toes! Do you need cash?"

"No, I don't need anything. I don't have the courage for this betrayal."

"What do you call betrayal, Pamela? Do the State a favour and help it rid society of its evils."

"No, you're wrong, Commissioner. If Cyprien really did this, there must be a reason. He's a worthy, honest and virtuous man. I've known him for four years. He wouldn't hurt a fly."

"What a bluff! Do you dare to defend a werewolf?"

"No, Commissioner, you are the real werewolf. You spend your life hunting down peaceful citizens, even the dead in the cemetery. Cyprien is a son of a king. Didn't the General Intelligence tell you that he is a descendant of Behanzin?"

"The French police do not care that he is descended from Behanzin. If a crook is descended from Jupiter himself, he is not exempt from prosecution on French territory."

"Are you serious, my Commander? Do you think you can capture the offspring of the Shark King with a horsehair?"

"It seems to me, Pamela, that you are not mentally stable. Excuse me for making this remark. I don't understand your about-turn."

"There you go! To crown it all, you're calling me crazy! Everyone has the right to commit mistakes and to make up for them. I made it up. I will not commit this betrayal. History must not be repeated because of me. The sad history! Do you understand? His ancestor, the Shark, died of treason by one of his own subjects. The treason itself was still a prowess of France. Today, the same France is tracking down even the descendants. Oh my God! What have I almost done! I'm a nasty piece of trash! I don't want to carry the curse fed by the pain of a whole nation. Have mercy on me, my God! Have mercy ..."

She cries.

"Be strong, Pamela. Calm down. Everything will be all right. We'll take you back to the Château immediately. You need to rest." He pulls out his cell phone and asks for a cab. Meanwhile, Pamela is shivering and grinding her teeth as they follow their footprints back to the street.

"Are you feeling better now?"

"No, not yet, Commissioner. But I'm not dying. I'll be all right."

The cab arrives instantly.

"Take the lady to the Château," the Commissioner says.

"Thank you, Commissioner!" Pamela says, opening the door.

While she is putting on the seat belt, the Commissioner dictates some instructions to the driver. Giving orders has become a reflex for him. Yes! His job always tries to take over him.

"Please drive the lady patiently, because she is not feeling well," he says. "Call me if you have any concerns."

He hands the man his contact. It is a booby-trapped card, inlaid with a tracking chip.

30

"Lieutenant," Fournier says, "we're on the verge of finding him. We've invested so much in this case that it would be a pity to miss the mark."

"That's encouraging, Commissioner!"

"Send two dozen men to sweep the woods before it gets dark. I want them to sift through the snow in Bois de Vincennes, flake by flake, to uncover the famous igloo. I also want you to dispatch a team right away to Pamela's house before she arrives. I think the box must be hidden there. We'll bust the thief and recover the loot simultaneously. I'll stand by to respond to any emergency."

Toulon calls his subordinates and gives them the necessary instructions. With his plan set in motion, he returns to his boss.

"No conversation in the cab, Commissioner?"

"No, nothing at this point!" He taps his forehead. "Oh damn! We forgot to activate the chip, Lieutenant!"

Calling the office, he asks the operator to activate the RCM-28 chip. Just then, his receiver beeps. He turns up the volume and listens to the end of a conversation.

"... Victor Hugo," Pamela says.

"What number?" the cab driver asks.

"87," she says.

"It's in the Sixteenth District!"

"Exactly!"

Silence returns to the cab. The Commissioner is not sure about the address. "Do you have an idea where 87 Victor Hugo might be?" he asks Toulon.

"Is it a street, a square, a boulevard, an avenue, a residential complex ... ?"

"There's the dilemma. She changed her destination. The cab is now on its way to Victor Hugo located in the Sixteenth District. We still have to find out what the name designates among all those things you have just enumerated."

"I believe, Commissioner, that there is only one of all these things in a district."

"Not at all! You got it wrong, Lieutenant! Can you ignore Victor Hugo? He was an illustrious man. There are men like him whose names are splashed all over Paris, and even other cities of the world. If I had to name one, I would mention Leclerc for example. Maybe he is not the most representative, but who cares? Is it my fault if I choose a name from our profession?"

The Lieutenant is not impressed with this digression, but he smiles to show approval for his boss.

The teams assigned to Bois de Vincennes are already at work. The tourists, understanding that something is amiss, withdraw without further ado. Minutes later, reinforcements arrive, happily for the Commissioner.

"We are fighting on three fronts," he says.

"Trust me for the two I'm holding."

"I do not doubt your flair."

"No more conversation on the receiver?" Toulon asks.

"Nothing! If in five minutes we don't get words from them, we'll call the office to search that address."

"Right!"

"Damn! Here!" Fournier says, rejoicing. "Speak of the devil, and he appears."

His receiver has just beeped, drawing his attention. He listens, dumbfounded, his eyebrows furrowed.

"What, Commissioner?" Toulon asks.

"The cab driver has picked up another passenger," Fournier says. "It seems that Pamela is no longer on board. She got off well before the Sixteenth. We've lost her again."

"How is this possible!" the Lieutenant says.

"It is more than possible. It's a reality, dammit!" He stamps his foot.

The next few minutes are very hectic. While two teams of policemen comb Bois de Vincennes and ransack Pamela's apartment, the Commissioner goes back to the office to take care of his two cumbersome captives. Toulon, accompanied by two men, is on the lookout in front of the Beninese Embassy located at 87, Victor Hugo Avenue. His binoculars allow him to monitor the entries and exits of this Beninese micro-territory on French soil. Of the many things he has observed, the most remarkable is the ambassador's car. It is carrying a pennant flying like the big tricolor flag planted in the pediment of the embassy. Through the gate bars, he can see the vehicle parked in the courtyard of the residence adjoining the embassy. Suitcases are being hastily loaded into the back trunk. Toulon says to himself, *This looks like a trip abroad.* He calls the Commissioner.

At this same moment, Mr. Bartoli arrives at the police station. He looks a bit surly because of all the things he has on his mind and the grey weather the city has been having for the last three days. A few people are sitting in the reception area waiting for service. He sits at the end of the bench next to a woman who keeps looking at her watch.

"We'll be here all night," she says.

"Oh! You are right, ma'am!" Bartoli replies.

"I don't know if I'll survive today."

"Let's hope it won't be long. It's almost closing time."

"I don't have a good head on my shoulders, sir. I've been hit with a sledgehammer."

"So, you've come to lodge a complaint against the assailant?"

"No, unfortunately. I would have preferred that this blow was the one you imagine. It's my heart that has broken into pieces. A sword has split me in two. My daughter has left me forever."

"I'm sorry, ma'am! Be brave."

"Thank you, sir, that's kind of you."

"I hope she's not underage."

"Far from it. She's over eighteen."

"When children reach that age, you can expect anything. Our parents kept us on a leash until we were old enough to start a family. But our children come into their own on the eve of their eighteenth birthday. At that age, they even start forbidding our entry into their bedrooms."

"That story you're telling is exactly like mine! My daughter did exactly that. What saddens me is not that she rejected my guardianship. Everyone aspires to become independent one day. She left an ulcer in my heart when she disappeared from the house for two days and

I didn't know where she had gone. My only daughter stabbed me in the back!"

"I understand your distress, ma'am. It's nothing compared to my situation, which I haven't told you yet. If I tell you what my son is doing to me, you will feel sorry for me."

"What is happening to our children today? My daughter is hanging out with suspicious people. She has met a boy who is turning her crazy, and he is not a choirboy. I can't go two hours without having the police in my house. I think I'm living in a Paris under Vichy."

"What are you saying, madam! I too have a child who causes me the same misery. They are all the same, our children! Let me tell you that he doesn't suffer from loneliness either. He and his girlfriend have formed an army of two soldiers who defy the police. I've been summoned here because my car, which I thought was in the garage, has committed some serious traffic violations. He didn't even bother to call me. It's the police who did."

"How far will they take us, sir? I didn't tell you about the Research Brigade that came to ransack my house to find the cache of prohibited things. Do you understand me?"

"Up to that point, ma'am?"

"Yes, my daughter is suspected of belonging to an illicit trafficking network. I don't know what to think. I'm confused. This child that I used to take on my lap not long ago has become a monster. She got rich in two days. If you see the car she drives! She always manages to park it far from the house for fear that I might see it. But I saw it with my own eyes today! My daughter hides it at the house of the father of her accomplice, whom I don't dare to call boyfriend anymore. They are being arrested as I speak."

"Is that why you are here, madam?"

"Hell yes! For God's sake!"

Mr. Bartoli is sympathetic to this revelation. The woman looks at her watch again and makes a disgusted pout. Bartoli's gaze lingers on the coffee corner. He gets up nimbly.

"Would you like a coffee, ma'am?"

"Yes, sir, with cream and sugar. That's kind of you."

A visitor leaves the reception, another replaces him. Mr. Bartoli returns and hands the coffee to the woman while he sips his own.

"Why do young people look so strangely alike today?"

"You know, sir, the ability to communicate quickly has something to do with it. We standardize habits in society, especially bad ones. Do you still need to go down the street to discover the new fashion? It's served to you at your bedside on some small portable screen. My daughter doesn't eat my meals anymore because she is afraid of getting fat like me. She believes in the doctrine of *flatbellyism* relayed by the media."

"You are right, ma'am. We will have fewer and fewer young people who behave differently from others. I can't tell you how afraid I am that my son will also end up in a criminal network. The police have been searching my house lately because of a friend of his that he is protecting."

"Sir, parenthood equals problems. We have so much in common. I feel like one day we can form something called Association of Concerned Parents. I don't know when we will be needed to help each other. I'm giving you my contact, if you don't mind." She writes down her phone number on a sheet of paper in her notebook. Tearing off the page, she hands it over to Bartoli. "My name is Benaoui."

"Nice to meet you, Mrs. Benaoui. Me, I'm Bartoli." He hands over a business card.

"You are from the south!"

"Yes, Madam."

"Ah! What a nice surprise! A Bartoli constitutes the best memory of my early life. You can't imagine!"

He smiles.

"It's your turn, Mrs. Benaoui, a receptionist is free."

She stands up.

"Good luck with your vehicle, Mr. Bartoli."

"And you, good luck with your daughter. May she return home safely."

31

COMMISSIONER FOURNIER IS on his way to Victor Hugo Avenue. He left his office practically running. The Lieutenant, hidden in an anonymous car, or an unmarked car as they say, has made a good catch. He parked not far from the Beninese embassy where he saw Pamela enter after getting out of the cab. The surprising thing is that she is not alone, but accompanied by a person whose features he did not quite recognize. For Laurent Fournier, this individual would be none other than Cyprien Ghezo. This makes up for the unpleasant news he has just received from the men assigned to the search. No igloo found in Bois de Vincennes; no box hidden at Pamela's. The call from Toulon makes him feel like he's received an injection of adrenalin. He feels his lungs loaded with a burning breath. His morale is propelled by an impulse worthy of the last fights. He speeds through the snow toward the embassy.

"Anything new, Lieutenant?" he asks over the radio.

"No, Commissioner. If there was, I would have put you in the loop."

"Only five more minutes, and I'll be there."

His thoughts are filled with images. He envisions a quick action on his part. He sees himself, followed by his Lieutenant, bursting like a flash into the embassy without warning. Then he orders the diplomats to peacefully hand over the suspect they want to hide.

The Commissioner plays out a small altercation in his head: *This is the diplomatic representation of a sovereign country, Mr. Commissioner!*

This is not new information, Your Excellency. I knew it long before you were accredited to France.

We cannot hand over to you a fellow citizen who is suspected by the French Justice. He is here on Beninese territory.

I am sorry, Excellency! Benin is in Africa. France does not consider any territory inviolable when it feels attacked. Don't forget, your offices are two meters away from our symbolic Triumphal Arch.

Ask the relevant French authorities to submit an extradition request to Porto-Novo.

Okay, Excellency, the request will be submitted, but we're leaving right away with the suspect.

Things are happening fast. His imaginary altercation comes to an end before he has clinched victory. Toulon has just awakened him from his daydreaming, telling him that Pamela has reappeared. She is leaving the embassy alone, walking out without the unidentified person.

"Shall I arrest her, Commissioner?" Toulon asks.

"No, let her go. We know where to get her if we need to. Now that she is on the move, she helps to reveal things for us."

Toulon trains his binoculars on the loading diplomatic vehicle. With all their strength, two powerful men lift a heavy piece of luggage and put it in the trunk.

What the hell is that? Toulon wonders.

In the meantime, the Commissioner has arrived and has parked behind him.

"Did you check about a trip, Commissioner?" Toulon asks.

"Yes, the GI confirmed it. His Excellency is leaving this evening on a Paris-Brussels-Cotonou flight."

"What I fear is that the Beninese diplomats will refuse to cooperate."

"Things are moving very fast, Lieutenant. I have already asked the Beauvau Square to throw their full weight behind this final assault."

"Diplomatic representations are generally territories ..."

"What! I see you have doubts, Lieutenant. Don't weaken at the last minute. There is no sacrosanct territory in France. Don't the events in the Middle East mean anything to you? The International Atomic Energy Agency searched even under Saddam Hussein's pillows."

"The unfortunate thing is that they did not find any weapons of mass destruction."

"So what! Lieutenant? Did you want us to ask him by phone to reveal his weapons caches?"

"Commissioner!"

"Go ahead!"

"The ambassador is coming on board."

"I expected that. He's going to Orly airport. He will take the Ring Road South. Men are placed at Terminal 2 to welcome him. I want that car searched. If Ghezo's escape to Benin turns from a hoax into a fact, I will never live with it. I mean never!"

"The gate is opening, Commissioner!"

"Well, well, well! You're going to join us for this last hunt. Let your men watch the embassy."

The diplomatic vehicle exits. A tricolor pennant floats on the left corner of the hood. The smoked windows ensure privacy inside. Without delay, Laurent Fournier and his men follow in its tire tracks: Victor Hugo Avenue, Foch Avenue, Dauphine Gate, Ring Road Boulevard South, Speed!

Orly, the legendary Parisian airport now overshadowed by the giant Charles de Gaulle, is located in the southern suburbs of Paris. The GPS indicates a twenty-four-kilometer distance from the embassy of Benin to the airport. As the trip continues smoothly, the Commissioner falls back into his reverie. He imagines he is being received as a hero by the Minister of Homeland Security, then at the Élysée Palace. The President of the Republic congratulates him for having once again maintained his reputation as a great cop. On a solemn day, such as July 14, he is decorated with a star medal suspended to a red ribbon: the star of the Great Cross of the Legion of Honour. Fournier always aims very high. In the whole France, only a hundred lucky few have received the Great Cross of the Legion of Honour. He had just been decorated Great Officer of the same order not long ago. His dream is not to remain in this rank which he shares with five hundred people who are sometimes chosen by fate rather than by merit. War cripples have also received it as compensation for a torn leg. For what? Is getting blown by a mine an act of bravery? According to Fournier, there is an urgent need to revise the decoration criteria in France. He describes the police as the most beautiful profession. In the police force, you have to read imaginary maps, find tracks on a globe that is not round, invent days that do not have twenty-four hours, converse with the unknown, pass very close to a target, come back, then return to the charge ... That is why he declined his appointment to the Police National Headquarters. He likes to experience the excitement of tailing suspects, and the strong emotions associated with risky missions. It is different from an office job in which appetite goes away with eating.

Toulon, who had remained silent during the trip, now comes to his mind. And Fournier thinks: *Ah! my Lieutenant. He must get some stripes too. He deserves it.* But just then, the sight of his henchman causes him to snap out of his reverie.

"We are about to write a new page in the history of the French police, Lieutenant."

"I have a little problem, Commissioner. I notice that the Beauvau Square so far has not answered you. But we're almost at Orly."

"Don't worry, Lieutenant. We will have an answer by the time we get there. And if we don't, we'll decide what to do."

"Oh, yes, I understand, but ..."

"But what! Again, I see that you are having doubts, Lieutenant! If you're not determined to walk on thorns, what have you been doing in the snow for three days with a gun stuck up your ass? You should have stayed home and prayed to God that the runaway surrenders."

The Lieutenant calms down. After all, he understands the stubbornness of his boss. He imagines how his boss would lose face if the diplomat managed to board the plane with the wanted box, and who knows, with the suspect next to him in business class. Or what would happen if the illustrious personality were intercepted in absence of directives from a competent authority? His anxiety increases when, through a barbed wire fence, he sees planes lined up as far as the eye can go. Their tall tails look like crosses planted at regular intervals on invisible graves in a huge cemetery. As for the Commissioner, he doesn't seem to have much to worry about. He is burning with the fever of the triumph he is anticipating.

When they arrive at Terminal 2, they find that the agents placed on the airport concourse have done their job well. The ambassador and his driver were stuck in their car. The agents took them to park in a quiet place, telling them they have been instructed to do so. Arriving soon after, accompanied by Toulon, the Commissioner introduces himself to the diplomat. Then he gives him the bad news. He tells him that an investigation has been launched into a State affair that involves a Beninese citizen. According to well-informed sources, he adds, the suspect had physical contact with the embassy an hour earlier. The ambassador listens to the brief account of the situation and replies: "We have been informed of the case by our supervisory ministry. We admire your personal commitment, Commissioner, but we regret to inform you that Ghezo has not been received at our embassy and is not in this vehicle. Please take our word for it."

"How about putting our doubts to rest by letting us take a look at the luggage, Excellency?"

"How can you try to get into diplomatic baggage, Commissioner? There is no provision in the law that allows you to do so."

The Commissioner shakes his head, unconvinced. Toulon, who knows him very well, understands what this gesture means. Surely, his boss has got something up his sleeve. Laurent Fournier is stubborn. He is famous for what he did in his last position at the Central Office of the Border Police, where he was in charge of airport security. On several occasions, he got private planes of Heads of State searched at Bourget Airport. The searches led to the discovery of weed on the planes. His ability to dismantle various small and large trafficking networks earned him the medal of Great Officer of the Legion of Honour. He was also offered an appointment to the General Office, which he turned down. His position as District Commissioner allows him to do what he is passionate about—carrying out operational commands. What Toulon had silently feared the most is finally here: the decision to search the ambassador's car, which falls like a hammer blow from his boss' mouth. The Lieutenant shudders but doesn't let his dismay show. He wants to whisper the word 'Beauvau', but the look on his boss' face stops him. The ambassador lets his driver open the trunk. The big bag is there, inert. The Commissioner presses it with his finger. It is soft, he notices. He orders agents to open it. Inside the suitcase are T-shirts printed with the effigy of a presidential candidate in Benin, some personal stuff in bags, and of course, confidential documents of no importance to the French police.

"No cardboard box belonging to CARAN, Commissioner."

Fournier is disconcerted. "No box ..."

The driver puts belongings ransacked by the cops into some semblance of order in the suitcase. Then on the ambassador's order, he sets out back to Paris. Trip cancelled! The cops are left standing still, all too aware of the serious situation brewing from the search. They are waiting for orders from their boss who is himself petrified. The ringing of the Commissioner's phone breaks the heavy silence. The caller, he finds out, is not the General Officer of the National Police for whom he has nothing but contempt. It is the Minister of Homeland Security! With the answer for which Fournier has been waiting for an hour, the Minister instructs: "Stay away from diplomatic circles, Commissioner. Do not conduct any searches. Any incident from that kind of search would be unmanageable in these times of electoral campaign."

The Commissioner stays still as a statue decorated with stripes; his blood seemingly frozen in his veins.

32

Eleventh District, Dahomey Street. At medium Sahid's, the atmosphere is heavy. The spirits have so crowded the air that he can no longer contain them. Every time he sets up a communication channel, they gather around it like larks attracted by a mirror.

"Here we can already draw them by the shovelful," he says to Cyprien. "If you had eyes, you would see them floating. They're not asking for anything other than to communicate."

"How come they show up without being invoked?"

"The simple fact of my setting up this stage is an invitation I've extended to them. Among them are some who have been yearning to speak for hundreds of years but have not found a single channel to use."

"This way, you are offering them a golden opportunity!"

"A wooden one! Let me stress that. All material must be made of wood because metals rather attract evil spirits, especially gold. Gold is the devil's flower. Metals are meant to hurt and kill. They have never brought about healing, unlike plants. But you see, it is not because they are jostling for attention in the parlor that we will let them express themselves in a fussy way."

"How will you sort them out?"

"When the time comes, you'll see. It's so simple that it will seem child's play."

"You're apparently more forthcoming and less ceremonial than other mediums in Paris."

"Yes, many practitioners wrap their art in a gangue of showy ceremonies to impact your psyche and make more money out of you. Have you been to one of us before?"

"Not really, but I have tried to get appointments without success. I think I told you about the Kardecists."

"Oh yes! But as far as I know, they couldn't give you the service you wanted. They are hybrid spiritualists, halfway between Christianity and spiritualism. I have never been able to tell where they fall. Their faith in Christ is as firm as that of any practicing Christian. At the same time, they betray the Church by invoking the spirits of the dead."

"Are they really betraying the Church? I think it is the Church that sets the tone by making a long list of saints that the faithful must venerate. Aren't the saints also formerly living people who died?"

"That's a good point, young man! Let's just say that the Kardecists have done nothing but continue the treacherous approach of the Church towards the Bible. My words will seem slanderous to you if you fail to see what I mean. I am neither a catechist nor a Kardecist; I neither defend nor condemn, but I can tell you that the Roman Church has embroidered its doctrine around the animistic beliefs of its time. Its median position between the Bible and animistic practices was aimed at bringing the pagans into the Christian cause by preaching to them the beliefs that sounded like their pagan ones. They take Christ for a loser who can't even count to three. If Christ scheduled his resurrection to occur three days and three nights after his death, it implies that he rose on Monday night. But the Church celebrates the event on Sunday instead."

"Yes, this is odd. How can we explain that from Friday evening to Sunday early morning three days and three nights have elapsed?"

"Good question! But it's easy to understand. The resurrection celebration was moved to Sunday to attract the animists who celebrated their Sun god on that day. Sunday means day of the Sun.

"I'm confused," Cyprien says. "I thought that the Sun god was worshipped in Egypt."

"Yes, originally. But remember that the Israelites had lived in captivity in Egypt for centuries under the pharaohs, before Moses led them back to the Promised Land. Back in Israel, they had not abandoned the Sun worship inherited from the Egyptians. This is why theocriticism questions whether the Roman Church worships Christ or the Sun."

"I can't pretend to answer you. Let's admit that this is where the Church has sinned against the Bible. And the Kardecists, how do they compare with the Church?"

"One says tomato and the other says tom-ah-to. Kardecists used the same strategy as the Church. To reconcile Christianity and spiritualism is to forge a middle ground that unites both beliefs. You see that? People join spiritualist seances because they find the precepts of their religion there. In the process, they don't realize that they have changed course."

"Is this good or bad?" Cyprien asks.

"I am not making a value judgment. I am merely commenting on Kardec's strategy. Here I'm doing spiritism without religion. You will see that I do not resort to the Holy Scriptures. And while we're at it, make up your mind about contacting your friends without further delay. I hope they are not praying in a chapel before joining us!"

"No, they aren't into biblical discourse. I trust them, they can't stand me up. They must be having transportation issues."

"You must act, young man! Sitting idle will do us no good. The air is already loaded with too many spirits eager to make themselves heard. If your friends don't have phones, how do you communicate with each other?"

"We use the Internet."

"Not very practical, is it?"

"We have no choice."

"Then send them an email!"

"That's a good idea." He is suffocating with fear at the thought of touching a computer.

"Go ahead, you don't need a password."

"Can't we start the seance with two people and wait for them to show up?"

"Have you ever seen a table on two legs?"

"How many people do we need to start the seance?"

"At least four."

"Four is great. I'm waiting for two friends."

"Nothing is guaranteed."

Cyprien knows the risk that writing to his friends would entail. The nosy Commissioner would send men to pin him down in the medium's house before he even had time to take one step down the long staircase. Suddenly he thinks of Bonnot. Contacting him would pose less of a risk, assuming of course his phone number has not been bugged yet. But alas! Cyprien doesn't have time to carry out this thought, because Sahid interrupts him again.

"I suggest you call other friends, or would you rather pay me for the thirty minutes you have already spent with me?"

"No, that's a bad alternative! Let's wait another five minutes, please. If they don't come, I'll call someone else."

"I can do it! But you should know that my meter has been running since 6 pm!"

"There's nothing to worry about."

"While we're at it, can you pay me an advance?"

"We'll write you a blanket cheque at the end of your service."

"Why can't you do it now? It's six hundred euros."

"I still think your bill is pretty steep."

"Steep, you say? Medium Ribanna would give you the same service for a thousand euros. Can you believe that?"

"We'll pay the six hundred at the end of the seance, don't worry. The checkbook is with one of my friends."

A brief period of silence follows, time for Sahid to calm a budding nervousness.

"Excuse me, young man," he says. "One can never deal with spirits without suffering a hit. Everything depends on which one arrives at any given moment. Right now, I feel as if a rather agitated spirit has just passed by." He pauses to listen. "In fact, I think it's still there. Look at what's happening. Do you see these cups here quaking?"

Cyprien stares at the two empty cups next to the teapot. They are visibly shaking and tinkling as if from a small seismic wave.

"Of course, I do! I see that."

"This is the effect of an impatient spirit. I wonder if we can be here another five minutes before they have thrown us out of the window. Do something, call someone else. Call whoever you want for support."

Cyprien gets up and walks briskly to the phone, determined to act despite his fear. He dials Bonnot's number. Because Bonnot hasn't picked up, Cyprien leaves a message on his voice mail. "Nobody at the end of the line," he says to Sahid.

"What?" Sahid exclaims.

Seeing how visibly annoyed Sahid is growing, Cyprien quickly says: "I will try something else."

He pulls the computer keyboard, and connects to the Internet, aware of the risk he is taking in contacting Jules and Yasmina.

"Hold on! Don't try anything further," Sahid says. "I think they're here."

"Who, the detectives?" Cyprien asks.

"No, your friends." He laughs. "Your friends are detectives?"

"Hmmm ... yes! I call them that because they always know where to find hidden information."

"Hahaha! You're in good hands. So, they're the ones who recommended you to my office?"

"Yes, we can say that."

"It doesn't matter who sent you! The main thing is you have found me, and you will get satisfaction."

He opens the door to the two friends before they even have had time to ring the bell.

"Come in, young ones. No need to introduce yourselves. Your friend and I have been waiting for you for three quarters of an hour."

Cyprien gives Yasmina a hug, then bumps fists with Jules.

"I am glad to see you finally, my dears. What happened?"

"Ah! We went through hot and cold. We will tell you everything in detail in good time."

"Take your seats," Sahid says. "I can see that you need tea to fight the cold." Jules and Yasmina nod. Grabbing the teapot, Sahid heads for the kitchen.

33

Cyprien is alarmed at learning about his friends' arrest. He's surprised not so much that they were arrested as at how promptly they were released.

"Let's keep in mind that this release may be part of the enemy's strategy," he says. "Did you cover your back? Do you think anyone followed you here?"

"Let's hope not," Jules replies.

Sahid's reappearance brings the conversation to a stop. After the tea, Sahid serves an elixir.

"While you are sipping this hot drink," he says, "try to think of the deceased. Fix your gaze on a specific spot and think of him in silence. This will help you focus quickly."

Everyone falls silent. Soon afterwards they put down their empty cups in turn, struggling to empty their minds of diffuse thoughts. The medium lets this silence last for a few minutes before he speaks again.

"Let me explain what is going to happen. We have the choice of communicating with our deceased through a process called 'turntable' or through a Ouija board. The first process consists of a stylus and a tablet. Use the stylus to write on the tablet, letting the impulse of a spirit move your hand. This way, the stylus will form words or sentences on the tablet."

"How can such a heavy table turn?"

"No, it is not the ceremony table that turns, but the small, wheeled tablet placed above it. This may seem strange to you because you're thinking physics and rationality. Physics only recognizes what is perceptible and measurable. How do you expect uninitiated physicists to perceive these fleshless hands wielding the stylus? Spiritual phenomena cannot be studied in labs, dear friends."

"That's obvious," Cyprien says. "Tell us about the second method, please."

He is in a hurry to finish with the preludes and get to the heart of the communication. Behind his eagerness is his anxiety brought about by his awareness that he's a fugitive. If his friends' short stint at the police station has changed the course of the events, he is not aware of that yet.

"The second method," Sahid says, "consists in making the spirit speak through writing too. Look at this board and this planchette. The board has all the letters of the alphabet and numbers zero to nine. The letters and numbers are enough to deliver all kinds of messages. In addition to YES and NO, you see the word GOODBYE. If the planchette stops there, the GOODBYE means that the spirit has withdrawn. Some more gifted mediums practice automatic writing on paper with a pen slipped into their hand. With other mediums, and these ones are rare, they can obtain direct writing from the spirit without using their own hand. Those mediums are called pneumatographic."

"Which of the two possibilities should we choose?" Cyprien asks.

"The Ouija board!" Yasmina proposes. She doesn't give the others a chance to think.

Sahid looks at her and smiles.

"You are inspired, my dear!" he says. "Is everyone for the Ouija?"

Jules shrugs. "Why not?"

"Let's go with the Ouija," Cyprien says, nodding.

"Well then! Get ready for the big encounter of your lives. Each of us should put two fingers on this planchette, the index and middle finger. Do not apply any force to it, so that it can slide easily on the board. Let your fingers be led by the movement of the planchette without resistance. Before invoking the spirit of the dead, we will mark out our magnetic field with purifying words to protect ourselves from attacks."

Jules' eyes grow wide. "Attacks?"

Yasmina caresses his cheek comfortingly.

"Let me explain to you," the medium says.

But before he can say anything more, a bell chime interrupts him.

"Wait, there is a visitor," he says. He apologizes, gets up and goes to open the door. At the sight of Bonnot's face in the doorway, Cyprien explodes with inner joy. He approaches Bonnot, introducing him to Sahid.

Sahid holds out his hand to Bonnot. "I'm Sahid, the medium."

"I know about you, Mr. Sahid, from the flyers you send."

"My pleasure to have you here. Take a seat."

Bonnot studies Sahid, who is tall as a Goliath, easily one meter ninety above his heels. The medium is wearing a sky-blue gandoura with an arabesque embroidered collar.

Another man has accompanied Bonnot. Bonnot takes a seat at the table and introduces Andy. He is an old friend of his from high school, a journalist at *The Canard*. He is the vitriolic columnist who hides behind the pseudonym Pierre Ciseau. It is under this pseudonym that he slashes French political personalities on a daily basis in his caustic papers. Many victims of his pen have sent him anonymous letters that have gone straight into the trash can. Because he is presently on leave, a lull has silenced his columns. His being here has come about through a call from Bonnot.

"I have a friend two blocks away who urgently needs to see me," Bonnot had told him on the phone. "Can you be so kind as to drive me there?" Andy did not hesitate. "Dear friend," he replied, "consider yourself already at your destination!" Then, they hit the road, and now, here is Andy, with Bonnot, and his three friends. Andy is still wondering how things have unfolded to get him around this table.

Sahid gives the two newcomers brief explanations on spiritualist communication. Andy listens bug-eyed. Not long ago, all he was planning was to drop off a friend at a destination before going for a drink and some billiards. Now here he is, with his right hand resting two fingers on a planchette. Cyprien is thrilled to see Bonnot here at this crucial moment in their quest. He wasn't sure Bonnot would get his voice message and act on it.

"Now," Sahid says, "if we are all ready, let's breathe in deeply, then breathe out, as we empty our minds and connect."

This is a moment of high concentration. The medium whispers words of purification, after which he invites Cyprien to ask his questions. Tired of waiting for this moment, Cyprien plunges into the task.

"Is there a spirit here?" he asks.

The planchette lies motionless. A dense silence dominates the room.

"Spirit of Louis XIV, are you among us?" Cyprien asks. As he does, he feels a blockage of his respiratory tract. Andy feels a tingling on his side, which he scratches.

The silence persists, but the occupants of the room experience strange sensations. They feel like they are descending into an abyss.

"My hair is standing on end," Jules whispers.

"I hear footsteps," Yasmina says.

"Me too," Bonnot says.

Sahid looks unblinking at them. The steps quickly intensify, until they sound like the stamping of a horde of wild animals. And just then the door bursts open, violently slamming against the wall. Jules dives under the table crying, "We are toast!"

Sahid pulls him out, seizing him by his shoulders. "Are you okay, Jules?" Then he turns to the others: "Is everyone all right?"

They all say they are all right, some less assuredly than others. Shadows with flashlights have invaded the room. Sahid talks to his teammates in a reassuring voice. "Stay cool. Stay cool, everyone."

34

FOURNIER IS BACK in his office. He is waiting for the Lieutenant to report. He does not believe his ears when he learns that the last raid has drawn a blank.

At eight o'clock, the night is already well underway. Fournier has his organizer open before him. He gives it an annoyed look. He lowers his pen to the last item on his to-do list. He draws a thick line across the item. Contrary to his habit, he keeps crossing the item out until he ends up with an ink stain. Only Toulon's entry into the room causes him to stop.

The Lieutenant sheds and hangs up his coat. "We've never had such bad weather in Paris as in the last few days."

"I believe this weather is the source of our misfortunes, Lieutenant. But what about the rest? It wasn't only the weather that stood in the way of our success. I still can't understand what just happened. You say that our men have lost the accomplices' tracks!"

"Exactly! I supervised the operation myself."

"Our greatest hope was based on this raid, a raid we missed carrying out. It was one of the last opportunities to restore the reputation of our corps. I don't know if we'll get another one before the deadline. The calendar is pressing us, time is running out. After midnight, everything will be ruined."

"Commissioner, our men did not lose out, no matter what. We have never run like we did tonight, but we have also never been so pinned down."

"What can we say to explain how suspects held in the crosshairs get lost in a disused apartment in the heart of the city?"

"None of us understands anything about this mystery. I still wonder how the City could let stand an apartment in such an advanced state of disrepair. Politicians are only too happy to dictate their will, and the people are too quick to blame us."

"It is unbelievable that we are being made to release accomplices, merely to maintain social peace. This only emboldens suspects to offend again. In the midst of all this, the police become the butt of jokes. When we randomly stop a suspect in the streets, we're accused of restricting freedom. When a freed suspect two blocks away commits a crime, they say we're unable to prevent crimes."

"This is what it comes down to, Commissioner. Our suspects have vanished into thin air. I would say in an apartment!"

"Tell me, what was the interior like?"

"Weird, Commissioner! Cracked and mossy walls; a non-existent ceiling, or rather one reduced to cobwebs; gaping windows; and what do you know! This house seemed to have been occupied for the last time twenty years ago! The roof has collapsed in one corner of the living room, allowing rainwater to come in through a hole. The water has caused a heavy bush to grow in the house. Soon the vegetation will spread across the entire living room."

"A bush in an apartment in Paris, you have to see it to believe it!"

"Commissioner, what I'm about to say will seem like the stuff of fantasy! The most curious thing in the room was an old table with six rickety chairs around, a porcelain teapot and dusty cups containing long dead cockroaches. But that's not all … In the middle of all this—hold on tight Commissioner—we found a Ouija board with its planchette!"

"This apartment would have been used for the last time by a family of spiritualists, but that's not the point. We are not interested in the fact that its inhabitants came down from Mars. What intrigues is why Bartoli and his girlfriend chose this place for refuge."

"Well, we thought that Cyprien Ghezo was hiding there. Naturally, his accomplices would come to visit him. What is disconcerting is how they got away."

"No back door?"

"None at all."

"You said the windows were open. They must have jumped out that way. No?"

"No, Commissioner. We found the windows still shrouded in cobwebs."

"Is this Mohammed's cave, or what?"

The Commissioner holds his chin in his hand, immersed in thought. A minute of silence later, he asks: "Did you take pictures, Lieutenant?"

"Unfortunately, not, Commissioner. We did not consider that to be urgent."

"We'll go back right away. I'll take a look at it. I can even promise you that I'll show you where those two assholes ran off to."

They leave.

35

At Sahid's place, serenity has returned. His customers have recovered from their fright. An impromptu visit from the police interrupted the seance. And who knows, it may have stopped Louis XIV on his way down to Paris, after about three centuries.

"We were surrounded by good spirits," Sahid says.. "How then can you explain how this horde of animals who broke in on us could have their hands brush against us without seeing us? You saw that they carried flashlights. That means their eyes saw only darkness in the room. And did you see how they walked with their feet raised high as if they were moving through tall grass?"

"And what was it about our presence that did not allow them to see us?" Cyprien asks.

"Look, Cyprien, they had no idea of our presence. We were concealed by our invisible friends who surrounded us. At that moment of danger, they lent us their perispirit so that our physical bodies would not betray us."

"I'm interested in that perispirit thing," Andy said. "What is it really?"

He sits back in his chair, thirsty for an explanation from Sahid. The change in Andy pleases everyone. The sound of the strange footsteps left him shaking like a dead leaf. He has now regained his journalistic curiosity. The mortal fear the footsteps induced in him has completely gone.

"The perispirit is the invisible ethereal envelope that covers our physical body," Sahid says. "You can see it by looking at your finger."

"How do you do that?"

"Move your index finger slowly between your two eyes. When you feel that you see two fingers, stop the movement, and look carefully around the finger."

Everyone tries it immediately.

"What do you see?"

"A thin transparent layer," Cyprien says. His friends echo his reaction.

"Good job! That is the perispirit. When unbodied spirits show themselves to us, they put on this body to make themselves transparent."

"Does it mean that the perispirit does not perish at death?"

"Do you see that this ethereal substance is putrescible?"

"I don't think so," Yasmina replies.

She has been trying in vain to touch the perispirit around her finger.

"What we have just experienced," Sahid says, "far from breaking our morale, should rather strengthen our confidence in the protection of good spirits. We can resume the seance without worries. Let's focus once more. It is up to you, dear friend Cyprien, to resume when you feel sufficiently ready."

Shortly afterwards, Cyprien again asks, "Is there any spirit here?" The planchette moves to YES. Cyprien asks,

"What is your name?" The spirit writes "Louis B". Cyprien interprets B as an abbreviation of Bourbon, to Jules' dismay. Jules voices his skepticism of Cyprien's interpretation. No sooner has Jules done so than the planchette goes sliding to the GOODBYE position. And no one in the room needs an explanation of what has happened. Jules' attitude has offended the spirit.

"I wanted to hear 'Louis XIV'," Jules says, defending himself. "I regret having put the spirit to the test. I take back what I said."

"Too late," Sahid says. "The spirit has gone. If we're lucky enough to have him back, don't offend him again. Any disembodied spirit is sensitive to humiliation like the human person it belonged to. Would you have dared to tell the Sun King, while he was alive, that you doubted his word? Remember this lesson which is dear to us in spiritualism. Always treat a spirit exactly the same way you would have treated the human person to whom it belonged. I want to point out one thing for the benefit of all. Spirits have emotions. So, when you humiliate them, they will withdraw quietly, if they are the good ones. Let's try again. Hopefully he will be gracious enough to return. Cyprien, you have the floor!"

As Cyprien repeats the question, the medium suddenly lets go of the planchette. He seems to be dizzy, or in a state of ecstasy.

"What is happening to you, Mr. Sahid?"

"I don't know how to explain it. My head is splitting."

"Is there any way we can help?" Cyprien asks.

"No, there's nothing you can do," Sahid says reassuringly. "I know what's happening. The spirit wants to be incarnated in me. It's trying to take possession of my body so it can speak to you directly. It is a tremendous sign of esteem that it has for you. Ouch! My head is splitting, oh God! My head! My head!"

"I know something about this phenomenon," Andy says. "I have heard about it in Kundalini-Yoga. It happens at the top of the head, at the crown chakra. It is there that the entrance and exit door for the spirit in the body is located. It is where the child's fontanel plays as a baby, because the baby's spirit is in constant communication with the beyond. Have you ever felt this door opening and your hair standing on end when you are frightened?"

Sahid continues to weaken like a malaria patient. He pushes aside the Ouija board and rests his forehead against the table.

"Are you all right Mr. Sahid?" Cyprien asks.

The medium no longer deigns to answer.

"He's gone," Bonnot says.

Everyone stays quiet. The silence reduces communication into a telepathic one among the occupants of the room. Andy turns to Cyprien and gives him a glance as if to ask: "What are you waiting for?"

Cyprien turns to Sahid with another question: "Is there a spirit in this body?"

The medium slowly gets up. From deep in his throat comes an articulate answer. "Aye."

"What's your name?"

"Louis."

"Are you a good spirit?"

"Aye, I am."

"Are you Louis XIV, who was King of France?"

In a hollow voice from the depths of time, the voice says, "Aye, I am. 'Tis me Louis XIV, king of France."

"Majesty, we are sorry for pulling you out of your royal resting place."

"Why dost thou calleth me Majesty? Don't calleth me Majesty anymore! I am not majestic."

"What should we call you, Majesty?"

"Louis is mine name. Mine mortal name. Calleth me Louis. The present day, I know who the true Majesty is. The true Majesty is the One who sitteth on the Throne, the Throne on which I, miserable wretch of Versailles, am unable to prostrate myself."

"We're sorry to hear that, Louis! You were powerful, you were the sun! How come things turned out so badly for you?"

"'Tis because of the beggars of the Kingdom of France & the corrupt officials of the State. Those gents hath called me all the slam-bang names to benefit from the largesse of the court. Those gents hath called me 'Sun King' at the time I didn't deserve to beest a crescent moon. To top it all off, Rigaud gaveth me a deifying representation under his brush whither he hath dressed me in a long ermine robe, with one foot on the earth globe & looking down on the universe. That wast so blasphemous. 'Tis only the present day that I can see all mine misery at the top of this false divinization. The sun hath betrayed me. I've lost mine way. I regret mine faults & all mine excesses. I regret the dragonnades & the bloodshed of the saints. I regret the crusades against the Jansenists & the Huguenots. I am in trouble. How could anyone imagine me as Almighty God trampling the globe? Listen to me, I order Rigaud to beest quartered at daybreak."

"Rigaud died more than two hundred years ago!"

"Two hundred calendar days already? That's big lie! In this case, may his body with heart & guts beest carried to the mountains to beest devoured by vultures!"

"I am sorry for your pains, Louis. I believe that at the end of your penance you will find your way. Now, can I ask you some questions?"

"Of course, thou can! Thou hath already asked me six. May I ask thee just one, Prince?"

"Yes, kind Louis, go ahead!"

"Art thou willing to risk thy life to findeth out the truth?"

"Hmmm ..."

"Ah, thou art hesitating, Prince."

"Yes, I can, Louis."

"Then, if thou art ready to row against the waves, if thou art ready to square the storm, go to Moret right hence. The grave thou art seeking is in Moret-sur-Loing. Jump on a horse at once & go thither at full gallop. If thou waste any more time, the enemy wilt precede thee to the city gates & wilt defeat thee with the flaming dagger he carryeth in his belt. He wilt taketh thee back tied up in his carriage to Paris whither thou wilt perish in the dungeons of the Bastille."

"The Bastille no longer exists, Louis."

"Hath the Jesuits already bought 't to turn 't into a factory?"

"What business can we do in the rubble of the Bastille, Louis?"

"One example is that of employing Bastille prisoners to grind wheat into flour on millstones. That could bringeth in a lot of wage. The Kingdom is hungry."

"No, the Bastille was demolished, demolished together with all the symbols of the monarchy. Today we have the Republic."

"Who is the King of that Republic?"

"The next president will be elected in a few months."

"Ah, I understandeth. But all this in one night?"

"That was centuries ago, Louis."

"I admire the French people. At the hour those gents art thirsty for something, they keepeth demanding 't until they receiveth 't."

"Me and my friends will find the opportunity to pass on your admiration to the French people."

"Thou draweth me from a distant retreat. Mine night hath been so long, the path I've taken harassing. Thee, thou must get out of hither but beware of the traitor. Look around thee. Thou hath a traitor in thy midst."

"A traitor?"

"Aye! A servant of the enemy. That gent is asking for wage."

"We will find a way to settle this problem as friends. Can you tell me how Louise-Marie ended up in the convent, Your Maj ... Louis?"

"Twast Madam de Maintenon who, willing to save the soul of that unfortunate baby, tooketh the baby thither. The lady hath sent her to the convent so that the baby could groweth & taketh the cloth & giveth her life to our most Blessed Mother, the Virgin."

"What was so special about that child?"

"Why ask me what thou know, Prince? But I'll answer thee anyway. She wast dark, very dark, on account of which the whole court madeth me their laughingstock.

The embassies in Paris spoke of a scandal in the French court. I hadst planned to separate this child from the Queen, but Madam de Maintenon forestalled me."

"And her supposedly adulterous father?"

"Thou art ruining mine morale, Prince! Dost not speak to me anymore about that scrap of a nigger. Whither else would that nigger beest but in the darkness of prison?"

"All right, Louis, let's move on. But I'm worried. You're sending me to Moret at night without a compass. I need more clues to help me find my way."

"Thou can't get lost in a small town. At the hour thou get to Moret, look for the mark of the soldier who walketh on fire. Go now! Get out of hither right hence. Can't thou feeleth the smell of gunpowder? War is at thy doorstep. Go & beware of the traitor."

36

THEY RUSH DOWN the long staircase. Everyone clumps into Andy's car, which has trouble starting.

"Do you really believe that this jalopy will get us to Moret?" Andy asks.

"Please, we have no other option," Cyprien says. "Let's not be discouraged. We'll push the jalopy to the limit. How much horsepower does it have in its belly?"

"It is not powerful enough. I'm afraid it won't take the first step. We can't even start it! The ignition system was due to be changed last winter."

Cyprien gets out of the car to make a call to Sahid from a nearby phone booth. At this very moment, Sahid is already awake and, thinking about the type of customers he has just received. He swears at them, uttering insults like "sons of bitches," "miserable fuckers," and so on. He is thinking that they took advantage of his mediumistic sleep to head for the hills without paying him. But just then he finds a piece of paper on the table with the following message: "We are sorry to leave you without saying goodbye. We cannot wait for you to wake up. We found out we must leave your place immediately. Welcome back to earth. Cyprien and company."

Sahid keeps screaming in anger until he receives Cyprien's call. Cyprien takes the opportunity to explain to the medium that they have left in a hurry, leaving him half asleep. With his senses still blurred, it was not possible to talk about money with him. Sahid is not convinced that Cyprien is telling the truth, until the young man asks him to read the back of the paper. On the other side, Sahid reads a postscript telling him that the cheque is in the pocket of his thobe. He pulls it out. It is for six hundred euros! His eyes glow. His voice changes. From gall to honey. After this joyful turn of events, Cyprien tells him that on Louis XIV's recommendation, they are going to Moret right away. The medium learns all this in surprise. He only served as an unwitting instrument that conveyed the information. Wishing them luck, he invokes the good spirits to protect them.

Cyprien goes back to the car, which is backfiring, but still unable to take off.

Looking through the window, Jules notices something frightening. "Hey, I see something there!"

"Huh? What? What do you see?" Cyprien asks.

"Get in first. Close the door and sit. Quickly!"

Cyprien obeys without asking questions. From inside the car, he looks out. What he sees causes him to shudder. Commissioner Fournier and Lieutenant Toulon are ascending the stairs to Sahid's house. The car backfires more and more frantically. It quivers mightily, then starts. Hurray! Andy pounds the gas pedal and they take off. Toulon turns around, suspecting the strange car.

"Commissioner, a car just sped off. You saw it?"

"Yes, I have the same feeling, Lieutenant. But it's too late to do anything. It's already gone past the curve over there. Let's hope that the driver's escape is not related to our visit."

On Charenton Street, Andy and his company continue their race. The road is bumpy and crenellated with ongoing construction work. They suffer uncomfortable jolts as the car goes over the rugged road. Of all those in the car, Andy is the only one who is not aware of what is happening. But despite his complete ignorance, he has shown a particular interest in this quest. One can see that he has gone from Andy to Pierre Ciseau. Already in his mind, a breathtaking paper on the Sun King's reappearance has begun to germinate.

"Tell me. Who is this Louise-Marie? I thought I heard from the King that she was born of the Queen."

"You got it right," Bonnot says. "The strange situation we are facing tonight can only be matched by the birth of a mixed-race child from the womb of the Queen who was white. Curious! Isn't it?"

"What happened to her after her internment in the convent of Moret?"

"Now you're asking the key question," Cyprien says. "If we knew that, we wouldn't have taken the road to Moret at night."

"Where do the cops fit into all this?"

"Treasure hunting never takes place free of obstacles. Obstacles are what make a hunt and any resulting discovery so exciting."

"If pitfalls are what make a discovery exciting, I guarantee you that ours will be mesmerizing, since our obstacle is no less than a high government official coming down to the field in person at night. In this search for a grave, what is at stake?"

"The moral satisfaction of our unexpected reunion. Revenge for the royal blood that was shed. The appeasement of souls frustrated through the centuries. It is about exposing the wounds of a whole people. About bursting pockets of abscesses of their history to extract the pus."

"What do you mean by reunion?"

"Louise-Marie is my ancestress. She is Nabo's daughter, Nabo himself being the son of Houegbadja. Houegbadja is known as the founder of the Kingdom of Dahomey in the seventeenth century. Behanzin, from whom I am descended, was the eleventh king in the Houegbadja dynasty. After him came the flood, orchestrated by the colonizers."

"You're a descendant of Behanzin!"

"Yes, Andy," Cyprien replies in a flat tone.

"You're too candid to be descended from Behanzin."

"You're wrong!" Cyprien says laughing. "Candor does not diminish the extent of one's greatness."

"It's incredible! I know Behanzin. Besides, who in our time can be indifferent to him? I covered an exhibition not long ago on the Shark King at Quai Branly Museum. It was fabulous! Tourists from all around the world were there. Should I understand that it is because of your royal rank that Louis XIV chose to call you Prince?"

"That's the only reason, Andy."

"What a night! I thought I had met only one king, but I was actually stuck between two of them. Stuck between the sun and the shark. The sky and the sea. Fire and water. Tell me, what, after three and a half centuries, pushed you onto the path of this search? What is it? I want to know!"

He looks at his companions in turn, retracting himself in the position of a novice among initiates.

"It all started with an engraving that a prisoner had made," Bonnot says. "This engraving was found during restoration works in a dungeon at Versailles Castle. I'm sorry I didn't have time to tell you about it. You can read the message here, when we get to a stop." Taking a pack of cigarettes from his pocket, Bonnot throws it on the dashboard before Andy. Andy quickly picks up the pack, eager to read the text. He begins to decipher it, holding his steering wheel with one hand.

"Do you understand the message?" Cyprien asks.

Andy reads the text aloud, pausing now and then to digest the meaning: "IN MEMORY OF NABO AND HIS DAUGHTER LOUISE-MARIE BORN OF THE QUEEN, CONDEMNED BY THE COURT OF FRANCE AND DISPATCHED."

"An enigma remains, dear friends," Andy says after thinking about it. "What does 'dispatched' mean? Does it mean killing or exiling? Earlier, the King spoke of 'separating' the child from the Queen. Do you think he would have left her alive?"

"He is a treacherous and perjured king," Cyprien says. "He is a murderer."

"You were rather sweet with him," Bonnot says.

"You say 'sweet', but that's a strategy in spiritualistic communications. You can't catch flies with vinegar. Do you understand? Bastard spirits who are cornered flee into the darkness and never come back. To get them, you have to cajole them."

"You know what?" Andy says. "I'm now more skeptical than ever. This whole convent thing is just a royal smokescreen. I think we're wasting our time. We're going to Moret for nothing."

"Do you think we're going to Moret with the dream of meeting the nun in her convent, kneeling at vespers and saying her prayers? We're going to look for her grave!"

"Excuse me, Cyprien, I'm losing my mind."

Andy is again looking at the cigarette pack when Yasmina shouts: "Watch out where you're going, Andy! Hey! stop!"

Andy springs into action, slams on the brakes. The car comes to a halt just short of a ribbon around a pit, the engine silent.

"We were going straight down into the abyss," Yasmina says. Jules rests his head on his girlfriend's chest, shaking. She caresses his hair calmingly.

"Londoners are right when they say Paris is the city of blocked roads," Andy says.

He turns the key to restart the car. Nothing happens. He tries again, and again, unsuccessfully. The car doesn't start anymore.

"We have failed forever!" Bonnot says. "Let the traitor among us denounce himself."

One of them raises his hand in oath. "If I am the traitor, may my tongue stick to my palate and may I become mute."

They take turns speaking, uttering self-inflected punishments such as "... may God take me back into my mother's womb."

"... may the ground crumble under my feet."

"... may the devil take me to hell in business class."

Fifteen minutes later, they have tried everything to restart the car, but nothing has worked. Cyprien suggests they continue the journey by train. He says that if the whole group manage to get to Lyon Train Station, they could continue the adventure taking the RER line D. This proposal provokes an outcry among his friends, who think it is immensely risky. The RER network, like all other public transport, is at all times infested with controllers and cops. Taking a cab is not an alternative, because usually, cabs do not accept trips out of Paris at night. Moret-sur-Loing is in Seine-et-Marne, seventy-six kilometers southeast of Paris. Jules, who has remained silent until then, comes up with a daring idea. He suggests to the group to give him time to go home and convince his father to lend him his second car. All his friends discourage him, pointing out how crazy the idea is. If he sets foot in the house, his father would never let him go out again. While Cyprien is checking on a map a way to get to the RER D station, Jules slips from the group. A few steps away, he hails a cab. Yasmina goes with him.

In the cab, they take the back seat. Jules huddles against the car door, and holds out his arms, inviting Yasmina.

"Ah you!" she says. "You really want to kiss me here?"

"Look, my dear, when one is a fresh rose, one must expect to be picked at any moment."

"Okay, but an evening rose is not fresh! Two days of unremitting struggle have withered me."

"No matter, my dear! Happiness is a product of our minds. If I consider a faded rose to be fresh, then it will be fresh for me!"

"Yes, pick me then, my wolf."

He throws himself on her like a wild beast and starts to devour her lips.

37

"I DON'T UNDERSTAND, Lieutenant," Fournier says, "how you can't find your way anymore. You will end up ringing thirty-six doors! Remember, we started with this same one. You were so sure, but ..."

"Yes, Commissioner, this is the one. This is the place we are looking for. I recognize the stairs."

"I'm afraid you're wrong again. This is not a neglected apartment with heavy brush growing in it."

Toulon hesitates at first, then, assumes the boldness of a Lieutenant and pushes against the wooden door panel. Instead of slamming against the wall as it did during his first visit here, the door resists his push. Sahid has noticed the moving shadows through the door's translucent glass. Stealthy as a wolf, he creeps towards the door, keeping an eye on the intruders. By now, he is wide awake and clearheaded. There is no risk for him of confusing a pear for an avocado, or, as the Islam saying goes, confusing a white thread for a black one. And indeed, when he opens the door, the ones he sees are two uniformed men. One is wearing a navy-blue camouflage overcoat and a black kepi stamped with six laurel branches. With his duck feet, he can lay no claim to have the agility of a monkey. His companion looks rather like a gorilla. He too is wearing a black turgid jacket and a kepi. He's not in the mood of someone who has come to declaim a love poem. Glances and astonished frowns are exchanged between Sahid and the strangers. The parties trade more or less sincere good evening greetings.

"Am I under arrest, Commissioner?" Sahid asks.

Fournier regards Sahid with an ironic smile. "No, not yet! Don't worry, as long as we don't find anything wrong with a citizen, he can rest easy under his roof. It does seem we have the wrong door."

"What are you looking for?"

"Do you know of a disused apartment in your neighbourhood opening into the street?"

"No, I don't. With the housing crisis, the City would not keep a dwelling space unoccupied."

"You're not wrong, I agree with you. Look at these photos, sir, do you recognize anyone?"

The commissioner shows him photos of Cyprien, Jules, Yasmina and Bonnot. After hesitating, Sahid says, "Maybe." A moment later, he says, "No."

"We are offering ten thousand euros to anyone who can put us on their trail."

"That's a fortune, Commissioner!"

"Yes, it is worth it," Fournier replies. "Here, take my card." He hands Sahid the terrible thing. "Call me if you have some news to tell me."

The two cops leave. As they get in the car, the Commissioner calls the office and gets the RCM-32 chip activated.

On the platform of Lyon Train Station, Cyprien strolls along, looking around. He expects Jules and Yasmina to join him. He has already let several trains go by. The electronic board says the next train will come in five minutes. He doesn't want to miss this one. He will go to Moret against all odds, he has decided, alone or accompanied.

Andy and Bonnot are still on Charenton Street, patiently waiting for a tow truck to drag away the car. They will not be going to Moret. Theirs will be another adventure. Behind the wheel of the defunct car, Andy is already scratching the first draft of his paper on Louis XIV's testimony, while Bonnot is keeping watch. Finally, Jules appears. Bonnot is not surprised, as he is swivelling his eyes in all directions. Jules has woeful news. He has failed to get his father's Jaguar, as they had all hoped he would. Comforting Jules, Bonnot says, "At least you are here. We have been waiting for you for an hour. Convinced you would return without the car, Cyprien has gone on to Lyon Train Station. When time passed and you were not back, we just knew that your plan for the car didn't work out. Only an optimist like you would imagine that your father would help you go back out. No parent would encourage their child to take risks by lending them a vehicle for such a purpose."

"Relax," Andy says to Jules. "Drop your gloomy face. We're all reunited again."

"I feel bad," Jules says. "I touched a corpse."

"A corpse! Where, and how? Did someone die in your house?"

Yasmina irrupts into the conversation, "Shut up, Jules! We promised to keep the secret, and we have to keep it!"

Then, she says addressing the other two men: "He is hallucinating. There was no corpse. You haven't heard anything! Okay? We're running to Lyon Station to catch up with Cyprien before he boards the train." She hails a cab and hustles Jules and herself aboard.

As they get off at Lyon Station, they hear the long monotonous sound from the train horn. The ticket machines are there, cold, but quick to serve. After picking up their tickets, they set out to climb down the steps of the escalators, rather than only having this mechanical ladder carry them down. When they finish going through the maze of galleries leading to the platform, they can only catch sight of the last car disappearing into the tunnel. Yasmina swears at the train, curses its driver to hell, denounces the SNCF fares that she finds exorbitant ... The platform is a dark anthill, swarming with black coats. The people, mute, cold and all dull, avoid each other like cars on the roads. The eternal half-light of the train station seems to have turned them into followers of an initiatory ballad. Like angels of death, the greedy trains channel travellers in both directions through dark mouths of tunnels into entrails of the unknown. Towards Tartarus, one would say.

Before they have time to wonder what to do, Jules and Yasmina are surprised when Cyprien suddenly appears, joining them on the platform.

He hails them. "Oh well guys, here you are!" He holds his fist out to Jules, gives Yasmina a hug.

"You have been spying on us, right?" Jules says.

"Yes, my eye is everywhere. I'm your Fournier."

They all laugh at Cyprien's words.

"In that case, I will play the Lieutenant," Jules says.

He suddenly stiffens his neck, turning to Yasmina, and shouts in a deep voice: "National Police! Turn this engine off! Get out of the vehicle! That's an order! Where is the stolen box? Eh?"

Yasmina is not impressed. She says to Jules, "I would rather like to see you play Julius Caesar instead."

Mocking Yasmina, Jules replies, "Yes, impostor that you are! Because you want to pass yourself off as Cornelia Cinna."

The scene amuses Cyprien. "If you were here, I would not have been bored. I went to check the exhibitions up there while waiting for you to reach the Station. I was sure you would come back without the crate, believe me. Where are the others?"

"They're taking care of their scrap of a car. Andy is also starting work on his paper. He doesn't want to miss the opportunity to raise the profile of his newspaper and to enhance his own reputation."

Jules points at the electronic board, which is flashing. "Here comes the monster!"

The three of them head for different cars. Before the doors slide open, they flash each the V-sign with two fingers to seal their unity.

38

AROUND NINE O'CLOCK in the evening, the Commissioner and his henchman are still active on the field. To avoid total exhaustion, they need to get some result before midnight. The big cop refuses to adopt the attitude of some terminally ill who use their last breath to order euthanasia.

"The end of everything is programmed," he says to Toulon. "But it only happens if we don't put it off. So, let us work! Let's close our eyes to the minutes ticking away! Let's stretch out time! Perhaps we will earn a Jules Verne *ghost day*. The most exciting thing about our job, as you know, is that things happen on their own when you think everything is lost. We have not lost the CARAN archives, Lieutenant, let alone Cyprien Ghezo. It is nine o'clock. In three hours, anything can happen. Remember the battle of Aboukir against the Turks. Even after he had taken a bullet in the face, our General Murat had not even needed all that time to defeat the grandstanding Mustapha Pacha. As you can see, failure does not result from the immensity of losses, but from the waning of the willpower to win. To tell you the truth, Ghezo has nothing similar to the Pasha's bravery, nor are his accomplices worth a hair of a Mamluk soldier. They are three little cowards who do not hesitate to seek refuge in cemeteries when our men approach. They are dead men! All we have to do is bury them, Lieutenant, and not later than midnight! It is up to us to show that our *Fluctuat nec mergitur*, the motto of our capital city, rests on a solid foundation."

Toulon nods. The Commissioner continues. "I'm giving you this speech because I heard Sahid thinking out loud. His name is Sahid, the man on Dahomey Street. The GI sent me all the details about him. He's a fortune teller, a bit of a snob around the edges, or something like that. Some Parisians know him from his two-cent advertising. It is very likely that our criminals have passed through his house, for you see, they are all of the same ilk. I have a feeling he has just extorted six hundred euros from someone."

"Oh, really! Commissioner?"

"Yes, I'm pretty sure. I caught his monologue in which he makes an interesting calculation. He considers that six hundred euros plus ten thousand euros makes a fortune as a single day's income. He says he cannot trample on a windfall that comes his way. He will call us, I'm sure. Did you notice his gesture when I showed him the photos?"

"Yes, he hesitated pronouncedly, then he was quick to say no."

"Well, those who behave that way want to say yes to you while covering their backs legally. You know, in justice, there is no room for irony or the unspoken. It is what comes out of the mouth that matters. This scoundrel will call us back, believe me."

"I agree with you, Commissioner. No doubt about it."

The Commissioner's cell phone rings just as he is checking his watch to count down the minutes. The caller is none other than Sahid! He is asking if he could meet Fournier immediately. Great!

The two policemen head back to Dahomey Street.

Seventy-six kilometers away from Paris, Cyprien Ghezo, Jules Bartoli and Yasmina are struggling to find the convent of the nuns. It is night. A wall map placed at Veneux-les-Sablons Station leads them to Église Street. The town is cold. So are its monuments and its frontages visible from Samois Square. Moret is quietly sleeping. One can hear its breathing in the soft murmur of the river whose course goes through a medieval dam. By a pedestrian street at the mercy of snow, the three reach Notre-Dame church. Accustomed to modern and ancient monuments in three days, Cyprien explains to his friends that the church dates back to the 12th century. Just across the street, they see the house of the nuns which at one time was the convent of Moret. Now the building is no longer a convent, but it was deemed to be useful in another way. It now houses nuns. As they approach the gate, they notice the dilapidated state of the walls. The walls are entirely covered by creeping plants that must undoubtedly bear abundant foliage during the green season. Cyprien rings the bell, which likely doesn't work, because no one answers. After a few moments of silence, he knocks on the metal door. A bent old woman with square shoulders crosses the courtyard and opens the door. She does not hide her surprise at these three unusual visitors who have turned up at such a late hour.

"I thought it was my son, so excuse my surprise! What can I do for you?"

"We are travellers, madam," Cyprien says. "Our car broke down a few miles from the city.

"Where did that happen?"

Jules looks at the map and points. "Here! On Chamois Street."

"That's the Departmental Road No. 218," the old woman says. "I'm afraid I can't help you. Have you mistaken this building for a repair shop?"

"No, ma'am," Cyprien says. "We need a shelter to spend the night."

"You don't live around here, apparently."

"We're from Paris."

"From Paris, moreover! So, you expect me to open my doors to you as if you were angels of the Father!"

"Don't leave us in the snow, ma'am. We're in trouble. Not only we are unable to reach our destination, but we also have had our hearts broken. We have just returned from seeing a sick aunty in Ecuelles. She's in bad way and will probably give up the ghost this very night."

"Oh, poor children. Be strong."

Yasmina blows her nose with her scarf. Looking at her, the old woman notices that her eyes are already peeing. "Don't cry, my daughter! Come, come, all of you! Come where it is warm. God will not reject you from the bosom of his dwelling. You don't look like big-city blighters. Poor children!"

She takes Yasmina and holds her tight to her chest. She lifts the girl's face and wipes her tears with her palm. The girl hiccups and shivers at the same time in these arms with maternal tepidness. Her friends are stunned looking at this scene improvised by their teammate. They wonder at seeing how easy it is for her to pump out tears at will from the tank of her eyes. Once the storm has calmed down, Mrs. Mathilde takes them to an outbuilding of the old premises, dimly lit by a single sixty-watt lamp.

"This is where I live with my son," she tells them.

"Thank you for welcoming us," Cyprien says.

"You must be very distressed; I can see it."

"We can't hide it, ma'am. When you have an aunty who is on her way out ... When the car refuses to take you home so that you can collect yourself ... What do you expect? We are sure to return to Ecuelles very soon, even more distressed than tonight. The venom of death is working in her already. We beg you to join your holy prayers to ours for the repose of her soul."

"It is done, my children. Let's put ourselves in God's hands. Should I assume that you are also hungry?"

"Yes, hungry as wolves, ma'am!"

"Be assured. You will not lack anything here, my children. I will make you happy."

She serves them mint tea to warm them up, patties left over from the evening meal, and fresh milk. To the satisfaction of their benefactress, they eat with great appetite. A three-day guerrilla campaign with the police has left a hole in their stomachs. Although victory is looming two hours away, this campaign has no respite and is but a warm-up to further war. Because the Commissioner, instructed by Sahid, is picking up the pace with several measures. Barricades are put up on departmental roads; video surveillance in public places is enhanced; systematic checks at the Moret Station are implemented; plainclothes informers are dispatched at short notice to patrol the small town of the 77th Department.

39

Old Mathilde is a likable lady. She talks about her only son Jeremiah, who is a coast guard and who works as a patrol on Loing river in a boat that travels up to the Seine mouth. She talks about her late husband who fell under the flag, about her devotion to the church, and so on. The parish priest entrusted her with the upkeep of the house of the nuns. The house is a former convent of Benedictine girls which had become a museum since the convent moved to Provins, a neighbouring town, in 1781. We owe to these ladies the invention of barley sugar which has existed through centuries. These little caramelized candies are still eaten today in the form of boiled sweets at Puits du Four Street. She tells them many stories, one embroidered over another, with the intention of distracting the minds of these poor young people. She needs to unburden them of the weight that she believes has weakened their morale. From time to time, she puts a hand on Yasmina's shoulder, who is sitting next to her. She invites them all to come back to Moret when their hearts have grown calmer, to be charmed by the tourist attractions the town offers. She mentions the Barley Sugar Museum located a few steps away from the convent, Notre Dame Church, the house of the nuns itself, the mausoleum of the painter Sisley who gave his name to the town, the modest inn that is still famous for having welcomed Napoleon I back from his Elba Island, the tanning mill planted in the heart of the river … and before the mill, Quai des Laveuses where century after century, the Town has immortalized water levels as the Loing breaks out in deadly floods.

Sharing her stories, Mathilde soon approaches that of Louise-Marie's, like a hare innocently advancing towards a trap. Jules foot-nudges Cyprien. Everyone is all ears when Lady Mathilde broaches the subject of the daughter of King Louis XIV born of an adulterous relationship between the Queen and her black slave.

"I'm telling you that she actually lived here in Moret, in this old house that you see," Mathilde says. "She was devoted to God. Besides, she came into the world only to serve God and not earthly royalty. She had been brought here still in her swaddling clothes by a mistress of the King who had been kind enough to save her from a death planned by the sovereign."

"How can a king order his daughter to be killed?" Cyprien asks.

"I won't hide it from you, it was the child of shame that served as the signature of the Queen's infidelity."

"The King did not show a good example of fidelity either, since this girl had been saved by a mistress of his."

"How quickly you have understood! Louis XIV is the most unfaithful king in the history of France, and his wife the most candid queen. On days when the King devoted an entire night to her, she would proclaim to the court from the balcony afterward how her husband had honoured her. It was her way of getting back at Anne of Austria, the King's mother, who had been trying to turn her son into a bad husband with toxic advice. Anne had not given her consent for this marriage. To all this, the Queen responded with puzzling calm. Her naivety and the goodness of her heart loosened the knots of court intrigues. All this is remembered to this day. The Queen's unfortunate daughter Louise-Marie spent her whole life within these walls that you see. Without fail, her benefactress, Madame de Maintenon, paid her frequent visits. The Queen also knew how to elude the vigilance of her royal husband and come to see the fruit of her womb. She was deeply attached to this child, but the aristocratic system is guided by principles which are by far not based on feelings of the heart."

"Did the King know that the Mooress was alive?"

"No, of course he didn't! If he had, he would have had her killed in the convent. O my God! Praise be to you that such an aberration had not occurred in your house." She makes a sign of the cross and clasps her hands together, eyes closed.

"How did her days end?"

"The natural way, blessedly. She died a natural death and was buried here in Moret. People point to many places where she was supposed to be buried, but many testimonies point to Champ de Mars. I have never considered any other place but Champ de Mars as her burial place."

Jules has been listening wisely to everything without a word. Sitting back in his chair, he asks, "What is the legend of a soldier who walks on fire, madam?"

Mathilde's eyes grow wide. "Ah … I thought you were asleep, my son! Who did you get that legend from?"

She smiles. "Did you take a quick trip to the country of silly things; I mean the country of dreams?"

"No, ma'am, I wasn't asleep," Jules replies.

"I've never heard of that, my good man. Maybe when you come back here, the tourist office will give you an answer."

"We would like to visit Champ de Mars."

"Yes, it's good to do that. It's a stone's throw from here, at the end of Pecherie Street. But I wonder what you will be able to see there in this gloomy season. I suggest you wait until summer when nature has been resuscitated. Champ de Mars, like the whole town of Moret in summer, is fantastic. Its rusticity and its old ramparts contrast with the glitter of our time. Champ de Mars itself is a huge crown placed on the tomb of the Mooress. Tourists are wrong to take this work for a simple horticultural jewel intended to adorn the town. In Moret we know what it represents. It is much more than an ornament. It is a highly symbolic masterpiece. The largest wreath ever laid on a grave in France. Even the heroes of the Liberation, including my late husband, had only been honoured with twigs."

"We can't wait to visit this place," Yasmina says.

"Oh! You, my daughter! You are awake? I thought you were also gone to the country of silly things."

"No, not yet. We are so happy in your house. How can we sleep? You are our mother."

Mathilde looks fondly at Yasmina. "My son is just as endearing as all of you. He never sleeps early. On days when he is off the night shift, we stay up till midnight. But listen, this is not a good time to visit. What do you want to see in a town besieged by snow? If you go to

Champ de Mars, all you'll get is an ice field. If tomorrow the snow melts like the weather forecast says it will, you can take a walk around the town, then my son will take you to Paris. He will not refuse to do this favour to his brothers, I am sure. Let's pray and go to bed. You need to rest. Let's entrust our souls to God and let's put in his powerful hands all that afflicts us." She closes her eyes and starts to pray. No one really accompanies her, except to murmur the responses. When the prayer is over, Jeremiah knocks on the door calling out, as if he were the good Lord coming to answer the supplications the orants have made.

"My son is a prophet, let's not forget it!" Mathilde says. "I just blasphemed!" she adds, with her right hand covering her mouth.

She heads to the door with a big key in her hand, agile like a young girl.

Jeremiah comes in. He looks exhausted, but nice otherwise. He apologizes for his delay as he reveals that he was held up in an eternal traffic jam created at the town entrance by the Country Police. The patrol was patiently checking all the vehicles caught in the traffic jam, shining their flashlights on passengers' faces, opening and searching even the back trunks.

"Sounds like another foul murder has just been committed," his mother says.

"We can assume that mom!" he replies.

She introduces Jeremiah to Yasmina, Cyprien and Jules. When he learns from his mom what the three young people are going through, he is moved to the verge of tears. His mother asks him to think of them as his younger siblings. She asks him to help them return to Paris the next day after they have had enough rest.

40

OF ALL THE definitions we give to sleep, of all the lore based on it, this thought captures best what it is: sleep is half-death. Yes, to sleep is to die halfway. Sleep is the guest who one receives, who one sees off afterwards, but not ever knowing at what time he came.

Before the three friends realize that they have slept, Jeremiah is at their door to tell them it is daybreak. Jeremiah's action somewhat annoys Lady Mathilde. She wished to see her children stay in bed until sleep had drained out of them. But she understands and forgives her son. She realizes he has professional matters to attend to, besides fulfilling his mother's request in favour of his brothers.

The little family gets into action. Mathilde is preparing breakfast while Jeremiah rummages for life jackets in a jumble of sea equipment. The three friends are scouring a map for the route to Champ de Mars.

After breakfast, the family gather around Mathilde for a farewell. It is heartbreaking moment! Heartbreaking to part after a Providence-dictated night together under the small roof of this old convent in Moret.

"You cannot swear to anything with certainty until

you have breathed your last, but anything is possible," Mathilde says. "I never imagined I would be blessed with these many children in my arms. But now, in the twilight of my life, God has decided otherwise. My children, we are now united by this meeting that was ordained by Heaven. In you I find all the dreams of my youth and my life coming true. Let us never forget each other. We are now mother and children. May the Lord take away the worries that are weighing down your hearts this morning. If it is his will, may your aunt recover from her illness. If, on the other hand, he already wants her with him, my children, who are we to say no? Let's keep our hands together as we face these challenges. Get back to your trip and be at peace. I expect to see you happier and more relaxed the next time you come back to your house."

She hugs in turn Cyprien, Jules and Yasmina. Yasmina sobs and bursts into tears in her arms. This time, her tears seem real and sincere. The old woman presses her to her flattish chest and tenderly pats her back. The only thing she doesn't is to sing Yasmina a little lullaby. The girl cries grow louder. Her lips perfectly articulate the word "Mom!"

"Yes, daughter!" Mathilde replies.

Yasmina slowly lifts her head. She touches the necklace of false pearls that she wears year-round. Taking off the necklace, she gazes at it for a bit. Then, she puts it around the lady's neck, after which she hugs her again.

"What do you mean by this gesture, my daughter?"

"It means that you are my mother. You are the mother I didn't have at birth. You are the mother I have always missed. I have never heard a mouth say 'daughter' to me since I was born. No one has ever wiped my tears with their own very hand."

Yasmina speaks through her tears. "The few times people have wiped my tears, they have done so with a disposable handkerchief!"

"My daughter, am I to understand that you were an orphan before we met?"

"I'm not actually. The woman who gave birth to me and calls herself my mother is so in name only. I'm not her daughter in the way I feel I'm your daughter. I was born of an unwanted pregnancy. You are my mother. It was only last night that I heard a mother's voice say with real love, 'My daughter'."

Yasmina's words impose silence on the farewell gathering. Tears flow down several cheeks as they watch Yasmina and Mathilde entwined in an embrace. But filled with their pride, the men quickly stifle the outflow of their emotions. It is womanly for a man to get emotional, people often say. This has always been the motto for men: to face life's upheavals, you have to be as hard as a rock. Hold in your internal volcano until you can no longer stand it. Bottle it up, until a fumarole has pierced the side of the mountain to show the volcano is ripe.

Mathilde hugs her son last. He has been waiting for his morning kiss from his mother, as he always does before he goes to work.

The group takes leave of her outside the house. To hide a tear drop that has welled up under her eyelid, Mathilde quickly turns and goes back inside. She heads to a window. There, she pulls back the curtain and gazes vaguely outside, without interest, with no wish to see anything in particular. But to her surprise, she notices that normal weather has risen from the snow that had beaten the region for three steady days.

At Bourgogne Gate, Jeremiah shows his younger brothers the way to Champ de Mars, then he turns right on Grande Street. While they go to visit the place of their passion, Jeremiah will be preparing the boat anchored on the Loing near La Grange des Graillons Quay. The weather has strangely improved. The rising temperature has melted the snow. At night, Mathilde, who sleeps with one eye open, was able to hear the rhythmic drip-drip of the water drops falling from the roof. Now, the conifers are shining again, once more victors of this winter.

ℬ In this quiet-looking town, a secret recon activity has been launched since the night before. It is difficult to know which corners the recon team has already scoured and which the members have yet to visit. Maybe they are scouring the cemeteries and woods as they did in Paris, maybe they are still sleeping in the cozy rooms of their hotels waiting for the town to wake up. The A5 and A6 highways are still blocked, as well as the departmental roads that branch off from them. The Country Police agents spent the night sifting and re-sifting through incoming and outgoing vehicles. Result? They have drawn nothing but a blank! At Veneux-les Sablons Station, the National Company of French Railways, better known as SNCF, has activated all its artificial eyes to scan 360 degrees of the surrounding area.

ℬ Champ de Mars. The trio is already on the spot. A large circle protected by a grid delimits what, according to laymen, is a horticultural jewel in good season. For the initiated, this circular work is nothing else but "The biggest wreath in France". It is the crown that embroiders the tomb of Louise-Marie of Bourbon, known as the Mooress of Moret.

The three friends stand near the circle, their gaze fixed on a central point, training their thoughts on what lies in the bosom of the damped earth. Cyprien leans against the gate. "It's really here," he says. "Do you hear these whispers rising from the depths of oblivion?"

"I feel that this circle is a dwelling," Yasmina says.

"It is," Jules says. "My hair is standing on end at the thought that she is watching us from inside."

Cyprien climbs the gate and walks to the middle of the "wreath". No stele has been planted there to guide the visitor. But voices of the forgotten never die. They smolder under time like an ember under ashes, waiting only for a small breath to fan them into an immense fire.

As his friends let him, he falls on his knees in the snow that has not finished melting, his ear to the ground. Then, arms spread, he throws himself on the ground and kisses it.

Finally, Yasmina calls him out. "Eh Cyprien! Dear friend, do you think you are a bear? You'll catch a cold! Get up now!"

"Calm down, my chick!" Jules says. "If he gets cold, all three of us will become blocks of ice. Give him time to feed his soul with a much sought-after reunion."

Inside the "wreath", they see Cyprien raise his head. His face to the sky and lost in reverie, he shouts with all the strength of his lungs: "Ancestress! Here I am!" His thunderous voice produces an echo audible all around the town. Buildings are shaken. The echo spreads to distant mountains that ring the town. Unleashed like an invisible lightning bolt, Cyprien's voice floats away. Not like a bottle thrown into the sea that randomly lands anywhere, but rather like a letter that a carrier conveys to a precise location. From Paris to Abomey, royal palaces shake. The foundations of the Shark King's palace shake. The Versailles Palace shakes.

When Jeremiah joins the group at Champ de Mars, Ghezo has his head down, his nose in the snow. He does a long recitation in *Fon*, a Beninese dialect that his friends don't understand.

"What is your friend doing in there?" Jeremiah asks in amazement.

"Let's give him time to feed his soul," Jules says. "He's communing with the Moorish woman at her burial site."

"Does he have a genealogical connection with this black princess?"

"Connection is an understatement. He is a descendant of Behanzin, who inherited the throne from the King of Dahomey, from whom the Mooress is descended."

"That's a curious story," Jeremiah says. "I know many things about the life of the Mooress. My very indiscreet mother must have told you tons. Or am I wrong?"

"She did, clearly!" Yasmina says. "She is the one who put us on the right track. She is so nice, that dear mother of ours!"

"That's how a simple car breakdown leads you prodigiously to your roots," Jeremiah says, nodding. "When you get to Paris, make sure to visit Saint Genevieve

Abbey where the Mooress' heart rests. That heart will reveal many mysteries to you, I am sure. Here, it is the body and the guts that have been buried together. Because there had never been any intention to embalm the Mooress, it wasn't considered appropriate to separate the guts from the body. Also, don't miss visiting Saint Genevieve herself. It is quite fair that a heart that has experienced and given so much love, in return receives tribute from those who esteem it. You see, I don't want us to waste hours driving on the highway and getting searched up to our guts. I'll take you along the Loing and the Seine to Paris. I have a navigation license that covers the whole Region of Île-de-France."

In the meantime, Cyprien comes out of his retreat. He is weak and strangely distant, his voice faint.

Jules can't hold his satisfaction within. "Dear friends, we have won! We have set the elements in motion. What gendarme or policeman can square off with the outburst we have unleashed? For a moment we became the absolute Voice that dictates the fate of the world."

Cyprien answers him in *Fon*, in a dreamy tone.

Jules waves his hand over Cyprien's face. "Hey! buddy, come back to earth! I'm not a *Fon* speaker. How do you expect me to understand you?"

Cyprien translates what he just said. "I mean that we have not stopped being the absolute Voice that dictates the destiny of the world."

"Everything will soon be accomplished," Jules says. "But the closer we get to the end, the more complicated the journey becomes. Do you know the last revelation?"

"Yes," Cyprien says, his voice firm again. "The wind of fate is taking us to Saint Genevieve to see part of the relics of the Mooress."

"How could you grasp that, with your head stuck in the snow?"

"As soon as a thought is formulated in the mind, it can be picked up by other minds without the intervention of the organ of hearing. Jeremiah said that the body and the guts of the Mooress lie here, but that we must find her heart at Saint Genevieve Abbey. That will be our last win."

"Nature is working for us," Jules says. "Do you see how lucky we are? We'll be able to get to Paris navigating two waters, avoiding the cops swarming the roads in search of us."

"Jules, you are no longer afraid of being arrested. You and Yasmina have already won your judicial immunity."

"Pending last night's dead body case. I can't predict where it will lead me. At any moment, the police can ask for my head again."

"But you, you didn't kill him!"

"Sure, I found him already dead, but I have my fingerprints on his throat. The experts will determine he died of strangulation."

"Don't worry, buddy. The truth is king. It always gets to light through the darkest and most tangled situations. See how the sun is shining this morning. It's melting away the three-day piles of snow. That's the truth."

Jeremiah comes to invite them to follow him onto the platform. They leave the "wreath". At the other end of Champ de Mars, where Pecherie Street begins, Yasmina stops abruptly. Her eyes are bright, and her hand is on her chin.

"You know what?" she says. "Look, look at these vehicles! Do they not mean anything to you?"

The others look. They see nothing strange on this vast parking lot of Moret Fire Department.

"They're just fire trucks," Jules says.

"And you, Cyprien, what do you think about this?"

"I don't understand the riddle. Like Jules, I only see these three fire trucks, two small rapid intervention cars with flashing lights, and nothing else!"

"Well, well, well!" Yasmina says. "My two little jerks, I'll tell you what it is. We are at the camp of the 'soldier who walketh on fire'!"

Her friends are stunned.

"The King wanted to make us think," Jules says.

"No, firemen were not a reality in his time," Cyprien says.

Jeremiah heads to La Grange Quay, the others trailing him. He is walking faster and faster. Everyone puts on a life jacket and takes a seat aboard Galaxy. Jeremiah raises the anchor.

41

PARIS, NOVEMBER 26. Ten o'clock in the morning. It is a clear day, a beautiful day, with no exaggeration! A radiant sun is taking its revenge on three days of unremitting greyness. The snow which melted last night was trapped in a recrystallization process, leaving ice spikes hanging from roofs. And this morning, the rising temperature is diluting these crystals that still sparkle in the sun like rough-cut diamonds. Nature, beautiful, has made peace with humans. It allows the inhabitants of the big city to entertain thoughts of spring, which they have hardly done in this month known to be chilly. White tables are popping up on bar terraces. Restaurants are filling up. *Happy hours* are extended to all day, as a sign of gratitude to the Heaven!

Mr. Bartoli has gone to the repair shop to see the injured car that needs treatment. The beast is damaged on the bumper, on the tip of the hood, and more discreetly on the radiator, having suffered a light dent.

The man is trying to control himself. He is struggling to be patient, and to hold himself back from swearing. Crossing his arms, he lets his thoughts wander. He imagines his son having sex with his girlfriend at her house while he, the father, is waiting for the mechanic to knock him silly with the repair cost estimate. Well, what's strange about that? Doesn't his son have the right to do what he wants with his majority? The problem is that these kids, who think they are adults at eighteen months old, break pots and leave their parents to pick up the pieces.

A providential phone call interrupts his disappointing thoughts, nudging him out of his reflective mood. "Hello! It's me, your teammate of misfortune, Benaoui!"

"Oh! BB! How are you?" Bartoli shouts with ill-concealed joy.

"Hey! What do you mean by 'baby'? You, Mr. Bartoli, can't you see that I'm too fat to appeal to men?"

"No, ma'am, don't misunderstand my words. BB stands for your initials, Bouchra Benaoui, if memory serves me."

"Oh yes! I'm sorry! I forgot that I gave you my full name."

"There you go! Now you remember. I hope you have some good news for me."

"Nothing, Mr. Bartoli."

"She didn't come back, your daughter?"

"No! I haven't seen her anywhere, not even in my dreams. I'm devastated!"

"Be strong. Everything always works out in the end. Sometimes when you think all is lost."

"And you, have you heard from your son?"

"Yes, I can say I have. But I don't know if I saw him in my dream or in reality. He dropped by last night just for a thirty-minute visit."

"And you let him go, Mr. Bartoli?"

"I had no way of stopping him. Do you know why he came back? It's because, not content with having damaged my first car, he wanted to take the second one to continue his madness across the city. You can imagine my categorical refusal!"

"That's for sure!"

"Disappointed, he left with his girlfriend without telling me his destination."

"Ah, these children! I no longer know who to turn to about the matter!"

Bartoli sighs. After a moment, he declares: "To Saint Genevieve, ma'am! To Saint Genevieve! She works miracles in families!"

"Are you making fun of me, Mr. Bartoli? You dare joke while my heart bleeds?"

"No, I am serious, today is the twenty-sixth. Genevieve is the patron saint of Paris, don't forget! Patron of all its inhabitants, of all families in pain and of all contrite souls."

"I am a Muslim. How can that work for me?"

"Listen, madam, miracle is a divine matter, with God at the helm. Does the sun, in order to enlighten humans, cares about our beliefs?"

"Do you believe in miracles?"

"If you don't believe in miracles in this century, what will you believe in? Material goods are no longer a guarantee. Look at all these rich people who flee France at seventy years old to nest elsewhere because their fortune has started to get them into trouble!"

"I need your help. I need your advice. We absolutely must meet!"

After they got details about the plan to meet, she bursts into tears, leaving the telephone connection open. She weeps silently.

Returning home, Mr. Bartoli wonders whether to call for help or not. He has barely turned the key in the lock of his door when the police turn up.

He is caught by surprise. "What again?" he asks.

"Your son! We want him!"

"You've been singing the same song for three days! If you haven't found any evidence to charge him in the CARAN incidents, leave him alone once and for all!"

"No, this time it's more serious. He killed a man last night in a parking lot."

"I don't see him as a murderer!"

"That's only because he hasn't tried to wring your neck yet, sir!"

Showing him their umpteenth search warrant, they push into the house.

The father could not imagine that his son, on leaving the house the night before, attempted to get a car through a hold-up. He arrived at the parking lot of a mall that had just lowered its blinds. At that moment of the night, customers were scarce on the concourse shrouded in darkness. A few cars were parked here and there, exposed to a snowfall that had lent them its colour. Crossing the parking lot on foot, Jules told Yasmina he needed one of those vehicles. Without hesitation, Yasmina gave her consent, assuming that Jules would only be renting a vehicle from the parking lot for their transportation to Moret, and that he would return it afterwards. Thrilled by Yasmina's consent, Jules decided to snatch the vehicle from the first owner who would open their door. And why wait so long? On a blue spot, there was a running vehicle. It was the ideal opportunity, yes! Snatching a vehicle from a disabled person limits the risk of a clash. On a blue spot, the hijacker is unlikely to face an aggressive push back by an owner eager to defend his property tooth and nail. In most cases, when users of blue spots are thrown onto the pavement, face down, and their treasure gone, they have nothing left but the clothes on their backs. With Yasmina keeping watch, like a hawk Jules pounced on his prey. His attack was made easier by the fact the door was not locked. Jules had no trouble with the driver behind the wheel. Grabbing him by the collar, he shouted: "Get out of that car, you bastard! I want it! It's mine now!" His victim showed no fear. In fact, no reaction from him was noticed. Jules furiously repeated: "Get out, before I throw you out with my own hands!" He raised his fist. His victim kept his eyes shut, not daring to respond. When Jules let go of the man, his forehead fell like a rock on the steering wheel, causing the horn to blare. Jules, suspicious of this deeper than normal sleep, removed his glove to feel the temperature of his victim's body. He placed his hand around the victim's neck. The body felt cold, the skin hardened. The man was dead! Jules ran back to Yasmina, aware that he had just left his fingerprints on the body of a man he did not kill. He and Yasmina took off instantly, cutting the parking lot diagonally.

His father, now struggling with the police about the revelation of this new chapter, accuses the investigators of acting on extrajudicial motives. He says, without ambiguity, that he is persecuted for the simple reason that he presides over the Association of Corsicans in Paris. The arguments he employs in defense of his son are not far-fetched. He tells the police his son has an alibi. How could his son, the father asks the investigators, have killed a man in a parking lot at eight in the evening when he was at home at the very same time? In conclusion, Mr. Bartoli says, if the experts can't point out another time or another culprit for their crime, they should leave the innocent boy alone. Before the police leave, he promises to lodge a strong protest about this incident. His words, as expected, do not go unnoticed in governing circles.

42

GALAXY HAS JUST entered the port of Montebello. It is a small port located in front of Notre Dame Cathedral. Its purpose is to welcome riverboats intended to carry tourists along the Seine. Before leaving his passengers on the quay, Jeremiah asks them to promise they will visit Saint Genevieve Abbey. He draws their attention to the fact that the abbey itself no longer exists, as it suffered the fate of many religious premises in France during the Revolution. The building, since then demolished, has only its library remaining today. Its famous Saint Genevieve Library in the heart of the Latin Quarter, which boasts of spreading knowledge to many neighbouring universities since the Middle Ages. Jeremiah displays a broad knowledge of religious history. When he was young, his mother pushed him into a career in theology. He did not last long in the field. He realized his heart was not in theology. Nevertheless, he left the seminary with a pronounced interest in all things ancient and in the contemporary history of the Church in France.

With a smile on his face, the trawler waves goodbye and makes a wide turn to starboard. The small boat draws a large white semicircle on the Seine as it moves away southbound on its way back.

The three friends move on the quay of Montebello up to the stairs which lead to the street. Walking in front, Yasmina sees three suspicious men approaching. Before she is able to turn around and warn her friends, she sees an avalanche of policemen springing from everywhere invade the footbridge. Other police, who were hidden in barracks on the quay and playing ticket salesmen, come running. Three unknown agents stop Yasmina and Jules. One of them shouts with satisfaction: "We have him! Here is the murderer!" When Cyprien Ghezo tries to run back to the platform, it is too late! His momentum is stopped by two policemen who block him in a pincer movement in the staircase. Cyprien judges the situation to be even more hopeless when he notices Fournier's big face, flanked by two big eyes, a thick bushy moustache, and a reassured mouth saying, "Calm down, dear hero. The race is over!"

"Not yet, Commissioner!" Ghezo replies.

"And how do you expect to escape from two cops who have you cornered on both sides in this staircase?"

"Like this!"

As Cyprien replies, one of the cops sees his handcuffs fly into the air under the strike of a two-footed leap which seems to have been set off from a tiger trap. This unexpected back flip has allowed the fugitive to throw himself over the railing. He lands on the platform, four meters below. A daring cop tries to make the same jump, but he ends up with a knee dislocation. His colleague rushes down to help him. Laurent Fournier arrives breathless on the platform. He has aged several years since midnight. He now knows what the politicians are planning to do to him for not bringing back either the stolen CARAN archives or the thief. He knows no one doubts his experience and tact, but that won't save him. It is a well-known fact that, every time the Republic sinks, politicians will find an expiatory victim to sacrifice to the popular monster. This thought makes him feel that he has suffered a reversal of roles. Now he is the victim, the one chased down by Ghezo and his people. Who would be his people in this case? His people consist of students, associations, human rights groups, and surely, these traitorous politicians!

He goes by the water drawing his gun. "I must defend myself," he says to his henchman.

"Against whom, Commissioner?"

"Against this negro," Fournier replies. "If I don't kill him, he'll kill me first. I saw him dive into the water. In that icy water, go figure! He has the ability to appear in your plate while you are eating. I can see bubbles rising from there!"

He points his gun at the spot.

"Are you really going to do that, Commissioner?"

"If he wants to play Wesley Snipes, we'll see who dies."

"Are you really determined to send him to the bottom?"

In response to the question, Fournier fires two shots at the bubbles.

"Let him die. He has to die. The Seine will carry that garbage to the Channel, and the Channel to the Atlantic Ocean, which will dump it on the coast of Benin."

43

SITTING IN AN armchair, stroking his goatee with his left hand and holding a newspaper in his right, Mr. Bartoli asks himself many questions. He knows that he defended his son out of pure paternal instinct, out of duty. For the last three days, he has been finding out things about this son whom, it appears, he barely knew. If Jules has really committed a murder, it would be the final disaster for the Bartolis. Everything is possible. In their quest for personality and balance, once children have grown up, they end up putting the earth above the sky. They live in a tumultuous world that tries to excrete everything bearing the mark of their parents, the way a tissue rejects a transplant. But instead of wisely and patiently easing themselves out of the parental imprint in the same way the tissue separates from its transplant, they explode like a river flood bursting the dikes placed to guide its course.

Mr. Bartoli examines his conscience. Has he failed in some way? Has he not exercised the necessary vigilance to keep his offspring from becoming a delinquent? In any case, the presumption of innocence prevents whoever to judge people guilty, even if all the evidence pointed towards them. Jules can still be exonerated. The man drops the newspaper he has just received from his housewife onto a pile of old issues accumulated through the years. The phone within reach of his right hand allows him to make a few calls without moving. He contacts the association's office, his business partners, and some old friends working in various sectors of society. He tells himself to start organizing his defense before the vice closes irrevocably. But then he gets confused! He hasn't read the latest economic chronicle. He has also failed to take note of the latest movements of the stock markets. As a result, his heart is far from settled. He realizes that this woman, Mrs. Benaoui, whom he already regards as a friend, is not the only one who needs a miracle. He too feels that he is hoping for something that comes from an unknown source, from a hidden power.

He calls the lady to make sure everything is okay. Yes, it is! Of course, it is! She has been in good shape, since she heard about the miracle of the *Burning Ones*. She can't wait to meet Saint Genevieve in her earthly home in Saint Étienne-du-Mont church. It is there that she will unload into the hands of the saint the painful burden of her life, the continuous pain of her childbirth nineteen years later.

The miracle expected by Mrs. Benaoui is only a fragment of the one that Andy and his friend Bonnot are about to offer the city. From his manager, Andy has obtained in extremis the right to insert his special story in the pages of the weekly newspaper *The Canard*. The mere fact that his proposal was received favourably is in itself a miracle. It is nothing short of a miracle indeed, when a journalist on leave bursts into the newsroom at midnight with a hot story when everything has already been wrapped up and formatted, and when his find in the end makes the front page of the next day's issue! Besides, who could resist this breathtaking tale: an ancient king stirring up the meanders of forgotten centuries to reappear in modern times against all odds? The words of the character, quoted in extenso, defy any rational judgment.

Will Paris, born of enlightenment and reason, believe this story in this digitally driven century? No! Certainly not! But why not? Paris will perhaps believe it. In these times of post-modernism, virtual reality reigns supreme. Since the new theory considers the word as independent of the speaker, it is possible that Louis XIV's words assume their autonomy to come and address Parisians without the King. This is the only advantage that these strange theories wield nowadays. They help to explain the inexplicable and to complicate the indisputable.

Whoever thinks that Paris is too skeptical or too credulous is mistaken. It achieves its balance between the mythical past of its antiquity and modern sciences, between the brightness of its face and the desolation of the surrounding ghettos, between the archaic devotion of the Middle Ages and modern avant-garde thoughts. It is Paris that combines the encyclopedic knowledge of the academies and the massive ignorance that secretes small, short-sighted doctrines. It is all certain, Paris will believe! And if it does, it is in order to understand things better. Besides, everything is played! The name of the Black Princess and the reappearance of the Solar King are two stones thrown in the Seine. They will make waves!

44

AND WHAT A turnaround! What a reversal of fortune! How to explain why the inspector in charge of questioning Jules, until now very fiery and surly, has suddenly taken on a lamb's gentleness? A conversation he has just had with a boss is the only explanation to this change of attitude. He has received a phone call from the Beauvau Square urging him to moderate his ardor. He was cautioned not to kick the anthill in this election period. Day after day, the polls consolidate the Minister of Homeland Security in his position of potential winner of the Élysée. Letting a sordid affair of an alleged crime throw thousands of students into the streets one more time would not be very smart. The right strategy should be to put a bushel on the case and acquit the accused. That's easy! When you're a professional tracker and stalker, there are times when you have to put water in your wine. Is it for not having understood this lesson that Laurent Fournier is in a bad situation? For some hours now, unconfirmed rumours have been circulating about his dismissal.

The inspector, who has become an ally in spite of himself, explains to Jules how the anti-crime brigade is sorry to have mistaken him for a neck twister.

"I already told you," Jules says. "I found him dead and cold."

"That's what a counter-expertise has just confirmed."

"May I use your phone, Inspector?"

"Go ahead, help yourself."

"No, I need an Internet connection instead."

"Please go help yourself to it in the meeting room."

Accompanied by Yasmina, he goes to a computer and logs on. He will send a message to Cyprien to ask him whether he is free or not. As he accesses his account, his eyes almost pop out of their sockets. Unbelievable! Cyprien has beaten him to it! There is an email from him! Besides, his friend has not used the coded language they have been using since the beginning of the guerrilla war. He has written in French to say that he is sorry for the events at the Montebello Quay. He was able to get away and would conclude their mission on his own in honour of them all.

What Cyprien did was prodigious. After diving into the river, he swam under water holding his breath along the coast to a riverboat where he hung on to wait for the anchor to be raised. A bit strange all the same, but isn't he the prince of waters? Jules leaves the room through a wide-open door, pushing Yasmina before him. They depart hurriedly, as if escaping.

Jules looks around. "It is nice today," he says. "The wind has stopped, the snow has melted, so we can take our motor scooter again. It will allow us to join Cyprien quickly."

"If the scooter is still ours," Yasmina says.

"You mean that someone may have borrowed it?" She laughs to dispel fear.

They get to Saint Ouen by subway, free as butterflies. From afar, they see the motor scooter waiting for them, under a protective plane tree. No one has cut the chain binding it to the tree. Jules lifts the seat and takes a look at the loot in its cage.

"It's still there!" he says. "You know, to hide it better, just deposit it in the street."

"We have no helmets," Yasmina says.

"Ah! Listen, darling! Our heads have endured plenty so far. They are now hard enough to take any kind of shock."

"My hair will float!"

"For your hair, I have a remedy! I'm making you a bun right now." Facing her, he takes her head in both hands, digs his fingers into her abundant hair while he nibbles her lips.

"I think the bun goes in the back of the head, Jules."

He doesn't say a word.

Mr. Bartoli and Mrs. Benaoui have gone to Saint Étienne-du-Mont church where Saint Genevieve worshipers gather for their annual celebration. People also go to Notre Dame Cathedral of Paris, where the miracle of the *Burning Ones* took place. It was in this cathedral, eight centuries earlier, that the reliquary shrine of the saint was transported to save Paris from the *Burning Ones* epidemic. It is said that those who looked at the shrine with faith were healed. Neither Paris nor France let the centuries get the better of this miracle. Genevieve is rightly declared the saint patron of Paris. If since antiquity Paris has been assaulted by numerous waves but has never sunk, it is thanks to this powerful protective hand which, at the age of 12, had repelled Attila's terrifying assault with a simple prayer, as she kneeled, joined both hands and looked up at heaven! Some humans claim a medal of longevity on the strength of the few hundred years they have lived on earth. On this matter, Saint Genevieve lets two eras tell her story. Born in Antiquity, she died in the Middle Ages. This fact alone is a miracle. If you needed to see to believe, she opened the eyes of the blind, who saw and believed. Every November twenty-sixth since 1130, churches and chapels dedicated to the Saint are filled with worshipers who gather to pay homage to her and ask for more blessings.

On this 26th in Paris, a devotee from the north of Spain, all gnawed by cancer, has been in Saint Étienne-du-Mont church the living testimony of the Saint's power. After touching the shrine, he has felt young, regenerated and free of his tumors. It is Mrs. Benaoui's turn to place her hand on one of the sides of this magic rectangle. She is followed by Mr. Bartoli who admires the artistic conception of the work. Deep in his heart, he is talking to himself. *This metal is pure gold. Unalterable! Immortal! How much is a bullion this morning in London? Hard to tell without reading the stock market news …* Benaoui bends both knees. Her descent shames Bartoli out of his speculation. He sees her on her knees, with her hand gripping the side rail still. She starts whispering inaudible words. Bartoli does the same but is unable to focus. In his mind, he is hearing the voice of a columnist as he compares indexes or counts points gained or lost since the opening of the stock market. Oh well, that is life. The meditation continues, interminably.

What a beautiful experience!

45

Cyprien arrives at 10, Pantheon Square. It is the Saint Genevieve Library, formerly used by the abbey of the same name. From outside, it has a falsely contemporary face. Its well-polished and shiny walls made of white ashlars are able to conceal its age. Its presence in the Latin Quarter gives it the status enjoyed by a central library surrounded by a myriad of universities. The other side of the coin is that the large spaces enjoyed by other popular facilities in the outskirts are only a dream here.

He knows what libraries all are about. If you're not a subscriber, you buy a daily pass, invariably. That's what he has just done at the front desk. Instead of going to the reading room and sitting under one of the white mushrooms like all the other readers, he asks to meet the curator of the monument.

"Why?" a lady asks him.

"I doubt you can help me with that, madam. I am asking for access to the urn that contains the heart of the Moorish woman."

"Hmm. As far as I know, we have never kept an urn containing the heart of the Moorish woman in this place. If you want to visit her sepulcher, go to Moret where she lived."

"I've just come back from there, madam! The tourist office of Moret mentions that the heart of the Mooress is here since the convent was moved in 1781."

"You are teaching me things! Out of curiosity, are you an archaeologist?"

"No, biologist."

"I am deeply sorry to disappoint you. I have never heard of an urn deposited anywhere in this building. What colour is it?"

"It is the colour of the heart."

"Well, let's suppose it exists. In what capacity are you doing this research?"

"We are of the same lineage, the Mooress and I."

"I remind you that the Mooress was the Sun King's putative daughter. Aren't you thumbing your nose at the royal genealogy with your statement?"

"I know her origins. I can even give you more details. You are right to note that she was a putative daughter. Her biological father was Nabo, the Queen's slave."

"Oh, yes! Her biological father ... Since you are a biologist, right? Ah, that's what they've always said, but who knows? What surprises me in this story is not the birth of a black princess to the French court. It is your appearance here, more than three centuries later, to claim a blood link with her. Isn't that disturbing?"

"Madame, the curator might have a different opinion."

She flinches at this remark. She realizes that her curiosity has snared her into this confronting conversation. It is not her intention to divert a visitor from her boss.

Now, she announces Cyprien's presence, then tries to be nice to correct her poor performance.

"I'll come back to you, sir. The curator will see you in a few minutes. But in the meantime, I'll suggest something that surely will interest you. Do you know that we have a picture of the Moorish woman in this library?"

"No, you're just talking nonsense to keep me going. Where would you have found it?"

"Well! Look at the back wall. What do you see?"

"A painting. It looks like a nun. Oh yes! A black nun! Is she the Mooress?"

The woman nods and lets Cyprien exult with emotion. He goes to the foot of the painting. It is a work that an unknown artist who had sheltered himself from persecution had skillfully executed. No authenticating signature.

"O my God! It is you, Louise-Marie? Here you are at last in the guise of the heroine of Dahomey! If the French court in its time had rejected you, Dahomey today rolls out its most beautiful red carpet for you."

All library employees and users stare at him. He begins to declaim verses in a dialect that only his interlocutor immortalized on the painting understands. Meanwhile, the curator has come down from the second floor where his office is located. The receptionist points to Cyprien while saying a few words to her boss. The latter approaches the young man.

"Are you the one who wants to meet me, sir?"

"Yes, yes, yes, if you'd like to make this finding full, sir, take me to the urn. Here I have the image, show me the flesh."

"What do you mean by 'flesh', sir?"

"The urn, Mr. Curator, the urn! The urn that contains the heart of the Moorish woman."

"Are you the one claiming to be descended from the Kingdom of Dahomey?"

"It is not a claim, sir. Look at our features, the Mooress and me. See how we are shaped."

He embraces the picture.

"You are here in a library. We do not keep relics among books."

"Is there no written documentation on her?"

"Damn! written documentation ..."

"Yes, handwritten or printed sources."

The curator is silent for a few seconds, during which time he takes psychological stock of his interlocutor. Having felt the need to empty himself, he decides to be forthcoming with the young man. "Listen! The documents sent by the convent were stolen. To tell you the truth, the folder that once contained them is now empty. Do you understand? Empty! The leaden screed that covers this story not only aimed to hide the love affair of a queen and her slave, or, of a white woman and a negro. The birth of that little girl had colossal political implications. At the death of Philip IV and the heir having died, the throne of Spain had sat without a sovereign for a long time. As a result, the Spanish people had to wait until 1700 to see the great-grandson of Louis XIV take power in Madrid. If the French court had not decided to ostracize Louise-Marie from birth, she could have taken power south of the Pyrenees. She could have, because her mother had renounced the claim to the throne in her own country, by linking her destiny to that of France. Can you imagine a black queen reigning over Spain!

This is how the French Court succeeded in changing the destiny of the black race in Europe. The present kings of Spain are French Bourbons by virtue of that historic succession. They could have been Dahomeans, if fate had not decided otherwise. While Spain was looking for a sovereign, Louise-Marie was the only living child of the French royal couple. Unfortunately, she was held prisoner in Moret."

"Let's just say that, after the long regency, the Spaniards had finally received the sovereign they needed. And to return to the urn, can I count on your help, sir?"

"It is obvious! I have already helped you enough and there is no reason to stop now. I could have reported you to the police, you know, because for three days now they have been monitoring the entire library system. My instinct tells me you are the man they are looking for. But don't worry. We'll stick together. It's not every year that I get to serve attentive visitors to whom I can tell my little librarian's secrets. I won't report you. These are the same document thieves and destroyers of archives who have been operating and stalking researchers century after century. Do your research here without fear, but don't click any electronic catalogues."

"Thank you for your help, sir."

"I'm the one to thank you. It was my pleasure to speak to you."

The curator makes a U-turn to head back to his office.

"And the urn, sir?"

"The urn ... The famous one! You won't believe your ears when I tell you where it is. You are standing less than forty meters away from it."

"Forty meters!"

"Well, well, well! At Louise-Marie's death, her heart found a place of rest in this abbey, while her body was buried in Moret. At that time, the new sanctuary of Saint Genevieve was under construction across the street. The abbey, already threatened by the republican mob, was evacuating all its precious belongings to a safe place. It was in this mess that the urn was taken out in a hurry by a Benedictine priest and was hidden in the new abbey church still under construction. I'm referring to that building in front of us, the one called Pantheon. The priest had placed the urn in a formwork, knowing that the next day, the concrete would be poured over it and it would be blocked in forever. This was his radical attempt to save this unique earthly and heavenly royal relic. The priest knew, according to the murmurs coming from the Republicans, that the new building would no longer serve, as it had been planned, as an abbey church. It would be transformed into a tomb, whose only vocation would be to house the remains of the great men of the nation. The revolutionaries no longer wanted to hear talk about churches or God in France. Aware of this plan, the Benedictine priest had therefore very deliberately wanted to include the Black Princess among the great men and women to be immortalized. What am I saying! He had offered her precedence over all the others. It was not Voltaire who vied with Mirabeau for a first place in the Pantheon as people wrongly believe. Neither one nor the other got this honour. The honour to rest in the Pantheon first went to the Black Princess Louise-Marie of Bourbon, daughter of Nabo and Queen Marie-Thérèse of Austria, Spanish princess. When years later, the Benedictines revealed the presence of the urn in a concrete wall, they decided simply to erect a memorial in front of the place, dedicated to THE UNKNOWN MATYRS."

"Is this memorial still there?"

"Of course, it is! Where else would it be if not in the temple of the immortals?"

"Why wasn't the urn recovered from the wall instead?"

"By breaking the concrete, of course, they were sure to reduce the urn to rubble. That would have been the saddest result. In my opinion, it is where it belongs. Let us accept verdicts that do not fall under our sublunary justice."

"You know, sir, I have visited all the libraries in Paris. I should have started here. I am conducting this research with a group of friends who will be very happy to see what I've seen. The Mooress in a picture! She is imposing, tall and beautiful. She could have succeeded Philip IV of Spain. But you see, history is like a diptych. It only evolves alternating between injuries and amends. Neither side of the diptych can stand without the other. Today, November 26, Paris is celebrating Saint Genevieve, its patron saint. At the same time through this devotion, France is celebrating the anniversary of Louise-Marie's birth, the Black Princess. These two events are incorporated like Russian dolls, one trying to hide the other, but to better protect it from wear and tear."

He picks up the wall phone and calls Bonnot.

The curator gives him a hug, then a pat on the shoulder, wishing him good luck. He takes the exit door. As he reaches the stairs that lead to the street, his gaze strikes the Pantheon like lightning falling on a treetop.

He now sees an inscription that he had never seen before, and yet that has always been present in large golden characters on the pediment of the monument. FATHERLAND'S GRATITUDE TO GREAT MEN. He had always looked at this writing, but he had never seen it. It is obvious! When you look with your eyes alone, you see nothing, until you learn to look with your mind. He crosses the street. With a sure and measured step, he moves towards the Pantheon, to meet the immortals.

46

JULES EMERGES FROM Clovis Street after skirting Saint Étienne-du-Mont church. Yasmina has clung to him to protect herself from the wind. A large lock woven over her nape is rubbing her back. The scooter is running at low speed. The street is narrow, like other streets of this area of the Latin Quarter. Originally intended for carriages, streets have never been enlarged, despite the automobile revolution. From the corner of the perpendicular street, Jules moves along the cars parked in a crenelated pattern. One of them, a dark blue one, catches his eye. He slows down.

"Look at that!" he says. "Doesn't that car look familiar?"

"It looks like your father's *Jag*!"

"Yes, it does."

He brakes sharply and feels the weight of his companion pressing his back. They like this game with its erotic overtones. Yasmina has already described it in her diary, under the title "The motorcycle and us." In her description, she personified the scooter as the author of this brief but intensely happy contact between her and Jules. They look at the car. The license plate confirms their initial feeling. They make a U-turn, come back and park close to the car.

What can my dad be doing here? Jules wonders.

They get off the scooter, then look through the car windows like people with bad intentions.

"What exactly are we looking for? Are we kids?" Yasmina says annoyed.

"This is what I'm looking for!" Jules says, pointing to a bunch of flowers on the back seat.

"What is it?"

"Flowers! My father is having an affair. The bastard is having one!"

"Having an affair makes one a bastard?"

"No, not everyone is, but he, yes! I want to see this woman he's paying attention to. I'll kick her in the ass." He tightens his lips, clenches his fists.

"You're not going to do that, Jules!"

"This is the fucking crate he denied us last night! Because he was saving it to go see that *floozy*!" He kicks the car door.

"You'd be wrong to attack a woman who keeps your father company."

"I do not condone that! He's the one who made Mom leave. She never got his attention for a minute. His credo is the casino and stock market. That's it! How can I be proud of someone who took my mother and my little sister away from me? I learned that the judge had divided the children and that I had fallen into this man's basket. I haven't got a mother ..."

He suddenly goes from aggressive to weak. He has turned pale.

"You are not going to cry in the street, Jules! If a classmate sees you crying here in front of a chick, you would be completely burnt on campus. On campus you have to stay strong even when things aren't going well. Otherwise, you would be flushed away by the law of natural selection." She holds him, her hands knotted behind his neck. He shudders, trying to calm down. "Jules, why tell me that you are without a mother? Anyone can find a mother in any woman."

"What do you mean by that?"

"Look at me. I mean that, despite my young age, I am your mother. Show me your baby smile, if you agree with me."

He laughs. As she tickles him further in the sides, he literally exults. "I love you, mom."

"Listen, Jules. Consider this woman who accompanies your father as a saving soul. If she can come in and humanize his existence a little bit by giving him the opportunity to think about what all men think about, I mean a pair of buttocks in the back and a pair of boobs in the front, what's the harm? Besides, your father has always been careful not to embarrass us. You in turn, leave him alone. Let him do his own thing. If you happen to meet this woman, be nice to her and mind your own business. Will you do that for me, baby?"

"Of course, I will! For you, yes! I've always done everything for you. I don't exist!"

He grows angry.

"Stop it, Jules! You can't blame me for that. Calm down, my treasure." She pats his hair.

"All right! Whatever you say! I'll leave his fucking mistress alone. I promise!"

"Alright, let's move on. Back to the Scooter!"

"Our route has ended. We are very close to Saint Genevieve Library."

"In this case, let's proceed on foot. A little walk will relax you."

"Exactly, sweetie!"

They walk up to the library, buy a twenty-four-hour pass and go to the research room. There is no sign of Cyprien. Nonetheless, they are careful not to ask any questions. They go to the reading room. There, enormous white mushrooms overhang the tables. Cyprien is not under any of them. They leave.

47

BARTOLI AND BENAOUI leave the church. She is assured she has obtained all the graces from the holy shrine. On his side, Bartoli is happy to have helped her assuage the pain in her soul.

They move around talking about the pomp of the celebration. From time to time, their conversation turns to the skepticism of the century and the power of money that the woman denounces. Bartoli, on the other hand, claims that no century has ever been as fruitful as the current one in terms of religiosity. The lay happiness promised by the Renaissance, by the Age of Enlightenment, by the republican revolutions, has not been achieved. The two world savageries of the 20th century came to crown the decay of modern societies. The immediate consequence was a massive return to the religiosity of the Middle Ages. Enough to convince the lady!

As he speaks juggling keys, he arrives close to the Jaguar unaware of the hundred or so meters he has covered to get there. He stops abruptly with a look of astonishment. Benaoui has noticed something is wrong.

"Why are you frowning at your car?" she asks.

"No, not my car. It's that motor scooter. It belongs to my son."

"Your son!"

"Yes, the license plate says it all. I don't know why he parked near me."

"I suspect he's looking for you. Don't you carry a cell phone?"

"I don't have it with me."

"He must have an urgent problem that he wants to bring to your attention."

"Like what, in your opinion?"

"You were telling me about his troubles with the police!"

"And how would he have spotted me in this place? I don't understand." He turns to look around on all sides. He doesn't see anyone who looks like his son. He takes out a cigar, but refrains from lighting it, remembering he is not alone. The lady notices his discomfort. She tells him encouragingly that she doesn't object to tobacco use.

After the first puff of his cigar, Mr. Bartoli spots a boy with a familiar gait at the end of the street.

"There he is!" he says. "The boy in the khaki coat."

"He is accompanied."

"Yes, he is always accompanied. He never separates from that girl."

The young couple hesitates, then turns around and stops. Jules has noticed someone is following them. It is a stranger who accompanied them to the library and came out at the same time they did. They suddenly know they are released to trap Cyprien. Classic move! They stand still for a few moments, just to check suspicious movements in their surroundings.

"They have stopped," Benaoui says. "Hmm ... I see something strange." She rubs her eyes to clear her vision.

"What do you see?"

"It looks like the one keeping your son company is ... none other ... than ... my daughter."

"It can't be. She probably only resembles your daughter. My son has been involved with this girl for a long time. I know her very well."

"I recognize her clothes. Can you tell me the name of your son's girlfriend?"

"Her name is Yasmina."

"Damn! It's her! That's my daughter! Unless I'm on the wrong planet."

Bartoli's eyes widen. "Your daughter! You mean that my son and your daughter are ... ?"

The cigar falls from his mouth.

"So, this is the boy who damaged your car yesterday?"

"Sure! That's him!"

"Does it imply that the sedan my daughter is secretly driving and that might belong to her boyfriend's father is your car?"

"Yes, I had it towed to the repair shop this morning."

"Unbelievable!"

"And I also understand that it was for her that you were at the police station yesterday. See how it all comes together."

"My God! Our children open our eyes to things! So far, I have one problem that worries me: how are we going to look them in the eye? But, Mr. Bartoli, you know what? It's destiny. Praise the Lord! Praise be to Saint Genevieve! Praise be to her holy shrine. I have barely crossed the portico of the church when my daughter returns to me."

Bartoli, who has been petrified until then, recovers. "And praise be to Allah who has opened your mind and allowed you to take this decisive step."

"You were right! Miracles are still possible today. Let us rejoice. Let us not disappoint the Most High who has sent us this sign."

Across the street, the young couple approach, slowly, hesitantly. Jules has noticed his father near the Jaguar.

"There he is!" he says. "There he is with his … I don't know who!"

"You promised me you would be good with her," Yasmina replies. "But … Look, Jules! I am stunned. Do you know who that woman is?"

"I'm not interested in her."

"It's my mom!"

"Your mom! Did you say your mom?"

"Yes, it's her! Do you see how they are looking at us?"

"It's so strange. What brought them together here?"

"I don't know."

"Everything is clear, sweetie. Do you now understand the story of the bouquet in the back seat?"

"My blood runs cold at the thought, Jules! That my mom and your dad are … lovers!"

"What fate has brought us all to this place?"

"You can find a bitch anywhere, you know that! My mom is a bitch. She wanted to liquidate me from the womb to be free to roam around like that! You see what I always tell you? I am very unwelcome in this world." She takes out a handkerchief.

"Don't cry, sweetie. If only you knew how the rain

of your eyes drowns my morale. Besides, my dad is watching us. He has great regard for you. You know what he said to me one day?"

"What?"

"One day when he was in a spin, he called me a muddle-headed boy. Then he said that he didn't have a son, but rather a daughter-in-law, talking about you. Do you think he was wrong in his anger? It is in rage that we say without reservation things that are on our minds. My dad adores you."

She smiles. "Jules, we won't stay here."

He snatches off the handkerchief. They head towards the scooter. As they reach their parents, Mr. Bartoli greets them. No answer, whatsoever! Yasmina looks at her mother and turns her head. Mr. Bartoli asks Jules, "Are you looking for me, son?"

"I don't need to look for you, dad!" he replies.

"I'm very happy to see you again, daughter," Benaoui says to Yasmina. "I'm so sorry. It was me who called the police to prevent you from jeopardizing your future. Here, before you, I confess it. I think I did the right thing. But this attitude you're showing prevents me from exulting in joy. I know how hurt you are because of my report to the police, and because of what is happening now. None of us arranged this four-way meeting. But, despite your disappointment, turn towards me and say you forgive me."

The girl dares not open her mouth.

As the four look at one another, an old car signals and enters the parking lot, going past them. The driver who gets out notices nothing. It is only when he has slammed the door shut that he notices Jules and Yasmina with two older people and with the scooter among them. The driver is Bonnot, who approaches smiling.

"Hey! Jules and Beautiful Yasmina!" he says.

"Hello Bonnot, good to see you here," Jules replies.

"What are you doing here? Did you also fail, as I did, to find a parking spot in front of Saint Genevieve? I thought the three of you were in the library! Cyprien gave me a call twenty minutes ago. You know, Andy's coming by cab. He doesn't trust his own car anymore. So I took the opportunity to use it."

"We'll be right with you," Jules says.

"Oh, dear! You are in a family gathering, it seems to me." Addressing the two older people, he says, "Excuse me, ma'am, excuse me, sir. I didn't notice that you were together. I'm really sorry!"

Without wasting a minute, Bonnot leaves. Jules and Yasmina follow him.

48

IF YOU WANT to lose your mind, take a tour of the Pantheon. This giant with a cheerful look viewed from Luxembourg Garden, is not quite the same when you get into its belly. It is like a dome sitting on a triangle, with a finishing that consists of a sort of hourglass topped with a cross. Its architecture displays all artistic styles that have ever existed. Everything is made to unsettle, to torment. This hourglass lantern, what is it for? How could you use an hourglass to measure eternity? And the cross, what an ambiguous symbol! The cross is an omnipresent object that maintains a hold of you everywhere. It is invoked for you at birth as you get baptized. It assists you when you are injured. And at the end, it serves as your antenna when you get buried. The cross of the Pantheon is very much an antenna planted on the underlying necropolis. Go figure if it preaches life or death. The Pantheon has the glory of embodying everything at once. It is a church sitting on a tomb.

Cyprien comes in through the left door. As soon as you enter the monument, the smell of death reaches out to you, seeking to seize you. It holds out its arms to you. Yes, if you want to lose your mind, go to the Pantheon. Blood, that of the decapitated, is still dripping on the left wall. His blood is still fresh on the floor, while the blade of his punishment lies at his side. Many visitors find the presence of this fresco of Saint Denis in the sanctuary of Saint Genevieve incongruous. Fortunately, a guide is always at hand, smiling, ready to answer any question. He will tell you, for example, that Saint Denis basilica was constructed on the recommendation of Saint Genevieve who had felt that the Dionysian work was worthy of recognition. Because King Clovis held Genevieve in high esteem, the sovereign accepted her recommendation and ordered the construction of the tomb which is now a basilica. This fresco, the guide would conclude, is the ultimate tribute being paid to Genevieve's initiative.

Looking at the fresco, Cyprien feels he has already seen it somewhere else before. But no, he is remembering it from a visit to the crypt of the basilica in Saint Denis, when a live voice told them the story of the Saint's martyrdom. He moves forward for a closer look. At this monument, everything looks strange. Looking up at the top of the dome, he sees a large central ogive with a hole on top. Daylight pours in through this opening. From outside the monument, a cross can be seen. But from the inside, only a void exists. How disconcerting! From this sky window comes a long wire which supports a clock. The shining ball, invented by Foucault, oscillates in all the splendor of its amplitude. Ah, Foucault ... Master of scientific insolence! Instead of building a clock with hands that turn around a fixed dial, as all the whipsters of his time did, he arrogantly forced Earth to turn around his needle pointed toward the ground. Yes, his twenty-four time zones turn around the oscillating ball.

A technical arrogance indeed! He ended up with a petanque ball on a wire that would revolutionize astrophysics. This provides proof that to have the ability to conceive simple things, one must be a brilliant scientist!

Behind Foucault's clock stands the monument to the National Convention. Cyprien walks around it, furtively admiring its refined features. In the gallery that opens on the left, tourists rush in to respond to the call of the famous dead. The hallways are filled with trestles, coffins and statues. He is looking for the memorial dedicated "TO THE UNKNOWN MARTYRS". In this dimly lit gallery, there is much to read. Here, the body is immortalized along with the ideas. Thoughts, maxims, axioms, both intelligible and meaningless, are engraved near the mouths that once uttered them. Cyprien ignores this literature. After exploring the remaining galleries, he finds no trace of the memorial. He returns to the main hall, where Foucault's clock indicates that Earth has rotated one hour since he entered. He thinks of his friends waiting across the street in the library. As he walks back towards the door, his eye catches a monument with a very broad base, which bears no statue. Its corners are smooth, filed away by the touch of many hands day after day. Approaching, Cyprien is welcomed by "TO THE UNKNOWN MARTYRS" inscription. The inscription, executed in low relief, has been tarnished by time. He feels a bewitching force from the monument bear on him. With the maximum span of his arms, he embraces an angle of the monument, holding it for a long time.

As he holds on to the monument, a truth that seems to have been compressed into it attempts to push through the concrete and the frames to make itself heard. The monument walls tingle with a light current that seems to be flowing through them. Electromagnetic waves radiate from the opposite wall and fill the perimeter. It is the radiation of the heart, the message of love. Cyprien expects the ground to shake again. Going to the wall, he feels the radiation intensify. It is there, it is indeed there the urn containing the heart of the Moorish woman. The message that this heart communicates is not available in the catalogue of human wisdom. It defies description. It is a flow of happiness which can only be felt and lived but cannot be expressed. Is it for this magnificence that the Benedictine priest chose to lose his terrestrial life to save this heart? Probably!

Having sufficiently fed on this happiness, Cyprien leaves the wall invigorated. He is filled with a plenitude he cannot explain. His soul is renewed. His mind now contains only one thought: forgiveness. He must forgive everyone and everything. At this moment, two time zones have just elapsed on Foucault clock. He walks slowly towards the door.

49

PANTHEON SQUARE. MANY vehicles are parked. One of them is a police car. Stuck to the steering wheel, Toulon the driver, stares at the entrance of Saint Genevieve Library. Fournier, standing and leaning against the car door, has his eyes riveted on the library entrance too.

To his amazement, Cyprien spots Jules, Yasmina and Bonnot coming out of the library in single file. He is amazed to see them all at once.

"All are here, but the Black. Where is he?" Fournier says to Toulon.

"Let's wait and see, he'll come out eventually," Toulon replies confidently.

Cyprien approaches the two cops. He's right behind the Commissioner, who has not seen him.

"Commissioner, the Black is behind the Toubab," Cyprien says. "Right behind! I have the feeling that you need me."

Fournier whirls around, his duck feet swivelling.

"So, it's true that you are alive!" he says. "I thought I had shot you on Montebello Quay. Have you come for revenge, Mister Ghezo? Are you carrying a gun? Here to kill me?"

"Why would I kill you, Commissioner? Each human holds in his hand the scythe that serves to reap his own life."

Toulon bursts out of the car, unhooking a pair of handcuffs. The Commissioner slows him down and keeps him away from Ghezo.

"You have wrong-footed us, Mr. Ghezo. It would be cowardly if I let someone who has walked to me get handcuffed. Just tell me why you are here."

"I'm here to surrender. My mission is over, and so is the guerrilla warfare. You can now take me wherever you want, because the newspapers are already on the stands with news."

Suddenly, they are surrounded by the group that just came out of the library. The police car has drawn attention to their presence. This white car with blue and red stripes and a flashing light has always drawn attention, even when there is nothing to blame. In the meantime, Mr. Bartoli and Mrs. Benaoui who have been trailing their children, have turned up and joined the group.

"This time, I have not come to arrest you, Mr. Ghezo," Fournier says. "You and I have very contrasting plans. When I wanted to nail you, you escaped me. I've come with the sole purpose of seeing you with my own eyes before I believe that you've escaped two bullets. But now you want to surrender."

"If you ever aim at a submerged human target from the dock again, don't shoot at the bubbles. Shoot some ten feet ahead of the bubbles, assuming that this distance will create an angle big enough to send your bullets deep onto the target, not onto the surface."

"Thanks for the reminder. I already remembered that we only shoot at the bubbles from a helicopter. But, like I said, I don't intend to arrest you anymore. No one up there wants you arrested. You now belong to an untouchable fringe of society. The same goes for all your accomplices. Politicians do not want to attract anti-racist associations to the streets. They know such groups have huge power. If the Association of Corsicans is set in motion in Paris, they will be supported by the separatists. Then again, we will be risking a resort to the Vigil Pirate plan. It would be the worst thing if the ETA gets involved and comes to reinforce them."

Bartoli understands these allegations targeting him. His response to Fournier is a silent pout.

"Explosives have just been stolen from an army powder magazine," Fournier says. "I'm not talking about Christmas firecrackers, but Semtex. A single kilo of Semtex is enough to reduce Paris to ashes. The authorities have been wise to limit the things to the campus. They don't want the crisis to escalate beyond."

"That policy is generous," Cyprien says, "but segregationist at the same time. I plead guilty to the CARAN incidents. I need to take responsibility for my actions, without colour as a factor. I want to be judged the same way as anyone."

"No, they know how it will end, Mr. Ghezo. They don't need riots. If you want to spend two nights of penance in a cell, the Lieutenant can arrange it for you. By this evening, I will have been sacked. But I intend to make the first move. I've already initiated the procedure for my resignation. You and I are all victims of the same system that is crushing us. It's a good thing I didn't kill you. We are manipulated in some way for shady purposes, down from an attendant right up to the most senior officer. We never know why we kill. But we kill anyway, for politics' sake." He takes a deep breath. "One last thing! I want to know this. What's being protected in this Pandora's box? What is it that has been protected so relentlessly throughout the centuries?"

"It is a State crime. Every human of any colour should be concerned about the fate of this princess. Misfortune is colourless."

All of a sudden, Jules returns on his motor scooter. He has disappeared somewhere all this while. He stops before the group. He gets down, lifts the scooter seat. From under it, he brings out a strapped cardboard box. He gives it to Cyprien, who hands it to the Commissioner. "Here is what you were looking for."

The Commissioner takes the box, opens it without a word. It contains a pile of yellowed documents. He looks at it. "I'll make sure they are safely returned to where they belong. But this is now only a squeezed orange. You have sucked the juice that had rendered the archives a treasure." He closes the box.

"No, Commissioner," Cyprien says, "we haven't done it for ourselves. We have done it to give France, which is ashamed of its history, the courage to assume it. When pages of history are dumped in the trash, they come out one day, not damaged, but enriched with the halo that centuries give to all mysteries. The Mooress is out of her prison today. She is stronger than ever. Because, as I am speaking to you, thousands of French people have her story before their eyes. It must not be long before it goes around the world. You will soon see myriads of foreigners coming from distant countries to be touched by her heart of love."

Bonnot's phone rings. It's Andy, calling from the newspaper's headquarters. The first print run of *The Canard*, he says, has sold out. They are currently resetting the press to increase the next run by two-fold, three-fold, or even four-fold, if need be!

This issue of the weekly newspaper captivated Parisians with its front-page headline: *"Return from the Beyond"* and its subtitle *"Louis XIV confesses to our editorial staff."* The new issue will have an insert with a portrait of the Black Princess provided by Saint Genevieve Library. Many homes in France, other parts of Europe, Africa and elsewhere will feature this portrait as their best discovery of the year.

At this point, Fournier only has one question in mind: "Did *The Canard* say anything about me?"

"I don't know," Bonnot replies after some hesitation.

He has the newspaper in his jacket but refrains from showing it to him. The Commissioner has in mind the story of a diplomatic incident. He figures that, if he is dismissed, it will be primarily because of the violation of the Beninese diplomat's immunity. But he is wrong. There was no diplomatic incident. Not in the least! The ambassador did not report the facts to his bosses. Everything remained between him and his driver. He did not want the Beninese authorities to realize that his heart was with the opposition and that he was supporting the president's opponent in the elections from behind the scenes. The bundle of T-shirts he had in the car was in fact intended for that candidate. Knowledge of such duplicity would not result in a simple dismissal by Porto-Novo authorities. The sanction would further be a Ben Barca-like disappearance in a street corner in Paris.

The real incident, the one that Laurent Fournier did not think about, was a statement made by the General Officer of the National Police. He portrayed the Commissioner as a vacationer who fools around in the woods while the Republic burns. This allegation was accompanied by a photo taken with a telephoto lens, showing Pamela in the Commissioner's arms in Bois de Vincennes park.

Cyprien tells his friends of his visit to the Pantheon, revealing his experience in contact with the Heart. As a result, the three of them, in turn, rush to the temple to touch this reality. Cyprien is happy to see them running to meet the Mooress. He knows how much Jules and his girlfriend dislike their parents. He hopes that a visit to the Pantheon will renew them, and that the scales of resentment will fall from their hearts. No one can approach the prodigious urn without giving ground on their human pride.

With the children gone, Benaoui whispers to Bartoli: "What do we do next, BB?"

"Ah, ma'am!" Bartoli says. "I am delighted with this little name that you just gave me! I didn't expect it so soon. But who would refuse an unexpected fortune?"

She laughs. "No, you misinterpreted my word, my dear sir. I did not say what you thought I said. BB is Bonaventure Bartoli, if I have to teach you your name." Then she grows serious.

"Okay, let's follow them. We must seek immediate reconciliation."

While approaching the stairs, she breaks into a light smile. It is the first smile she has given him since they met. As they walk up, a thought strikes Mr. Bartoli.

"Maybe our children are not wrong," he says. "Somehow, we must admit that one only exists by rebelling, by breaking the mold. Have you ever visited the Tower of Pisa? It is famous only because of its inclination. If it had stayed upright as its builder expected it to, it would be just another tower in Europe. Our children have understood this. They want to make their lives useful and visible."

Benaoui nods, her face now relaxed. They walk side by side after their children, who have already disappeared into the Pantheon.

The Commissioner notices the void surrounding him. "I won't even have a rabbit to chase anymore!" No one reacts to his joke. He becomes serious again. He looks at Cyprien, staring at him as if he has never seen him, as if he never drew a gun on him.

"Mr. Ghezo," he says, "I'm not the same anymore. I have changed my way of looking at the world. I have changed the way I regard you. Nobody could imagine that royal blood flows in your veins. I realize now that all those who relocate from their home country to ours, have a story to tell. I want to proclaim it loud from the top of this monument. Foreigners have something to share with our people as equals, because since the dawn of time, only equals go together."

"Forest people have their own way of saying that: 'Only trees of the same height exchange monkeys.'"

"It all comes down to the same thing, my dear fellow. Take note that I am transformed. You have opened my eyes."

"And I would say that you have had the right reflex, Commissioner. A wise man is one who gives up his prejudices."

The Commissioner opens the car door. Before taking his seat, he pauses, then he says: "Today I understand you better, Mr. Ghezo. I did not realize that we were both hooked to the same holed parachute. You have touched the ground, but I haven't. Stand firm!" He holds out his hand to Cyprien. Cyprien does not hesitate to do the same. They shake hands.

"And you, Commissioner," Cyprien says, "your bloodhound spirit finally enabled you to find the right path. Renunciation. It is only by throwing away our weapons that we can easily reach the heart of the enemy's fortress."

The car door slams shut.

Acknowledgements

My thanks go to Elsy Temfack and Gideon Lambiv for their valuable input by reading the story and offering their insight. Special thanks to Tololwa Molell for his unparalleled editing on this English version. Thank you to all the institutions that contributed to the achievement of this work by providing essential information and archives, especially The Spiritualist Studies Center Brotherhood of Montreal, The Saint Genevieve Library of Paris and The Barley Sugar Museum of Moret. Finally, a thank you to Guernica Editions for publishing the English version of this novel.

A big hug to Caroline, Alex and Indira.

About the Author

Roger Fodjo is a native of Cameroon and a resident of Edmonton, Canada. He dedicated a decade to teaching the Spanish language before moving into translation as a profession. Following *J'ai six fois vécu* (Edilivre Editions, Paris, 2007), Fodjo wrote *Les poubelles du palais* in 2011 and *Prête-moi ton destin* in 2021, both published by L'Harmatan Editions, Paris. These books are works of fiction strongly rooted in historical facts and social reality that emphasize the author's clear stance in favour of marginalized groups.

Printed by Imprimerie Gauvin
Gatineau, Québec